Round and round
run the Gashta.
Small ones,
big ones,
golden ones,
and the pale-furred ones.

We laugh and push,
tripping and scrambling.
When we play hide-and-find
we are happy.
But we must be cautious
or we may die . . .

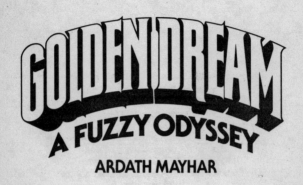

GOLDEN DREAM
A FUZZY ODYSSEY

ARDATH MAYHAR

ACE SCIENCE FICTION BOOKS
NEW YORK

This Ace Science Fiction Book contains the complete
text of the original trade edition.
It has been completely reset in a typeface
designed for easy reading, and was printed
from new film.

GOLDEN DREAM: A FUZZY ODYSSEY

An Ace Science Fiction Book / published by arrangement with
the author

PRINTING HISTORY
Trade Original / October 1982
Ace Mass Market edition / September 1983

ISBN: 0-441-29726-9

Ace Science Fiction Books are published by
The Berkley Publishing Group,
200 Madison Avenue, New York, New York 10016.
PRINTED IN THE UNITED STATES OF AMERICA

To H. Beam Piper and William Tuning, without whom this book would have been nonexistent.

Note on Gashta Songs: The Gashta sang in the "upper mode," meaning ultrasonic range. Though each Gashta invented his own melody as he went along, the words were always the same, as long as memory of the song survived.

Foreword

One dreadfully gray and frozen February day in early 1982, the telephone rang. This is more of an occasion for me than for most, as I live at the back of beyond, almost on Sam Rayburn Lake in the Big Thicket area of East Texas. My contacts with the world come, principally, from telephone and mailbox. It was one of those mornings when the feet are so cold that the brain works only spasmodically, so that ring interrupted nothing earth-shaking.

And it was an editor at ACE Books, Terri Windling, telling me that her copies of my first-ever paperback had just come in and were stunningly beautiful. After mutual congratulations and a modicum of small-talk, Terri asked, very diffidently, "May I ask you something?"

Anybody can ask me anything. Of course, some things bring about black eyes, but from Terri I knew that would not be a problem. And the thing she asked was this: Was I familiar with H. Beam Piper's books about the Fuzzies? And might I be interested in writing a new one . . . from the Fuzzies' viewpoint?

I was, on both counts. Later, when Susan Allison called me there was instant rapport. Particularly when she said (not in so many words—she is far more tactful than that), "We were knocking the problem of the new Fuzzy book about the office one day, asking who was very *fast* at writing, and who was partly alien, and

ix

naturally your name popped into our minds.''

Being both very fast and partly alien, I was charmed.

Then and there I agreed to reread my copies of the books (of course my personal Gremlin had devoured one of them, so Susan had to send me another post-haste), and to try writing a segment, both to see how I fit into a Fuzzy-skin and to see how well the result suited ACE. For my part, I found that golden fur and a two-foot-high elevation are strangely familiar. I hope that ACE was at least as happy.

I hope that H. Beam Piper, in whatever dimension he now exists, is happy, too. I found that he had given fascinating clues to both Fuzzy language and development in his books *Little Fuzzy* and *Fuzzy Sapiens*. Moreover, I felt, more than once, that the Father of the Fuzzies might be standing at my elbow, reading over my shoulder, and giving subliminal suggestions.

To Mr. William Tuning I also offer thanks for his interesting deep background on the Fuzzies, revealed in *Fuzzy Bones*. Without his concepts of the Valley and the Ship and the buried cavern, this history of the Gashta would not have been possible.

For anyone interested, I will insert here that I am well over two feet tall (my husband would chuckle and say that five-feet-two isn't all that much over, but I ignore such snide remarks); my fur, what there is of it, is gray, not golden. But I think I'd swing a mean zatku-hodda, given the chance.

Personae

THE GASHTA
Book I
i., ii.

Breaks-Twigs, Teacher
Sun-Blossom, his daughter
Speaks-Well, his permanent mate
Stargazer (formerly Root-Digger), his brother
Fire-Bringer, a young hunter

iii.

Fears-Nothing, former leader
Fast-Foot, his mate
Big-Voice, present leader
Many-Winters, Teacher of this village
Cricket-Catcher, who spoke in the Circle

iv.

Sun-Blossom as an adult, now Teacher in the Valley
Stargazer, son of Root-Digger, now Haigun

v., vi., vii.

Bad-Thing-Killer, great hunter
Sharp-Teeth, his mate
Axe-Maker, his brother
Snail-Catcher, Axe-Maker's mate
Nut and Shell, Bad-Thing-Killer's sons
Fruit, daughter of Snail-Catcher

viii.

Zatku-Cracker, who learned that he must go home
Fruit-Finder, his mate
Seed, their son
Spear-Maker, Fruit-Finder's brother

ix.

Teacher, daughter of Sun-Blossom

Book II

i.

Stargazer, descendant of the earlier Stargazers
Cord-Maker, young Stargazer-in-training

ii., iii.

Remembers-Things, patriarch of his family
Climbs-Rocks, who has traveled in the south
Runs-Fast, his mate
Sees-Far and Pulls-Weeds, son-in-law and daughter
Petal, child of Climbs-Rocks and Runs-Fast

iv.

Root-Grower, discontented gardener
Leaf, her daughter
Swift-Stone-Thrower, her mother, now dead
Climbs-Swiftly (who was later called Silver-Fur)

v.

Stands-Fast, leader of his family
Golden-Eyes, his mate, Net-Weaver, his second mate
Knows-Much, his grandmother
Hunts-Zeeto, his brother
Weaves-Cords-Together, his grandfather
Sprout, his son
Plum, his daughter

Book III
i., ii., iii.

Leaf, now an adult
Whistle, her baby son

vi.

Dark-Fur, who later became Little Fuzzy
Mama-Fuzzy, his mate (Gashta name "Tells-Things")
Baby

ix.

Mike, Mitzi, KoKo, the other members of Dark-Fur's
   family

xii.

Golden-Fur (later Goldilocks)
Soft-Voice, her sister (later Cinderella)

Book IV
iii.

Silver-Fur, Root-Grower's long-ago mate, father to
   Leaf, now patriarch of a family
Bud, the only female in the group
Ku and Ik, the other two males in the family
one black and white kitten, who became Bud's very own

Book V
iv.

a family whose names are not mentioned at their own
   request

THE HAGGA
Book III
ii.-ix.

August and Lemuel Mirabeau, family of Leaf, squatters
   on Beta Continent

Jack Holloway (Pappy Jack), prospector, champion of Gashta, and later Commissioner of Native Affairs

x., xi.

Bennett Rainsford, naturalist, later Governor of Zarathustra

Two policemen

xii., xiii.

Ruth Ortheris, Lt., j.g., Navy, on secret duty, working for the Zarathustra Company under Ernst Mallin

Gerd Van Riebeek, Company scientist, later married to Ruth

Leonard Kellogg, who kills Goldilocks

Kurt Borch, gunman killed by Jack Holloway

Juan Jimenez, Company employee and scientist

xiv.

Augustus Brannhard (Unca Gus), lawyer and friend to Jack Holloway and preserver of Baby from the sack

Book IV

Ernst Mallin, charged with proving the Gashta nonsapient

Victor Grego, President of the Chartered Zarathustra Company

Leslie Coombes, Company attorney

Book V

i.

Pancho Ybarra, Navy psychologist who worked with Gashta on Xerxes

Alex Napier, Navy Commander on Xerxes

iii.

Luis J. Camber, Chief Petty Officer, T.F.N., hearing-aid expert

GOLDEN DREAM: A FUZZY ODYSSEY

BOOK I.

The Valley
of the Gashta

~~~~~~~~~~~~~~~

Ja'aki-fessi—I was hungry
   T'ho! T'ho!—Yes! Yes!
Zatku bizzo keef-i—A land-prawn came quietly
   T'ho! T'ho!—Yes! Yes!
Zatku-hodda ne'ti—My weapon talked to it
   T'ho! T'ho!—Yes! Yes!
Hoksu zatku-fusso!—Wonderful zatku-food!

PROLOGUE

i.

Breaks-Twigs (*Etza-T'ra* in his own Gashta tongue) climbed into the feather tree, found a comfortable spot, and settled himself to his task of watching the young ones. He was grunting with effort, and his old heart was patting in his chest as he looked downward, through the concentric layers of plumed branches that rayed, spoke-like, from the treetrunk. His daughter sat directly below him.

Sun-Blossom was making a beautiful thing. Though all the Gashta spent some of their precious time at such things, she seemed most preoccupied with the activity. The sun touched her golden fur, her bare pink ears, and her tiny hands as they moved surely to place bright pebbles, green and gold leaves, and bits of moss and twig in the pattern that she was forming.

Breaks-Twigs could see, even from so far above, that her version of the Spiral was more accurate than most. It was strange, he knew, how the shape of the Home System remained in the minds of its children, even on this distant, alien world. Even stranger, it continued to persist, even after memories of the ship and its equipment became dim among the elders and entirely lost among the children.

He looked away from his child, out into the glades of the forest. Only here in the valley could the young be

2

allowed to roam at will, and even then one adult must watch over them. The *gotza* were sharp-eyed, even from the high places where they flew, and could swoop, unseen, to grab an unsuspecting Gashta who wandered into a clearing. And the *toshki-washa* prowled even here, though hunters kept their numbers down as best they could. So he counted his charges and reminded himself that he must give a lesson, when all paused in their mushroom-eating and insect-catching. They were forgetting how to count, among many other things that were slipping away from his kind.

Breaks-Twigs mused, as his eyes pierced shadows and studied motions. So many things were going, since the earthquake had covered over the cave and the ship. But it was so very hard to live here, with only bare hands and natural things and what could be managed between the two. Even their language . . . the piercing voices from the wood irritated his sensitive ears . . . was going. The necessity for raising the pitch to levels that the predators couldn't hear had made a change in the tongue itself.

He stilled, his head cocking, his eyes focusing upon a movement in the brush off to his left. Forgetting his age and the awkwardness at hunting that had given him his name, he slipped down the tree silently, retrieved his wooden *zatku-hodda* from the low branch where he had left it, and dropped beside Sun-Blossom.

She looked up from her patterning. Her eyes went even wider, their jade-green depths sparkling with fright. He tossed her up into the tree, gave an ultrasonic cry that warned all the frolicking young ones, and slid into the brush, moving at an angle toward the spot that had roused his suspicion.

The young Gashta froze where they were. The wood was suddenly filled with plump golden-furred statues, for the danger might be anywhere. To hide might be to go into the waiting jaws of a *toshki-washa*.

Breaks-Twigs was no longer the clumsy-foot that he had been in his youth. No leaf flicked against another as he snaked along the pathways that his people had worn into the lower fabric of the forest. His small hand was steady on the haft of the *zatku-hodda*, though the longer hair of the golden mane about his head and neck was standing out from his skin in response to the danger-impulse.

The sound of the beast's breathing was clear, now, in his ears. He could hear the thumping of its heart and the faint riffling of its fur as it moved to scent him. His voice rose in a shout for assistance, for the creature ahead of him was at least four times his size. To its ears, he knew, that shout was inaudible, and he heard a distant answer with much relief. He slowed his pace, waiting for the other hunters to draw near enough to be of help.

There came a tiny clicking sound. Others were in position. He lifted his *zatku-hodda* and rushed toward the big, hot body of the animal, driving the blunt, paddle-shaped weapon ahead of him as if it were a spear.

With a yelping grunt, the beast broke from cover. Concentrating on the young Gashta beyond the bushy place, it had not heard any sound to indicate the approach of the hunters, and the wind had been in their favor. Now it was surrounded by small warriors wielding an array of wooden tools and weapons. As it charged one of them, that one retreated and those on either side attacked, piercing the beast's hairy hide with pebble-tipped spears or beating at it with the thinner edges of the *zatku-hodda*.

It was too big and tough to be killed with such instruments. The Gashta knew that. But it didn't like being hurt, and that was the thing they counted on. After a dozen or so charges that ended with bruised ribs and sore hide, the thing howled and leaped into the forest. The warriors could hear the rapid patter of its paws, as it ran toward the mountain that flanked their valley.

Breaks-Twigs had been flung down in the act of prodding the animal in its flank. Its break for freedom had caught him unaware, and the heavy body had flattened him as it turned. Now he lay there, panting. One of the young warriors came to hunker beside him.

"Is it that you are hurt, Old Teacher?" he asked. "Is

it that I might help you to rise up?"

"This one is unhurt, Fire-Bringer. This one is merely old and very tired. It would be well if you helped me back to the young ones. They will be frightened. It is well that this was a *toshki-washa*. The *gotza* are not so easily discouraged."

The old Gashta struggled to sit up, and Fire-Bringer caught his hand and tugged him to his feet. Now that the danger was over, Breaks-Twigs felt as if his strength had turned to water and drained away through his toes. The quiver in his bones was a reminder . . . and a warning.

"Our ways change, young one," he said as they trudged through the brushy ways again. "We, who are old, die, and you who are younger must keep the people safe and feed us and yourselves. Already, the ship is only a tale, even to us who are old. The old skills are dying, even among the *Haigun-sha*. And the *Kampushi-sha*, who were never trained in the ship-ways, are beginning to look away from the valley, even though we have been taught that we must stay near it."

He paused, his big green eyes narrowing against some internal pain, and the younger Gashta looked at him with concern.

"It is that you are hurt!" he said firmly. "It is that you must be taken to Speaks-Well. One of the hunters will watch the young."

Breaks-Twigs had begun to suspect that this might be true. He made no protest, but he called to Sun-Blossom, who ran to follow them to their hut beneath the thorns.

They followed the maze-like pathways, hidden here from any flying creature, and long before they neared their hut, they could hear Speaks-Well singing.

"Oho!" said Breaks-Twigs. "That is the proper use for the high-mode. In the old days, I was taught, it was used only for music, never for speech. Hear how she trills! Though she does indeed speak well, my mate sings even better."

The singing broke off abruptly. The rounded shape of Speaks-Well appeared in the opening of the hut. She was of a height with her mate, but her eyes were a darker green, her silky fur a more sunlit gold. Now those big green eyes darkened with worry, raking over the approaching group, assessing the reasons that might have brought her mate back from his duties so soon.

Fire-Bringer helped Breaks-Twigs into the wicker-like house and stood over him, his face concerned. Breaks-Twigs sank onto his bed-pile and sighed. Then he smiled up at his wife and daughter and friend.

"This one is not really injured, I think. Though a pain sits in the breast, it is only a bruise. One gets old. One cannot bounce up from the ground as the young ones do. I am grateful, Fire-Bringer. As you go to join the other hunters, will you tell Stargazer that I would talk with him?"

The younger Gashta nodded, accepted the thanks of Speaks-Well, and left about his errands. Speaks-Well, freed of the need for dignity before one not of the household, knelt beside her wounded mate and touched him gently, probing for broken bones. At the center of his chest, she found a spot that brought a gasp of agony from him.

"Ribs," she said, forgetting and speaking in the older, deeper, speech-tones. "It is that they might be cracked. It is that they might be broken or crushed. It is that you will remain quiet for a time to let them heal. *Aki-noho-so!*"

When she used that tone, he knew that obedience was the easiest way. He and their children and her children by the other male Gashta that the *Haigun* had assigned to her over the years of her fertility understood fully the extent of her flexibility. Once she spoke with this firmness, appeal was useless.

"When you tell me, I always heed," he said mildly, though that was by no means entirely true. Only when he heard that particular note in her voice did he agree so readily. "But one must watch the young. Hunters cannot be spared for long. Is it that you could watch on this, my day, instead of waiting for tomorrow, your own?"

She rose to her feet. Only then could it be seen that she was as old as her mate, for she moved with some stiffness, and the faint popping of her joints was quite audible to the quick ears of her family. She took her own *zatku-hodda* from the corner set aside for their tools and returned to his side.

"Sun-Blossom will stay," she said. "If there is a need, she can come into the forest and call. I will watch this day and tomorrow also. And the day after, if it seems that there is cause. Meat-Bringer came early. Fire-Bringer will come before I return, and Sun-Blossom can set the meat over the fire-pile and strike the spark. Do not move!"

Her small form darkened the door-hole for a moment, and Breaks-Twigs gasped his dry chuckle. She knew quite well that he knew the household schedules and methods as well as she. After all, on alternate days those duties were his, as his were hers. She was the sort of Gashta who worried about small things and large ones, things that needed worry and things that did not. Yet she was his choice, and they had spent their adult lives together, interrupted only by the mandatory periods of her matings and his own with those the Haigun assigned to them.

Lying upon his pile of dried grasses, he considered the lives that his people now led. Far different . . . oh so far different from those that the ancestors had thought to establish for their descendants. The traditions that he had been taught and that he, in turn, taught to the young ones were taking on, even for himself, the dimness of dreams and legends. Yet he could remember the cavern in the mountainside. He had seen with his own eyes those instruments and machines that his ancestors had rescued from the ship, after it had crashed into the mountain.

His own family had been ship-people. For that reason he and his mate, together with Stargazer and his, had inherited the tasks of teacher and watcher-of-the-stars. Even after so many generations it was easy to see which of the Gashta of the valley had descended from the ship's crew, and which from the colonists who had been its passengers.

Already the *Kampushi-sha*, inheriting the restlessness

that had sent their ancestors out to colonize other
worlds, were pushing outward from the valley. There
had been no word from those who had gone southward.
The group that went north sent messengers to the valley,
from time to time, giving word of their progress and
inquiring after family and friends. The last two such
communications had not been cheerful. They were not
prospering as they had hoped. And too many of their
young were stillborn.

The descendants of the ship-people clung stubbornly
to the valley. They had been told to remain here. Help
would come. A message had been sent, out into space,
that would bring their own to their rescue. "You must
watch the stars," the old ones had said. "Stay in the
valley and watch!"

But it had not been easy.

He turned on his bed, and the pain of his chest
brought a moan from him. Sun-Blossom, his *Fe'ha-
Hok'e*, came and knelt beside him. "*Pa-ha-izza*," she
shrilled in the high mode, "Can bring you *waji?* You
have thirst?"

He patted her little hand, and the warm fingers closed
about his. "I would like water," he answered, more to
make her feel useful than because he was thirsty. He
heard her take the shell from beside the door and make
her way down the path outside to the pot that Water-
Bringer kept filled from the stream.

Even though the maze of paths beneath the thorntrees was hidden from the air and inaccessible to the big
predators of the forest and the grasslands, he listened
with attention until she was inside the hut again. There
were so many things that hunted the Gashta and savored
their flesh!

That had been one of the things that made life more
than difficult for the survivors. Sometimes he thought
that those who had been trapped inside the caves, buried
along with all the supplies of food and equipment and
weapons and tools, had been more fortunate than those
who had been hunting and gathering roots and watching
the young ones play and romp in the sunlight. They, at

least, had not been left to cope with a hostile world filled with predators many times their size and weight. Aside from a few tools and weapons that the food-gatherers and the hunters had had with them, there had been nothing left but the stunned Gashta.

He could remember standing with his father, gazing at the dusty rubble that made a long slant where the steep cliff had been. They had known, without any doubt, that there was no way in which to clear away half a mountainside in time to save those trapped in the caverns. Or, indeed, any way to clear it at all. They were few. They had no tools. If there had been ten times their number, the task could not have been accomplished.

The pain of that moment of understanding had never left him. His mother had been inside, as had his siblings, except for the one now known as Stargazer. Then he had been Root-Digger.

Sun-Blossom touched his shoulder, and he sat up with a groan. The water was cool to his lips and his throat. He must be fevered, though he had not thought so at first. It was best, perhaps, that he lie here quietly for a day or so.

As he settled back into the bed-pile, he heard Stargazer's distinctive footfall on the path. Soon he would come, and they would sit together and talk, remembering things that they alone were old enough to recall.

"The Haigun, my uncle, comes!" said Sun-Blossom, going to the door-opening to look out. "I may sit on the path and make *shokka-washa,* when he is here?"

"You may," he said. He closed his eyes. Even then, he could see the glint of the sunlight on her fur, her small, smooth face amid the bright waves of her mane. She was so beautiful, his daughter. He wondered what time held in store for her.

ii.

Stargazer found Sun-Blossom beside the door, busy with her patterning. He bent to touch her sunny head as he passed. As always, he marveled at the accuracy of her racial memory. The Spiral of her design was a duplicate of that on the star-maps that he had seen in his youth. He shook his head. The Way of Things was always a puzzle. That was the one thing that did not change.

He found his brother lying on his bed-pile. The fact that he had not risen to sit, once Sun-Blossom's watchful eyes were turned away, told him much about the pain of Breaks-Twigs's injury.

Stargazer squatted comfortably on the floor beside the bed-pile. "The *toshki-washa* treated you badly, then?" he asked. "And what can you expect? Those as old as we cannot go attacking such big beasts with only a *zatku-hodda* and expect to come out of the encounter without a scratch!" Though his words were stern, he found his heart warmed by the bravery of this brother, who, though unsuited for such work, did not hesitate when there was necessity.

A dry chuckle rose from the quiet figure. "Indeed, my brother, I forgot for the time how very old I am. For that short while I was young again, my blood hot in my veins and my heart full of lust for the blood of anything that threatens our young. I was reminded quite soon that things are no longer exactly so." He coughed a bit, and Stargazer lifted the water-filled shell to his lips and helped him drink.

"I was thinking," the teacher said, once he was settled again, "of all the ways in which our lives have changed. What sort of world do you think it might have been . . . that one the ship was supposed to find? Could it have been as hostile to our kind as this? I dream, sometimes, of what might have been, if . . ."

Stargazer looked sharply at the face, dimly lit by the light from the doorway. His brother looked very thin, very fragile, as he lay on his bed-pile. The aura of strength and competence that had always surrounded him seemed thinned to nothing. The Haigun felt a jolt of sorrow beneath his chest-fur. But he answered calmly.

"I have so little time for dreaming. Life is so hard, so dangerous. I cannot seem to glance away, even for a moment. At night I look up at the stars, watching for the promised configuration. By day I worry about the Gashta. And about my foolish brother, who attacks *toshki-washa.*"

The Teacher sighed. "It would have been so much easier, if only the caverns had not been covered over. The Oldest Ones knew many things that we lost when the side of the Mountain collapsed upon them. The tools and the weapons, there in the caves . . . they would have given us some defense against *toshki-washa* and *gotza* and even, perhaps, *so-shi-fazzu.* Though it might, indeed, have been worse. If our father, the Haigun, had been inside the caves—even the star-secrets would have been lost. The memories of the ship's crashing into the mountain, the sending of the signal for help . . . all those would have been wiped away from the memory of our people. And you would not have known all the things that a Stargazer must know."

Breaks-Twigs pushed with his arms, sitting up in his pile of grass, his breath coming in gasps. "But I am wandering. Fever, perhaps. I did not call for you to take you with me into the past."

"It is a good thing to go back, at times," Stargazer said. "There is need for this one to sit quietly and to talk with his only brother about the things we remember. The things that *only* we two remember. But what did you want to tell me?"

The Teacher sighed. "We are losing so much, day by day. The young ones must work so hard for food, must watch so closely for danger. Survival takes so much of their time and strength that they are losing the skills that made our people able to travel between stars. There

is no time to teach them the difficult things that we
learned in the caverns, when we were young. Our children are forgetting how to count beyond the fingers of
their hands. The calculations that guided our Ship are
lost even to you and to me. Even the mathematics to
begin forming them has been lost to the young of our
kind.

"And the ways our people lived, before the catas-
trophe . . . they also are being forgotten. The young
ones think that Gashta have always mated as directed.
When I try to explain genetics and the facts of inbreeding to them, they fidget and make patterns with
stones. I find that nothing that I have said enters their
heads, for they are watching *zatku* in the clearings or
scanning the sky for *gotza*. It pains me that we are losing our heritage."

Stargazer grunted. "Other things are vital now. We
have taught them so well the need for speaking in the
high modes that the youngest have lost the ability to talk
in lower registers. Yet it is a necessity, if we are to survive. This one has thought much on these things, my
brother. What is lost is the culture that formed us and
sent us here. What is developing is a set of habits and
abilities that may keep our descendants alive. When old
things are lost, it is a sad thing. But better that they be
lost than that the Gashta themselves die away."

"But how tragic it would be for those from the home
world to come after us, only to find . . . primitives . . .
savages? . . . in the place of their kin!" Breaks-Twigs
had a mental image of those would-be rescuers standing
appalled at the thing that had overtaken their own kind.

Stargazer moved his fingers, drawing a pattern in the
dust of the floor. His gaze was not upon that, however,
but on the face of his brother.

"There was a thing that our father told me," he said,
his voice set low in the deep mode. Almost a whisper, in
fact. "It is not for the ears of those who do not lead. I
have kept it from you, for I disliked removing hope
from your heart, but if you are so troubled about what
might be in time to come, then you must know.

"That signal that we were told of, in our youth . . . the signal that keeps my eyes set on the night sky and your efforts concentrated upon teaching our past to those who must go into the future . . . was sent, it is true. It went out from the ship, just before the forces of this planet caught us and brought us down. But the power of the engines had failed. The signal could not be sent in the swift way it would have gone, had there been the power for that.

"I know nothing of the ways they had of such sendings. Our father told me that our people always had a second and a third method at hand, if their best should fail. That signal is still traveling upon its way. Not for generations will it reach that *hoksu-mitto* that was the birthplace of our people. Not for many-many years can any of our number expect another ship to come after us."

Breaks-Twigs pressed his hands together in his lap. Tears brimmed in his pale-green eyes. "It is so?" he breathed. "The hope that I have nourished in myself and in others is a thing so slender and frail that it is almost nonexistent?"

Stargazer looked down at his pattern in the dust. "It is true. Our father told me that this is not a thing to tell the Gashta. They need the strong hope that our knowledge of the signal gives them. And by the time it becomes clear that no answer may come for long—or at all—perhaps the people will be settled into this land and able to survive here."

"What of those who have gone outside the valley? Have they survived and prospered?" The teacher's tone was bitter.

His brother brushed the dust, erasing the Spiral that his fingers had drawn.

"No."

"I think that they will not. Do you recall what we were told about the years just after the ship crashed? Those first brave ones who moved out of the caverns into the valley and worked to live independently found that their young ones were born dead . . . dead, or so

deformed that they died. Only when they asked the
Haigun-sha in the caverns for food from our own supplies did they return to normal.

"Our father believed that there is something that our
bodies need that this world does not supply. Those who
have gone north are having stillbirths. You have told me
this. Those who went south—who knows? We have had
no word from them in the time since their leaving. I believe that they are all dead. Do our minds walk together?"

The *Haigun* shifted uneasily, his fur rippling in the
dim light.

"It is in my heart that we are trapped here in this
valley. We must stay here, for what we need is contained
here. And that is strange, for it was not here for those
who came first. It has come into being in the years since
the ship crashed. Could some element from the ship
have permeated the soil in the years that have passed?"

"So much of the knowledge has been lost," sighed
the teacher. "Yet it is possible. It must be so. And the
young still clamor to go out, over the mountains, into
the wide lands beyond."

The two old Gashta looked at one another in the dimming light. Their green eyes held a deep sadness, for
both knew that their life-sparks were flickering.

"Soon we will be gone," murmured Stargazer. "The
new *Haigun* knows what I could teach him, yet he dis-
believes much of what I say. Once we are laid in our
grave-pits, our people will be so much the poorer."

The old teacher reached out a small hand and grasped
that of his brother. They sat there, wordless, until the
sound of Speaks-Well's song shimmered in the air of the
hut.

She entered to find Stargazer standing, ready to leave.

"You find him well?" she asked.

"As well as one can be who is incautious enough to
attack a *toshki-washa*," he replied with gentle courtesy.
"Keep him quiet, Sister-in-law. I will be back tomorrow."

The Haigun went away up the pathway to his spot

atop a rock. From there he could see the stars that gleamed in specks and whorls and mists of milky luminescence. Obedient to his training, he set his eyes upon the proper spot in the dark vault above him. But the bright images swam in a haze of tears.

THE OLDEST SONG

Listen to the oldest song,
   half-forgotten, now.
The teacher sings of a Ship,
   a road across the sky,
a world filled with Gashta.

How wonderful!

He sings of a cavern
   in the Mountain,
fine-fine things,
   wonderful foods,
lost when the land shook.

How terrible!

He sings of things we never saw,
   do not remember,
things we have mislaid
among the years
   and the dangers.

How sad!

iii.

Clouds hovered about the hips of the mountains, dribbling rain onto the lower slopes and into the valleys that pocked the range. Fears-Nothing leaned on his useless *zatku-hodda*, dreaming of the flavor of the ugly landprawns that had been left behind in the valley from which his people had migrated.

In the years since leaving the home valley, the group that his father and mother had led had dwindled, instead of grown. That was a constant worry to the young *kin-sha*, along with the growing danger from *so-shi-fazzu*. The huge horned beasts had found an easy way over the lower ranges. Now they were grazing on the very edges of the village thorn-patch. And they were big enough to force their way into the thickets after tender green shoots and random patches of wire-grass.

Fears-Nothing huddled his shoulders together, shuddering to rid his fur of some of the damp. Even the rain had not deterred the movements of the *so-shi-fazzu*. He had kept one eye on the weather, another on the beasts, and wished he had still a third for the mood of his people. It would have been sensible to send them into the rough country high on the slopes. The *so-shi-fazzu* were going to come crashing through the thorn-scrub soon, and every one of the Gashta knew that. But the winter had been hard. They had lost several young hunters and a number of infants. Every temper in the village was frayed to the breaking-point, and he had not dared to order everyone out.

The *Kampushi-sha* were not the disciplined and obedient people that the *Haigun-sha* were. They knew their own minds, and if their ideas clashed with those of the one they had chosen to be leader, then they deposed him and put another in his place. So they had done, setting Big-Voice, with his short-sighted advice and his dangerous example, in the place of Fears-Nothing, who wanted only their good. He had a bad feeling, deep in his bright-furred body. This time his people had chosen badly.

So he crouched in the rain that fell harder than before, watching and listening. Even in the spring air, the wet brought a chill to his body, and to make matters worse he heard a movement in the brushy area at the forest's edge. A deep huffing of breath. *So-shi-fazzu*. There was no doubt of that.

The thorntrees in the home valley were thick and prickly enough to turn even such huge beasts. In this more northerly place they were thin and spindly. Fears-Nothing knew them to be too weak to stop beasts as large as the three *so-shi-fazzu* that now were splashing through the wet toward his village. He shouted in the high mode with all his might.

Wriggling through the bushes, he made for the thorny paths as fast as he could go. Once he reached the outer parts of the maze, he stopped and shouted again.

He could hear the leisurely plod of hooves in the mulch behind him. There was no doubt at all; the creatures were heading straight for the greening thorn-bushes.

They were thin with the winter's deprivation. That was the only reason he could find that might make them take interest in the tough vegetation of the thorns. Their ugly heads, with three horns, one at each jaw, one on the forehead, were aimed for the spot where he was standing.

"Run for the stream!" Fears-Nothing shrilled. "Leave everything! Run for the streambed!"

Many rustlings told him that the people, at last, were listening to him. But the beasts were almost upon him now. He turned and fled up the winding pathway.

A young Gashta, burdened with one of the few living babies born in the past year, struggled along ahead of him. He caught up the child and pushed its mother before him up the pathways. The rest of his people had evidently moved with much speed at his first shout. Most were well past the maze of thorn and were crossing the gardens. The stream was not far beyond them. Its rough banks could hide many of the Gashta among its boulders and flints.

He chanced a glance over his shoulder. The first of the *so-shi-fazzu* was wading into the thorn. It twitched its hide and snorted at the pricking thorns. It was browsing, nevertheless, on the mist of new green growth that the spring rains had brought to the tough and whiplike branches. As he watched, a huge hoof crashed through the wall of a house.

Now he turned back and chivvied the young female along at a fierce pace, overtaking the main body of his people as they gained the edge of the stream. They, too, had looked back at the havoc being wrought upon their village. They were wasting no time in scurrying down the rain-chewed cuts between stones. Though as individuals they might escape the notice of the big beasts, a large group of Gashta might well bring all three charging through the thorn. The creatures had no objection to a taste of flesh, now and then.

The Gashta poured down the steep cut, a flood of furred bodies, dark with wet. Some carried food. Most had their *zatku-hodda* or their stone axes. As they gained the shelter of the embankment, they melted from sight into crevices between boulders and rock-layers. Fears-Nothing saw his charges safely installed in a notch with his own mate, Fast-Foot, and snaked back up the bank to peer over the top.

The village was gone. He had no doubt of that, for the three *so-shi-fazzu* stood in a group at what had been the center of the huddle of wicker houses.

He felt a touch on his arm. Big-Voice stood at his side, in full view of the *so-shi-fazzu*. He was surveying the animals as if the streambed were some sort of impregnable protection. He swung his arms wide, his face angry.

"They are standing upon this one's house!" he shouted, his big voice sliding down into the deep-mode, out of the high range that the beasts couldn't hear.

Fears-Nothing kicked his feet from under him, bringing his surprised face down to ground-level. "Foolish Gashta!" he hissed. "Do you think that those beasts are so fond of thorn shoots that they would not prefer your flesh instead? You chance bringing them down upon all of us. We are far too few, as it stands."

Big-Voice narrowed his eyes. The smooth contours of his face turned a muddy brown, a certain indication of rage. "You were chosen *kin-sha*, to lead us wisely and to keep us safe. Now we hide in the rain, watching our homes destroyed. You have failed us, and so I will say to the rest of the Gashta!"

"Say it. Shout it, if you will. But you spoke loudly to them, persuaded them to stay in this dangerous place when I would have moved them to safety. You were loudest of all in protesting my notion of hiding the whole village, once we knew that the beasts were in our little valley. There are always Gashta who think that the loudest voice carries the wisest words. Disaster has come to the people, upon your words and your actions. And so *I* will say to the Gashta."

Rage was not a common thing with the Gashta, but Fears-Nothing felt something hot and powerful building beneath the fur of his breast. Big-Voice had chanced the lives of his people. He had frightened the timid and made the brave over-bold. The killing of Gashta by Gashta was a thing that happened only in myth, it seemed. Yet such had occurred in the long past, the Teacher had said. If all these damp and miserable people had perished beneath the hooves of those beasts, it would have been murder on a scale undreamed-of in all of Gashta history.

He felt within himself an urge to hurt Big-Voice. It shocked him. Yet the instinct that made him a natural leader told him that that urge was not entirely wrong. There was the seed of something useful within it. He wished suddenly that he could talk with old Breaks-Twigs, who had been his teacher. With Stargazer. With one whose solid good sense could be depended upon.

Fears-Nothing slithered back down the slope to a point from which all could hear him.

"The village is destroyed," he cried. "If it were not, there are such great gaps in the thorn-growth that any enemy might walk through at will. There is no thorn in any of the other valleys. We must go back to the valley where our people live. This land has not been good for us. Even the babies die at birth or within a few days."

Big-Voice jumped to his feet on the steep surface, almost lost his balance, and caught at a boulder for support. "We have planted our gardens! Would you have us leave them and waste the work of a spring? Our houses can be repaired. I am leader here, and I say that we shall stay. More will die if they try to cross the mountains now. We lost too many in the winter!"

Many-Winters popped out from behind a rock formation. He stood a bit creakily. He gave Big-Voice a measured look, and then glanced at Fears-Nothing. Then he raised his own voice.

"I have been Teacher here since we left the valley. I know the things that Breaks-Twigs taught, before he died. Many were strange to my ears, and I did not believe his words. As years go by, I understand more and more.

"He said that though we are an old people who have good judgment and kindliness in our heritage, occasionally one is born who is contentious and stubborn and wrong-headed, but able to lead his fellows into folly. On the old world such are treated kindly but are isolated from those they might harm. There they lived as they chose, without endangering their fellows.

"Breaks-Twigs was educated in the caverns, before the earthquake. He was taught there, his mother and siblings are entombed there. Those who still held a direct link with our home world cautioned him that our situation had changed drastically, once we were wrecked here. Instead of a whole world of people, we have only a few. Even after two generations, we are still pitifully few. Then his teachers told Breaks-Twigs a terrible thing.

"It is better to kill a Gashta who leads his people into danger than to allow his misjudgment to cause their deaths or their grave danger. One Gashta dead is better than many Gashta dead. That is the thing they taught him, long ago in the caves."

There was a stunned silence. Though he could not see the faces of his people, Fears-Nothing knew that they must mirror the shock that he felt upon his own. Yet there was a stirring within him, something like recognition of a thing he had tried to forget or ignore.

"You are saying that Gashta must sometimes deliberately kill Gashta?" His voice almost descended into the deeper mode, so great was his distress.

Many-Winters shook his damp golden mane. "This is a thing that a Teacher does not say lightly. Only the greatest danger, the most terrible need brings it to light. Yet here we have a very grave thing, indeed. Big-Voice has misused the trust his people placed in him. His wisdom has been proven to be faulty, and his judgment untrustworthy. What can be more dangerous for a people than to have such a leader? And Big-Voice can persuade people into his ways of thinking. That is proven by the fact that we are still in this unprotected valley, after our first *kin-sha* warned us of the danger.

"Talk to any who refused to go, who turned to Big-Voice for leadership. The mothers of the three babies who were convinced that exposure would destroy their young ones. The older who were persuaded that their ills would grow worse. The timid who were frightened. At the root of every dissent, when Fears-Nothing was set aside, you can find a seed planted by Big-Voice. After what has happened today to our village, that says one thing only:

"Big-Voice is a danger to us all. We cannot afford such danger. Already we number many fewer than we numbered when we came here. A journey back across the mountains, whose heights hold the nests of the

gotza, whose valleys and forests hold *toshki-washa* and
so-shi-fazzu, is dangerous enough in itself. We cannot
afford to make that journey in the company of one so
dangerous to us, and so full of guilt. Does anyone speak
to defend this Gashta?''

There was a long silence, full of unspoken things.
Gashta looked at Gashta, mate to mate, child to parent.
In the midst of all, Big-Voice stood as if stricken speechless. His large eyes roved from place to place, as if he
could not believe that not one of the people would speak
in his behalf.

Yet no word came. They were a gentle people by
nature. Though willing to fight, given sufficient provo-
cation, they had never in their experience been guilty of
the deliberate killing of any creature, except for food or
in self-defense. The killing-impulse had been weeded
out of their stock for generations. No Gashta ever went
looking for trouble, and only the *zatku* had cause to
fear them.

But they were by no means gentle to the point of fool-
ishness.

''Harsh words,'' Fears-Nothing said to Many-
Winters, at last. ''Still, my heart speaks to me. There is
a thing that must be done. I know of no proper way to
go about it. Come out, Gashta, from your hiding
places, for we must talk of this thing. The beasts are
busy and out of sight above the streambank.''

As if by magic, the steep was dotted with furred
bodies. Damp, frightened, and miserable as they were,
the thirty members of the village formed a ragged circle,
as best they could, and faced one another to discuss this
important question.

Now Big-Voice seemed to comprehend the thing that
was being discussed. The dark color faded from his
face, leaving it pale and cold-looking in the gray light.
For once his big voice failed him. He sat wordlessly in
the center of the circle, his eyes flicking from one face to
another as the Gashta spoke in turn.

''It is a terrible thing, indeed,'' said one.

"But we chose wrongly. This one is ashamed that she listened to Big-Voice," said Cricket-Catcher, avoiding his eyes as she spoke. "I can see plainly that there is danger. I say that we must do . . . the thing that Many-Winters said."

They spoke, one by one, going about the circle to the left, as was customary. No dissenting voice was raised, although some questions were asked of Many-Winters. But all had been endangered. The evidence of Big-Voice's dangerous incompetence was plain to any who peeped over the embankment to look at their shattered homes. They knew that if Fears-Nothing had not gone out into the damp and watched over his ungrateful village, they would even now be rumbling in those big bellies, along with the thorn-greens.

Fears-Nothing said nothing more, nor did Many-Winters. Big-Voice could not. There were thirty votes for death.

"Who will do the thing?" asked Fears-Nothing, his manner subdued.

"I told you the old words. It is my duty, as Teacher here, and as eldest," said Many-Winters.

Taking his *zatku-hodda* in hand, he motioned to Big-Voice. As if stunned, the burly Gashta leaned forward onto the wet rock of the streambed, exposing his neck. One sharp blow rendered him unconscious, and a second broke his neck. He jerked upon the flints, his eyes empty of the thing that had been himself. When he was still, many of his fellows turned aside and were sick, but all knew that justice had been done.

They put him into a grave-pit with all proper mourning.

"It is that he was sick," said Many-Winters, over the grave. "He was not a bad Gashta by his own will. Some strangeness twisted his thinking."

It was the only possible epitaph.

The remnant of the larger party that had come into the valley so hopefully set out to go home again. As they crossed the pass, that evening, the sun came out, lighting their bodies to a brilliance of gold. Fears-Nothing, at the end of the line of march, stopped and looked back into the valley, at the *so-shi-fazzu* still browsing among the ruins of their homes.

Then he turned his face southward, toward the other Valley where the rest of the Gashta survived on this hostile world. He was sad that he took with him so little of value to show for the time spent here.

Yet this straggle of Gashta bore with them a gift for their people, though none quite realized that. They had set a precedent that would remove from their bloodlines any individuals lacking in mental balance, and that was to prove a valuable thing for all the Gashta on Zarathustra.

iv.

Summer lay over the valley of the Gashta. In the forest that rimmed the clearing fruit-bearing trees were heavy, their branches drooping within the reach of even the youngest of the Gashta, and the tandavines were thick with their succulent beans. It should have been a season to fill the teacher of this generation of the Gashta with satisfaction.

Yet Sun-Blossom was filled with unease. In the years since Breaks-Twigs' death, the population had grown and grown again. Those who went north had returned to their home valley, and those who had gone south had not been heard of again. Births had been frequent, and the infants had been healthy. Few had been lost to the coughing sickness in the past winters. The valley was filled with the Gashta, and, even with the abundant harvest from the gardens and the native plants and trees, it would be difficult to store enough to bring so many through the winter. The last weeks before spring would be, she knew, very hard. Very hard.

Sun-Blossom was faced with a dilemma of great proportions. Once again the *Kampushi-sha* were agitating among themselves, gathering the courage to go out past the mountains, on their own. Groups had left all summer. Some had returned periodically, bringing word that the *zatku* had spread all through the country between the mountain ranges. Hunting was very good in the lands south of the valley. Others would go, she knew in her heart.

It was her duty to teach the *Haigun-sha*, keeping the people here in the place where the ship had come down. Only here could those future generations of the Home-World Gashta know to look for their lost kindred. It was her duty, written upon her mind and heart by her training and her heredity, to hold her kind together while they waited for rescue.

Yet she knew that such overcrowding must lead, in the end, to sickness, starvation, and death. And perhaps to worse things. Already, the *Kampushi-sha* were beginning to quarrel among themselves, and even the *Haigun-sha* seemed irritable and short-tempered. The discipline that had lasted through so many generations of hardship would crack, she could see plainly, beneath the weight of over-population.

The sun was almost down. She knew that the present Stargazer would be sitting atop his rock, engaged in his nightly duty. She wound her way through the maze of paths beneath the thorntree barrier and found herself standing at the foot of his rock.

He was there, his small face turned upward toward the spot where the blue star traveled its deliberate route about its white companion. He was a silhouette against the last-light of the sky, so still, so intent, that she was, at first, hesitant about interrupting him. But they must talk. Both had known it for some time.

"Stargazer!" she hissed.

He looked down, searching for her in the shadowy

place at the foot of the rock. "*Noho-washa?* It is that one who is teacher to the Gashta?"

"This one is here, Haigun. Will you allow this one to climb the rock and talk with you? There is that which must be said."

He breathed a shuddering sigh. "It is known to me. Come up and sit, Cousin. It would be well if we could talk, now, with our fathers and mothers. They were nearer than we to the beginnings, to the teachings of those who still had the things in the cave. We have lost much and will lose, I am afraid, far more. You came about that, I think."

"It is so. And all that we have lost is only a small-small thing, compared with the thing that now is happening, Cousin. Matters have changed in ways that our ancestors could not foresee. It is in my heart that we must now go against all the things that we were taught."

"And let them go out." His words were not a question.

"But what of the old teachings? What of the rescue that will come?" The words hung in the air between them. They sat silent upon the rock for a time, wrestling with their consciences and their training.

"Ahh, Stargazer," she said at last, "that is a thing that our fathers kept secret from all except those they trained to follow them. Only we two, in the Valley, now know that any who might come from the Home World seeking us have not yet been born. So many generations lie between the ones who must find a way to live now and those who may be rescued! It frightens me to think of it."

"It is a terrible thing to know. But this one has thought on this matter for many turns of the moons. Those who want to go southward know that the *zatku* have migrated in that direction. Wild foods grow in abundance, and even the winters are warm. Those who have traveled there have seen these things and brought back that word to us who must remain here.

"Look about you, *Noho-washa*. Gashta are not quarrelsome and petty. They do not duel over imagined slights or places on a feather-tree branch. Yet that has been happening, again and again. For two summers it has been true, and this warm season has made it quite clear that it will only get worse. When our people are crowded, they become unhappy. They must go someplace, and we know that north is not good for Gashta. Those who returned learned that."

"If any are to survive the long years as Gashta," the Teacher said slowly, "we must allow them to scatter. Indeed, we cannot force them to remain here. That is not the way of our people. It is only the long tradition of obedience to the *Haigun* that has kept them thus far. And yet there is much danger in that, also. Those who have left the valley for more than the span of a journey have learned, to their sorrow, that this world is unfit for our kind. The lack of children dooms any hope of making a real home away from this valley. What of that?"

He did not answer. She could see him now as only a shadow against the rock, dim in the starlight. One moon was down past the trees. The other was not yet visible.

She wound her small fingers in her lap. Her throat seemed too dry for speech, yet she managed to say, "We must stay here, you and I, together with all the *Haigun-sha*. We are the descendants of the crew, the technicians, the disciplined ones. We can and will hold to the old teachings. That is the thing that has held most of the Gashta here for so long as this. But the *Kampushi-sha*—I ache for them. Theirs is not a heritage of standing in place, obeying the dictates of duty. They are the children of those adventuresome ones who went out to colonize a new world. Their very blood forces them from us.

"We must let the *Kampushi-sha* go."

The sound he made was less one of disagreement than one of pain. His hand touched her furry shoulder, his fingers gripping hard. She understood. His distress needed company.

Yet when he spoke, his voice was calm and natural. "We have known for two years that this must be so. I have spoken with all of the elders, as you have. Some agree with this decision, some feel it a betrayal of all that Gashta believe. Yet only we can see the true picture. Only we know that our time here will be measured in generations rather than in years. And only we can send forth the *Kampushi-sha* in such a way that they do not go as exiles but as members, still, of the family of Gashta.

"For they must return, from time to time, to this Valley. For a summer, or a year. If they do not, it is possible that they may die away completely, and we must make this most clear to their minds. Their small ones will need the teaching that only you can give. They will need the thing in this place that makes our babies live and not die. We must gather them together and make this plain to them. Those who have been angry at being kept here when their instinct told them to wander will have the cause of their irritation removed."

"Or they will be angry at being sent away. Gashta nature is far from perfect, Stargazer." She patted his hand. Then she stood. "The time has come. This thing has troubled our hearts and the hearts of all the old ones for too long. I am relieved that you, too, see the need . . . yet I would wish that the need did not exist.

"I shall call the Gashta together, even the hunters who are in the mountains. The old habit will bring them at our word, for their deepest instincts bid them respect those who were responsible for their lives, long ago on that lost Ship. Their minds do not remember, but their hearts do."

He looked up at her, his big eyes glimmering in the starlight. "True. The Spiral—think how it persists, even in the youngest of small ones who have never been told of the Home System. There it is, the nebula that held our sun and our world, patterned in shell or pebbles or twigs. Other matters are also a part of our people. Let us hope that they will listen to our words."

His manner told her that he wanted to be left, now, to his watching. Sun-Blossom slipped quietly from the rock and turned her steps back into the thorn-maze. The task was begun, and this discussion of such a painful matter had been the hardest thing that she had ever done. All her instincts told her to cling to the old way, to hold to all the Gashta and the hope that might come from the stars.

THE NAMING OF BAD-THING-KILLER

It is that one hunter walked away across the mountains. He was called Strong-Arm, and he was large and brave and wanted to see the lands beyond the high places. He took his *zatku-hodda* and his net-bag made of bark fiber. He set a new handle into his stone axe and slung it from a cord on his shoulder. He said farewell to his fellow hunters and to the one who was his true mate.

This is the story of Bad-Thing-Killer!

He climbed up the ridge into the great trees, and he was all alone, for few of the hunters went there. He looked up and up into those tall trees and he saw Gozzo smiling beyond their topmost branches. Far away, he could hear a sound, the cry of a *toshki-washa*, and his heart burned within him.

This is the story of Bad-Thing-Killer!

Never had a single Gashta hunted for that beast. Never had any Gashta wanted to find it! But this one was dizzy with moonlight and with his own daring. He ran toward the spot where the cry had sounded.

And in a glade of moonlight stood a *toshki-washa*, standing above its prey. It snarled, tearing the meat of the *hatta-zosa* it had killed, and it expected no attack.

This is the story of Bad-Thing-Killer!

Strong-Arm ran through the ferns, his sharp axe ready, his heart prepared to meet death.

Ai! Ai!

And he crashed through the ferns and struck the *toshki-washa* a terrible blow between its eyes. Its dark-brown fur ran with blood, down its pointed snout, onto its teeth. Its claws were busy at once, but the Gashta was not idle.

He struck with his axe and his strong arms, again and

again. The *toshki-washa* staggered, its head dropping
low, its paws uncertain upon the ground. Then it fell at
the Gashta's feet, and he killed it with a blow to the
neck.

Never had such a thing been done! Who would
believe?

He took his flint knife from his net-bag. It was a
terrible task, yet he skinned that beast from paws to
head, from tail to throat. He returned to his village with
it and stretched that hide upon a rock to dry, so that all
Gashta might see.

This is the story of Bad-Thing-Killer!

He went out into the other lands. No one has done a
greater thing than this.

V.

There was much excitement among the Gashta. Seldom,
now, were they called together by the *Haigun*. The
word, coming from the Teacher, had held no hint of the
thing that brought them together, and many held anger
in their hearts, feeling that they were going to be instructed to stay here in this crowded place. All their im-
pulses rebelled against that notion.

Bad-Thing-Killer was angrier than most. He had his
family group convinced that they must go out over the
barrier-mountains, into those southern places where
zatku flourished and none disputed over a place to live.
Not that many disputed with him. He was some hand's
width taller than any of his fellows; as tall, the Teacher
told him, as the ancestors who had come in the ship.

He doubted the tale of the ship, that of the cave, and
more than anything else that of those who would come
from the stars to take the people away to some *hoksu-
mitto* in the sky. This valley, where his people had lived

for so many generations, was a poor, cramped place, far inferior to many that he had seen on hunting expeditions into the places between the ranges. And once he had gone, alone, over the mountains that crossed from range to range. The journey had been terrible, for predators were many along those steep slopes. But on the other side . . . there had been a *hoksu-mitto*, indeed! One that could be seen and enjoyed by the eyes in his own head, now, not in some magical time-to-come.

He was determined to go there. Sharp-Teeth, his present mate, was as bold as he, and as eager to go away from the thronging Gashta. His brother, with his mate and their little ones, and his own two, who were half-grown, made up a group of good size. He felt that they could live and flourish until such time as the younger would go off to form their own groups.

His family stood together, jostled by others taking their places in the wide space that stretched upward from the *Haigun's* rock. The air about them shrilled with comments and questions and exclamations, as the entire people of the valley squeezed together to hear Stargazer speak.

The *Haigun* climbed onto his rock, at last, and stood looking down at his people. His face was sad. His eyes, Bad-Thing-Killer thought with surprise, seemed filled with tears. Seeing him, the throng quieted politely, waiting for what he might say.

To the astonishment of all, the *Haigun* spoke in the deep mode. Unaccustomed to those tones, the listeners strained their ears and focused attention upon his words. They had almost forgotten, indeed, that the people could speak so, and some of the infants were frightened and had to be cuddled or fed to quiet them.

"For the first time in many passages of seasons," Stargazer began, "this one has called you into one place to hear. Some have spoken to me, over the past moon passages, of the problems that have come into being here in our valley. One of those has been the Teacher, Sun-Blossom. Yet I have known that something must be

done to aid our people. Something unusual. Indeed,
something that is against all the teaching that we received from our ancestors.

"We are too crowded. It makes not only for unrest
but for famine, when the winter grows long and supplies
diminish. We grew thin in the past cold season. There
are more of us now, and the very old and the very young
will not survive another like the last.

"Even worse is the quarrelling among ourselves.
Some have even raised their *zatku-hodda* against their
neighbors, and this is a thing that our people have never
been guilty of doing. In the Home-World, when the
people grow to be many, some have always gone away
to colonies among the stars. We are a people who need
much space about us. In this valley we no longer have
such space."

The crowded mass of furred bodies stirred restlessly.
This was not, indeed, the thing they had expected to
hear, and they were thrown off balance. Bad-Thing-
Killer was puzzled, his anger changing to something like
apprehension as the *Haigun* went on.

"There are those among you who have determined to
go out, with their families. Before this time, this one
and the Teacher have always tried to dissuade you from
such ventures. Our impulse was to do the same this
time. But it would be wrong. If some of the people are
to survive to meet our rescuers, we must disperse. We of
the *Haigun-sha* will stay here, and when our kinfolk
come to find us we will tell them that others live upon
this world. You know us. You know that we will abide
here, held by our duty, for as long as we exist."

There was another stir among the people. A voice
came from the crowd.

"You are sending the *Kampushi-sha* away?" Bad-
Thing-Killer found to his surprise that the voice was his
own. His heart, angry before, was now sore at the
thought of being sent away from the place that was,
after all, the home of every Gashta.

"No. Oh, no. Who would send them? Who could
send our own people from the place that is theirs? But

there are those who want to go, and I speak now to them. There are things that they must know, for we will not be with them to remind them.

"It was the thought of our fathers that something in the soil of this valley gave strength to us as a people. For that reason, it would be well for those who leave us to plan to return, from time to time. Spending a summer, perhaps. Visiting their kindred. Breathing the air and eating the fruits of the soil. Teach your young ones to do this, also. It may be most important to your families."

He paused, and the people spoke rapidly among themselves. The shrilling of their voices filled his ears, but most of the comment he could catch was favorable. He had taken the rebellious elements by surprise, and that was good.

He hated the thought of ever being forced to kill one of his people. But without relief this situation would lead to that, as the situation in the north had led to the death of Big-Voice. He wondered for the thousandth time if the action related by the people who had returned from the north had been the best of good things or the worst of terrible ones.

"Do not forget . . ." they quieted again as he spoke . . . "to teach your young ones that our help will come. It may be very long in coming. But it will come. When their hearts tell them to set the Spiral into their *shokka-washa*, that will remind them. Help will come. Help will come. We must continue the Gashta here, as well as we may, that there will be someone here to greet those helpers when they arrive."

He looked about at the different families, standing together in groups, their big eyes focused upon him. "There is another thing. A thing that we have almost lost. I will ask the Teacher to say it to you."

Sun-Blossom climbed onto the rock, as Stargazer sat. She took a deep breath.

"Gashta we all are. We have given ourselves names, according to the things we do best. Yet those are not the names of our families who came upon the Ship. Before you go out, those who are going, I will say for a last time the names of the families who came as colonists upon the ship of our people.

"The Family Ginzu.

"The Family Hashi-so.

"The Family Zashi. The Family Taki-yo; the Family Hasa . . ."

Bad-Thing-Killer realized, astonished, that that was the name of his own family. He did not consciously remember being told that his was the family Hasa, but it was there, inside him, as a seed is curled and hidden inside a nut. By the time that he remembered to listen again, the Teacher had finished her name-telling.

"These names will be forgotten, as time goes by. Perhaps even the names we call ourselves now will be forgotten. This is a large and dangerous planet. Almost every beast upon it is far larger and stronger than we. Life has been hard. It will probably become harder. But now, for this moment, let us remember our ancestors and be thankful for their fortitude. Without it, we would be one with those who perished in the ship and those who smothered in the caverns. We come of strong stock. Our people are wise and ingenious. We will live to greet those who will come. Be sure of that."

She stepped down from the rock. There was a moment of silence as the listeners thought upon what she had said. Then there came a swift hiss of approbation.

The *Haigun* rose again. "Any who want to talk with me or with the Teacher may do so. We will give aid and supplies and tools to those who are going. We will welcome back those who return. May you fare well, Gashta." He turned and was gone from the rock.

Bad-Thing-Killer looked about at his family. They looked as stunned as he felt.

vi.

It was a very strange sensation. Sharp-Teeth knew that
her mate and her children felt it as strongly as she did.
As the valley grew small behind them she found herself
looking back at every opportunity, and she noted that
Bad-Thing-Killer and Axe-Maker and his mate Snail-
Catcher did the same. Even the small ones peered back
over the shoulders of those who carried them, seeking a
last glimpse of the place that had been their home for so
very long.

The easy slopes were behind them now. Ahead were
steep cliffs rubbled with scree, planes of stone that lay at
precarious angles, and narrow ledges of flint that gave
only the most uncertain footing to those who risked the
heights. The older children found it all very exciting,
adding to their parents' anxiety, for they tended to want
to scamper ahead, their small feet certain on the uneasy
paths. As the party came out onto an apron of rock that
led, in turn, onto a terribly slender ledge-path, Bad-
Thing-Killer called them all to a halt.

"Now it is that we must go cautiously. Nut,
Shell . . ." his two sons came to stand beside him . . .
"you can no longer be children. The time has come
when we need for you to be adults, taking your part of
the responsibility for the little ones. There are only a bit
less than two hands of us, now. We need one to go
ahead to find the way and to warn of beasts or of *gotza*.
We need one to come behind, seeing that none of us
stray or straggle. The three smallest must now be carried
all the time, for a fall from these heights would kill
them. The six of us who are grown must be a whole
village, in ourselves.

"Remember," he looked into their big green eyes,
and the two stared back at him, awed by their sudden
elevation to adult status, "we must depend upon your
good sense and your courage. Can you be depended
upon?"

Nut scratched his diminutive nose. Shell rubbed one

foot against the back of his other leg, ruffling the fur.
They looked both proud and frightened, and Sharp-
Teeth felt a moment's pang at cutting short their span of
childish freedom.

Then Nut said, "We will do our best, *Pa-ha-izza*. But
we may forget, sometimes."

Their father nodded. "Then we will go thus. I will go
ahead, for I have slain the *toshki-washa* and am best
able to manage if I meet anything dangerous. Axe-
Maker will come behind, keeping watch over all. Sharp-
Teeth will carry the bundles and keep her flint axe in her
hand, for she is the best warrior of us all. Nut and Shell
will carry the smallest one, and Snail-Catcher will carry
her plump little Fruit. So. Take your places."

As unusual as it was for *Kampushi-sha* of any age or
sex to accept orders without question, these found no
cause for quarrelling with Bad-Thing-Killer over this.
He had traveled this path before. He had slain the
toshki-washa. And the arrangements were completely
sensible, a matter that all Gashta accepted at any time.
In a very short time, the line of laden people moved forward, following as Bad-Thing-Killer led.

Sharp-Teeth found herself very proud of her mate.
He had much more ability than had ever been needful,
back there in the safety of the valley. She felt that their
group would succeed in the southern lands, whatever
happened to those others that came behind them. She
would be a bit saddened when the time came for them to
go with other mates into other groups.

There came a shrill word from up ahead. Bad-Thing-
Killer had gone around a buttress of rock that kneed out
from the cliff. At that point the path was more a thing
in the mind than a certainty underfoot, and Sharp-Teeth
crept carefully to the spot and peered around it, looking
for Bad-Thing-Killer.

On the other side of the obstruction the path curled
back sharply into a hollow in the cliff-face. The ledge
was littered with loose pebbles and flints, and it seemed
to be crumbling a bit. She heard a click and looked up.

Her mate had gained the far side of the uncertain

part. Now he stood braced in a sort of chimney. In his hand was a ball of the strong bark cord they made from the under-layer that grew on the feather-tree. She understood at once what he intended, and she lay on her side on the path, curled partway about the stone barrier. Both her hands were now free for the catch.

The ball sailed across the space between them, to land in her grasp, and she slithered backward, sat, and turned to the rest of the family. One by one she saw them around the narrow spot, from which point they went forward steadied by the cord that Bad-Thing-Killer had anchored with a twist about a spur of stone at his side.

She could not see around the corner, and her heart thudded uncomfortably as she envisioned her two sons, burdened with the squirming young ones, making their way around the dangerous point ahead. But she snapped her small, sharp teeth together and endured, anchoring the cord at her end with the weight of her body and the strength of her grip.

Once there came a strong tug, as if someone had almost fallen. She hooked her toes around a small boulder and clung tightly. But the tug eased, and she was able to breathe again. Then there came two sharp jerks on the line, and she knew that she must go to join the rest.

When she reached the stone knee, she had the ball of cord rolled to that point. Bracing herself, she tossed it back across the dizzy space to Axe-Maker, who had relieved Bad-Thing-Killer at the other end of the cord. Then, sure-footed and fearless, now that she knew her children were safe, she crossed the crazy way, feeling loose rock slither under her feet and plummet down the side of the mountain. But now she was within arm's reach of Axe-Maker. And now she was safe on the wider area in which he stood. Beyond, scrambling up a wide sloping space from which the debris had washed or fallen, she could see Nut and Shell burdened with the smallest of the little ones. Evidently, the perilous passage across the spot behind them had frightened them into stillness. It was a good thing, for while the present path looked safer than that other, the drop below was even farther.

Bad-Thing-Killer was just visible at the top of the slope. He was clinging to a scrubby bush and watching the others make their way up to his level. Beyond him there seemed to be, once again, forest. Perhaps even a flat space on which to stretch themselves for some much-needed rest. Sharp-Teeth edged past Axe-Maker and went up the incline, her small fingers and toes finding cracks to cling to as she went.

When all had climbed out of the gorge and stood on the mounded crest of the mountain, Sharp-Teeth looked back. The valley was a tiny paler patch among the circling trees. Beyond it was the immense shape of the mountain beneath which the old ones were entombed. No person looking down from any peak about would have been able to tell, if he had not known already, that intelligent people lived down there.

The stream was a faint glimmer of brightness under the late-afternoon sky. She thought of the sharp tang of its water. Perhaps they would never again taste the waters of home. Almost, she regretted this terribly important step that the family was taking. Then she thought of the stresses of the crowded ways beneath the thorntrees. Not enough room for huts. Not enough food. Too many people, elbow-by-elbow. No, it was a good thing, this outgoing. Come what might, it had to be a good thing.

She felt a touch at her elbow. Bad-Thing-Killer was at her side, and she put her arm about his waist, feeling the crisp curl of his fur against her hand. He, too, was looking downward with sadness in his face. She smiled sidewise at him.

His hand moved in her mane, touching her ear, her cheek. They stood together at the edge of space, the dividing-place of two very different lives. The loneliness they felt was touched with a bit of fear. Fear of what might come. Fear of being forced to return, unsuccessful, to their peers.

Huddled into a mass of golden fur, the two little people looked back for the last time. Then they turned together and took their places in the line of family that awaited their coming.

The walkers trudged away in the dimming light of late afternoon. And Bad-Thing-Killer, at the head of the group, was smiling. Sharp-Teeth knew that, though she could not see him. She knew, for she was smiling, still, herself.

vii.

To a pair of eyes barely twelve inches above the ground, the world on top of the mountain-ridge seemed a terribly large place. Shell, being the younger of the two brothers, felt very strange at his new place in the family, his new place in the world, and his new sleeping-place beneath a bush. Not to mention the fact that he was used to sleeping by day, as was most of his family.

But Bad-Thing-Killer had explained, before their journey began, that the paths that they must follow, now, were steep and dangerous. Light was necessary, if they were to pass over into the gentler country beyond without losing any of their number. They would return to hunting at night and gardening by moonlight when it was safe to do that. For now, they must reverse their habits.

Shell should have been tired. He had walked and climbed and scrambled all day, most of that time carrying the heavy plumpness of little Pebble in his aching arms. They still ached, along with his legs and his short neck, but his big green eyes would not close in sleep. They stared upward, through the bush, at a small patch of starry sky visible through the distant branches of the trees that cloaked the top of the mountain. Those branches were touched with silvery light, for the moon that his people called Gozzo was high above, and Tansha, its companion, was low in the west.

The small person shivered. Summer or no, it was chill at night on this high place. Nut, huddled against his back, grunted and squirmed closer. His warmth was good, and Shell felt somewhat comforted. He would have preferred to burrow between his parents, feeling the greater warmth of their furred bodies, but he knew that they would not allow that. Once he reached his sixth summer, he had been firmly, if lovingly, ejected from that comforting nest. Now he nestled his back to his brother, turning onto his side in order to get the most benefit from their closeness.

Axe-Maker came into his line of vision. The eyes of the Gashta were keen, even at night, and Shell could see the lines on his face, the curly fur on the backs of his hands. Axe-Maker's eyes were closed, though he was supposed to be keeping watch for the first hours of the night.

Shell hissed. Nut, behind him, stirred uneasily, but Axe-Maker dozed on. The young one wrinkled his nose, puzzled as to what he should do now. It was not safe to sleep without a guard. Here there was no thorntree barrier. There were no flimsy but comforting wicker walls to protect the family.

Shell strained his ears. There were many hands-of-hands of sounds. Trillings of insects, abrupt cheerps from the smaller versions of the *gotza* that lived in treetops and ate seeds instead of flesh, crackles and crunchings from the forest about them that marked the goings and comings of small beasts at their hunting. And something else. Something that he had never heard in all his short life in the valley.

It was almost too deep a noise for even his acute Gashta ears to detect. More of a moan than a howl, less a cry than a grunt, it sounded through the wood, still far away enough so that its vibrations did not waken the adults from their exhausted slumber.

Shell stirred. Nut's arms tightened about his waist, and his sharp chin burrowed into Shell's shoulder, but his brother still slept. Shell knew that he must get up and wake the others. The sound was getting nearer, and, quiet as it was, it made his fur stand erect and bristly. This was no little predator. This was one of those that his kind still discovered from time to time on their hunting expeditions. New to the Gashta, perhaps, but all the same in their love of the flesh of the furred ones.

Shell could hear undisturbed breathing all about him. He was the only one of all the family awake, afraid. So afraid that he found it difficult to move. But he managed at last, drawing himself away from Nut's grasp and sitting up beneath their sheltering bush.

He had opened his mouth to give the cry of alarm when his eyes focused on a spot behind Axe-Maker. Two bright eyes, touched with moonlight, were also gazing at the sleeping shape of his uncle.

"Ayeeeeeh!" shrilled Shell, flying up from his crouch with his small flint-tipped spear in his hand.

Without thinking, he charged toward the beast, which had paused in its stealthy approach toward Axe-Maker and was gazing at its tiny assailant with surprise. Axe-Maker, waked too quickly and fuddled with sleep, tightened his grip on his axe and turned to follow Shell, as Bad-Thing-Killer and the two females woke and rose, within the same instant.

Shell, his shrill voice still shouting warning, was almost upon the beast. And it was a huge one, from the viewpoint of a Gashta. Eighteen inches high at the shoulder, it had a scaly hide that covered a stocky shape that must weigh at least forty pounds. Its leathery ears were cocked forward, and a mouth filled with white daggers was already opening to devour the rash young one who seemed so eager to become a midnight snack.

Axe-Maker, seeing the beast clearly for the first time, roared in the deep mode and dashed past Shell, swinging his axe to smash against the pointed nose. Shell, pushed aside by one brisk hand as his uncle passed him, sprawled into a bush. He sat up immediately and

watched what was happening, his huge eyes gleaming
green in the dim light. Before he was altogether settled,
his father, mother, and aunt ran past.

Now the strange beast had stopped, its head down, its
bright eyes glancing this way and that as the Gashta
circled it, pricking its tough hide with spears and
gashing it with blows of their axes. Every one of them
was shouting in the deep mode, which seemed to be-
wilder the thing. As Bad-Thing-Killer came near its
head, it swung toward him with unexpected speed, the
curved teeth reaching for the Gashta's shoulder. Sharp-
Teeth caught it behind the ear with her axe, stunning
it for an instant, and Snail-Catcher and Axe-Maker
attacked it from the other side with all their might.

Shell, excited beyond control, rose from his place of
safety and ran forward again, ignoring his mother's
sharp command to stay out of the way. Straight and
true, his small spear headed for one of the gleaming eyes
with all of Shell's weight and velocity behind it. At the
last moment, he leaped, and the point buried itself in the
socket, going through the eye and gristle, into the brain
behind.

The creature jerked, standing. It flung its head back,
throwing Shell, who still held onto the haft of the spear
with grim purpose, away into the bushes again. Then it
fell as if its legs had given way beneath its weight. With
a few more jerks and a spatter of blood from the head
that tried to toss once more, the thing died.

The family stood stunned at the suddenness of the
battle's end. Shell crawled out of a prickly growth, rub-
bing a long scratch on his cheek. He looked at the big
thing that he had attacked alone, then had been so
foolish as to attack yet again. He began to shiver. Then
he began to cry.

By this time all the children had waked and huddled
together into one furry heap. Fruit began to sob in company with her cousin, and the two babies looked as if
they intended to do the same. Nut crawled out of the
pile of young ones and went to his mother. But she had

already cuddled Shell to her side, and he was wiping away the un-Gashta-like tears on her fur.

Bad-Thing-Killer was examining the beast.

"What do we call this one?" he asked at last, looking about at the family members. "It is not a thing that we have seen before, and it is our right to give it a name."

There was no answer. Shell, speechless still, stared at the lump of dead flesh with wide eyes.

Bad-Thing-Killer looked at his younger son with both pride and disapproval.

"It is a good thing to be courageous," he said at last. "But it is not a good thing to be foolish. A loud cry would have done as well. So, for you I will name this creature. It will be called *nozzo-fazzu*. Always-Run. Remember that, Shell, until you are much older than you are now. When I asked you to be an adult, I did not intend for you to do such dangerous things."

He turned to his brother. "Axe-Maker, when we find a spot to stay for a time, I would take it well if you would make an axe for my son, here. It is time that he had a good weapon, a man's weapon. If he must behave as an adult, he must be armed as one. He must also be given the name he has earned. His blow was true and sure, and he did not falter. His name is Strikes-Well." Bad-Thing-Killer looked at his family, and all nodded their agreement.

Shell's heart thumped wildly. He could see the envy in Nut's eyes and the awe in the faces of the small ones. Filled with an unnameable mixture of feelings, he followed his mother back to the sleeping-bush, where she laid him down with Nut and the other little ones.

"Now sleep, Strikes-Well. It is good that you did not, before. But now you must, if you are to do your work tomorrow. *Aki-noho-so!*"

When she spoke in that tone, it was always best to do as she said. Strikes-Well closed his eyes. The warmth of the other children filled him with peace. Soon he slept.

viii.

Zatku-Cracker woke suddenly. *What?* His pinkish ears twitched as he listened intently for the thing that had pulled him from sleep.

Without moving, he looked about at his family. All were drooping, relaxed, in their various sleeping-spots. Not one had fallen from the treetop they had chosen for the day's rest. With a lithe wriggle, he turned and risked an eye's-width of himself to peer at the ground below. Except for dapples of sunlight, the narrow track below was empty. Not even a *hatta-zosa* rooted in the mulch of the forest floor.

The sun was high. Even the insects had quieted in the noonday heat, so Zatku-Cracker could easily detect every sound for more than a mile around his position. Only an occasional rustle as the little *zeeto* bustled through the underlayer of the wood, seeking for stray seeds and the smaller insects. Every sound he perceived he was able to identify as something not immediately dangerous to his family.

But what had waked him, here in the middle of his time for sleep? He sat up, very quietly so as not to disturb his mate, who slept on the other side of the slender bole of the feather-tree. His reddish-golden fur was rumpled with his squirming, and he began smoothing it with his hands, combing out any tangles with his nails.

His mind was not on what he was doing. He was no worrier. Indeed, Fruit-Finder, his mate for the time, thought that he worried entirely too little. Since the last birth, another stillborn daughter, she had been quieter than he liked, turned into her own thought. Thinking, he was certain, of something that would disturb him, once she made it clear to him.

He had to admit to himself that she had good reason to be concerned. In all the seasons that they had been together, only one child had joined them. Four had been dead at birth. One had been born alive, and had struggled for breath for a day and a night, then it had quieted and died. Only Seed had survived.

For some reason, the memory was more troubling now, in the heat-stillness of this day when he should have been sleeping, than it had seemed at the times of those deaths. He searched his memory. They had traveled a short space with four other groups of the Gashta in the past season. In those groups, only three young ones lived. But in the group that had no young alive at all, there had been a very old Gashta whose fur had become streaked with white.

Her name had been Fruit, and she had been skillful in many things that most of her people had forgotten. And she had told tales, to which his family had listened with awe as they hunkered in the circle about her.

"There is a valley," she had said, "where others like us still live. We were told, so my father and mother told me, that we who went out into the southern ways should return from time to time. There is something in the valley that is good for Gashta. And there is always welcome there for us. I am going back, if I live so long. Those in this group go also, for without offspring we will die away to nothing. It would be well if all of you who listen to me now were to tell others that you meet of this thing. In the north, past the mountains that block the wooded lands, there is a *great* mountain. The valley is at its foot. Remember!"

He knew that Fruit-Finder, his mate, had told the tale many times. He had not really thought of it again until now. And at this moment, safe in a tree while his family slept about him, he felt a compulsion rising within him.

That was what had waked him! The need to go back, as old Fruit had said. That valley was calling to him. It was filled with Gashta, Fruit had said, and that was a thing that he found hard to envision. Never in his entire life had he seen more than four or five hands of his people gathered together in the same place. Could there be many-many Gashta? He felt that he must see.

Once he realized that he had become determined to make the journey, he found his eyes growing heavy again. He lay back upon his comfortable branch and dozed. When he woke, the sun was down against the most distant treetops, and the rest of his family was stirring. Fruit-Finder had joined him on his side of the tree-bole and was sitting with her hand upon his ankle.

He looked into her face. Her big eyes stared back at him, sad, sad, in that smooth countenance. He touched her hand, laid his head against hers and touched cheeks.

Why had he not seen that she was suffering? Had he slept, even while hunting and killing *zatku* and climbing after the round-fruit?

"I am awake," he said, and she looked surprised.

"I see it," she answered.

"No. This one is really awake. This one has seen—or has been shown, something while you slept. You remember the tale of that other Fruit . . . the tale you tell all we meet?"

Her green eyes kindled with excitement. "This one does, indeed, remember."

"I woke while the sun was high, and that tale came back to me. And all our little ones, their faces came back to me, though I would have thought that ones seen so briefly would be lost with time. It came to me that our family does not grow. Only you and I and Seed and your brother Spear-Maker have hunted together for many seasons, and we gain no new members. It is time that we went back to that valley. If it does, indeed, exist. If we can find it. Something must be done, or we will find ourselves alone, when we grow old."

Though she had not moved, as far as he could tell, her entire body was different. Energy began to flow from her. Her very fur seemed to stand erect and alive. Her hands clutched at his arm, gripping tightly as she spoke.

"It does exist. It must, for where else could we have come from in the beginning? We do not prosper in these forests, as do the *gotza* and the *hatta-zosa* and the *toshki-washa*. Things thrive in their own places. We do not thrive, and so we are in a place that is not ours. Is that not good sense?"

He puzzled over her words for a bit. Then he nodded.

"It is good sense," he admitted. "Can we find that valley, do you think?"

She looked at him, surprised. "Have you ever known a Gashta who did not know where he was? Even Seed could lead us back over every step we have made since he was born. A Gashta can find what is needful . . . and that valley is known to many of our kind. We will find it. Be certain of that."

She took his hand again. Then she trilled to the other two, who came agilely through the branches to listen to her words.

So impassioned was she that they were on their way before Gozzo had reached the treetops. Having nothing except their *zatku-hodda* and their axes, they had no need for packing or house-minding. Where their wishes led them, they could go, and go they did. For such small creatures, they moved along the low paths made by the little natives of this world with amazing speed.

There was much sense in traveling or hunting or insect-hunting by night instead of by day. The *gotza* could not see well at night, and they seldom hunted then. The *toshki-washa* moved principally at twilight and at daybreak, and so were less likely to be encountered. And the *so-shi-fazzu* was strictly a diurnal beast. The lesser animals, the night-hunters, were the terrors of others of their own size or less, but the Gashta dealt with those without a problem.

Indeed, one such little predator made a midnight meal for the family that now was traveling northward. They did not even take the time to sit in a circle for their food. They chopped off portions as large as they could comfortably carry with their axes and gnawed cheerfully on the dripping bits as they went.

Once the plan had been proposed, it had been strangely easy to agree upon it, Zatku-Cracker thought, as he pattered along. In no other matter that he could remember had it been so easy to get his family moving together . . . and with so little delay. It was as if something had been calling to them all, though they had

not known it. Once they recognized that call, they had
turned to follow it without hesitation.

His *zatku-hodda* was across his shoulder, with his
axe. The meat was warm and full in his belly. He could,
he knew, go in any direction and find there more meat,
other families, trees to sleep in, streams to splash in, interesting things to do and to learn. Why did he now
trudge wearily along the paths that led most nearly
northward?

He had learned when very young that it was not a wise
thing to worry overmuch, to allow life to become too
serious. Play was as good as food, when the time was
right for it. Joy was better than worry and much better
for the digestion.

The stream that his feet splashed through—there were
long stretches of smooth soapstone in it, glimmering in
the light of the two moons, that now were well up the
sky. It would be fine to stop and slide there for awhile.

Yet he felt no need for that. And to his surprise even
Seed did not look twice at the tempting expanse. On any
other night, the young one would have howled at being
taken away from such a playground. Now he marched
on at his mother's side, his small *zatku-hodda* at a
jaunty angle over his tiny shoulder. He stopped, with
the rest, for just long enough to wash the blood from
their fur and to drink deeply.

When they were moving again, an amazing thought
came to Zatku-Cracker. If the valley of myth existed,
then it was possible—more than possible, perhaps—that
those fabled ones who were to come and take the Gashta
away to a *hoksu-mitto* in the sky might also be possible.

The valley, if it existed, would be the place where the
ship whose existence he had always doubted would have
crashed. It was enough to make his belly growl, just
thinking of that.

ix.

Flower sat high in a feather-tree, watching her charges as they skittered about after insects or burrowed for roots or climbed into the round-fruit trees after luscious snacks. There were so many small ones, now. More than ever before. It was such a strange thing.

She shook her golden mane so the tendrils that strayed into her eyes fell into place. Chip was straying into the open again . . . she shrilled a warning at the tiny shape, and he darted beneath the cover of the branches. One so young was barely a mouthful for the *gotza*, yet they didn't scorn to dive after such.

Most of the Gashta were asleep. More and more, her people were becoming nocturnal, she found, and though it had not been the way of their forebears, it was a sensible thing. Yet the little ones slept little in the daylight hours, so some few must stay awake to watch them. She, being too old for active hunting and too stiff for much farming, was happy to reverse her rest times. The hours spent guarding and the times of teaching were the most joyful of her life.

She thought of her mates of past seasons. Most of them were gone, for the life in the valley, while safer than that in the outlands, was no secure thing for Gashta. Only Tooth-Breaker survived, of all the fathers of her children. And those children . . . how many were left in the valley now? Few. Most had gone out southward, taking their family groups and venturing toward places with space and many *zatku*.

She glanced sharply about, noting the whereabouts of every one of her charges. A sweep of the sky showed no distant, wheeling shape of a *gotza*. No sound came to her ears that warned of *toshki-washa*. For the time, things were well.

She leaned comfortably into her tree-branch nook. The breeze was pleasant, riffling her fur and dissipating the early summer heat. Her mother had loved days like this one, warm and scented with water-smells from the stream, stone-smells from the Mountain, and growing-smells from the gardens.

Sun-Blossom had taught her children so many things. The teacher wished, for a moment, that she might talk again with her. Sun-Blossom had named her Flower. It had been many-many seasons since she had thought of herself as anything but teacher, and longer than that since her peers or her family had called her by that name. It was strange. Except for the small ones, who must be called back from harm as quickly as possible, most of her fellow Gashta seemed to be losing their names. Most were called, if at all, simply by the thing they did best. And with so many living in the valley, it would have been confusing, except for the fact that they dispersed at night into the gardens, the forest, and the mountains, as they went about their work.

From an old, old memory, Flower drew out a name. The Family Ginzu. Yes. Her mother had told her that that was the ship-family from which she and her father and his father had descended. A strange thought, keeping record of who your ancestors might have been. There was no time for such things, now. The search for food was all-consuming, as the pressure of population bore upon the valley's resources.

There came to her sharp ears a shrill call from the ridge just south of the valley. Incomers? It was likely, though fewer seemed to come, now, than had been the case when she was a young teacher.

She stood on her branch, caught the limb above her perch to steady herself, and shrilled a reply. Her heart began to thump. One day, she hoped, one or more of her own offspring might return to the valley, as all had been cautioned to do. She knew quite well that many hundreds now roamed the southern forests and meadows. It was unlikely that this group would contain any of her own. Yet all were kindred. Of the two-hundred-odd Gashta who had survived the crash, only a few more than a hundred had been outside the caverns when the earthquake came. From those few had come all those who now lived on this unfriendly world.

She shook her head. Even to her, who was the carrier of the Gashta's history, it had become dim. Almost a myth. It was no wonder that those not entrusted with keeping the story alive had stopped really believing in it. She wondered, herself, if she was passing on a reality or a dream-tale.

The call came again. Nearer. They were making good time down the cliff-face. It had not been so in the old days, before Stargazer had led the valley Gashta in making a better track up the mountain. The present *Haigun* and Watcher-of-Stars was wise, for one so young, but he was not the man his father had been.

She listened, then called again. Her thoughts returned to the past as she waited. It was truly strange to see the working-out of the bloodlines. Those of the young in whom the heritage of the ship-people was strong clung to the ways of the *Haigun-sha*. They hunted together. They kept a discipline. They obeyed the *Haigun* and the *Noho-washa* and seldom questioned their directions. Those in whom the blood of the colonists ran strongly, on the contrary, were restless, anxious to move out into the southern ways. They quarrelled with the *Haigun* and even with her, their teacher. She could see that, once they were away from the influence of the valley, they would fragment wholly into small groups, and even single members would be fiercely independent.

That showed in those who returned to the home valley. They straggled in, from time to time, and for a while all were suspicious of any who came too near their camping-spots or trees. It sometimes took an entire summer for those exiled Gashta to become easy in the old home.

Now the call came from the foot of the mountain, and Teacher slipped painfully down the tree and called her flock together. She could tell, even now, which would go out and which would stay, for the driving force of their blood was already implicit in the speed —or lack of it—with which they obeyed her call.

By the time she had them marshaled and moving

toward the huts beneath the thorntree barrier, Stargazer had come to meet her.

"New ones come," he said, looking across the cleared space between the forest and the foot of the ridge. "It is strange that the old ties still hold them, the old rules still find obedience."

"Not so strange," Teacher answered. "Think of those who come—all are worn by the life there. All have been saddened by the loss of many babies. They come home to heal themselves. It is true, the thing that the elders taught us. Something in this valley makes us strong. Think how many we are, here. How few there are in the little bunches who come back to us. And all of those go out, in a year or in two, with new babies in their arms and the promise of still others in the females' bellies. Healed. Happy again."

He grinned at her, and she thought how young he looked, for a *Haigun*. Her child, the present Stargazer. Strange how the functions of *Noho-washa* and *Haigun* seemed to cling to those of her family's blood.

Now a line of small marchers was visible in the cleared space. They looked very weary, terribly thin. Their very fur seemed limp, even from this distance.

Flower caught her son's hand. "Hurry!" she said. "We must greet them with joy, as our fathers and mothers promised theirs."

They scampered down the twisting paths, into the clearing. The newcomers paused, hands on *zatku-hodda* and axes, their expressions wary in their furless faces. Then the four came on, very slowly.

"One child," commented Flower. "A young male. And a mated pair. A small family, now."

She shrilled a greeting, and the wary faces relaxed a bit. Then the little one raised his head, sniffed deeply, and broke into a wide grin. Without waiting, he dashed forward and flung himself into her arms.

"Seed!" The mother and father cried together, but their child didn't heed them.

"A young one knows a Teacher, whether he has ever met one before or not," the teacher said, swinging the clinging child onto her back and settling his arms so they didn't throttle her. "Our kind need teachers as they need food. That is another reason for coming back to the home valley."

The male came near, looked closely at her, then caught her in a hug. His action was repeated by his mate and the younger male. The air of dejected exhaustion that had clung about them was dissipating, moment by moment.

Stargazer hugged them in his turn. "I am *Haigun* here," he said, when all had been greeted. "You are welcome to the old home of your kind. If you remember the old tales, I am he who is called Stargazer."

The male set his *zatku-hodda* by and gestured toward it. "I am called Zatku-Cracker. This is Fruit-Finder. And this small one is Seed."

"I am Spear-Maker," Fruit-Finder's brother said, his voice overly shrill with shyness. "This seems as good a place as old Fruit said it would be."

Teacher set Seed on his feet and took his hand. "You have met one called Fruit? I knew one such, long ago when I was a small one and she was tiny. She would be very, very old, now."

"She is older than that," answered Fruit-Finder. "But she is coming here, if her life lasts through the journey. It was that one who told us of the home valley."

Flower felt a tear at the corner of her eye. Fruit, whom she had last seen as a plump burden in her mother's arms, might come. Fruit, her father's child by Snail-Catcher. Though siblings were hard to keep track of, this one had been dear and very special. Perhaps the long wait for one she knew to return was almost over.

BOOK II.

The Dry Times Come

~~~~~~~~~~~~~~~

Stargazer sits on his rock in the night,
watching white-star, watching blue-star,
remembering the things
Stargazers know.

We trust him to remember.

When he sleeps we pen *zatku* by his door
and bring round-fruit;
he watches all night and cannot hunt.

We trust him to remember.

He will see when our help
comes from the stars.

i.

The sky was clear from mountain to ridge to slopes. Not a single cloud.

Stargazer found himself too warm, even beneath the coolness of the night sky, and he laid one small hand flat on the rock where he sat. But it was hot, still, with the sun-heat of the day. Not even a trace of dew had formed with the coming of darkness.

He had thought that the increasing dryness of the seasons would be a short-lived thing. Always, in the past, it had been so. But each summer brought less rain than that before it, and in fall and winter they found little relief. Even the trees were beginning to suffer. Some of the feather-trees nearest the rocky slopes were turning yellowish. He feared that they would die before this summer ended.

He wished he could believe that only trees would die of this drought.

The valley, sloping away to his right, was still watered by the stream. The gardens were lush, for the past years had taught the Gashta to make irrigation ditches for watering their plants. Those who lived from day to day were unworried. There had been dry years—even many at a span—before this, and always the rains had returned.

Yet Stargazer watched from year to year, not from day to day. He saw the snow on the peak of the Mountain, and saw that the winters now brought far less than they ever had before. The stream was fed by the snows. He knew that, as the long line of his predecessors had known it. If there came a winter when no snow fell, even at the top of the mountain, then what would happen to this valley?

The thought was a pain inside him. Only he, of all the Gashta, remembered why the wandering families came back to the valley for seasons of rest and healing. Once, he remembered having been told by the *Haigun* who had trained him, there had always been a teacher to share the burdens of remembering and planning and deciding. But the people had become so scattered, so busy with their hunting and harvesting, that no teacher had been wanted, and the place of learning had been filled by purest survival.

What might such a one teach? Even he, straining to remember every word of the old *Haigun*, had realized that he was receiving only the smallest part of what had been the truth of his kind. He watched the blue star move about the white one. He gauged the snow on the Mountain. He kept track of the coming and going of those who visited the valley. He appointed one to watch the little ones, decided among squabbling hunters as to their territories, and organized the parties that were needed, at times, to attack marauding *toshki-washa* or to hunt for *hatta-zosa*.

He was pitied by all the people, and with good reason. His was the hardest task of all. And now it had become, in the space of ten seasons, even harder. It was becoming almost impossible for the valley to support its population. The incomers strained its resources even more. This winter would bring starvation, unless many left for the southern lands.

It was in his heart that he would be forced to order most of the *Kampushi-sha* to leave by summer's end. Without the vine-beans, the round-fruit, and the insects and snails of summer, starvation would surely come to the Gashta. There was not enough for all.

And that was a thing that all his heredity and instinct cried out against. This was the home valley. Here was the place to which the families might come for healing and rest. Out there, beyond the ridge, was a world in which the Gashta died. Slowly, it was true, but a long death was no less deadly than a short one.

He sighed and looked up at the white star. The blue was behind it. The lights that he had seen, many seasons before, had roused in him a hope that the old tales might be true. That help would come from the spaces, out there, and kin would come to take the Gashta away from this world full of oversized beasts.

But now the lights came and went almost as often as the moons, and no help had ever come. He wondered, with his sharp and logical mind, why no such lights had ever been seen before. He had not seen them, and there was no tradition of any other of the *Haigun* ever seeing such things. He had no idea what they could be. He knew about stars and moons and planets. Even comets and meteors had been described to him and their traditional explanations drilled into his mind.

First came the lights. Then the drought came. Seasons apart, it was true, but still . . . neither had been to such a degree before. Could they be connected?

He shook his mane aside, trying for a cooling breeze. He had no way of knowing. And the causes were of no consequence. He was still caught in a dilemma unlike any that he had been taught to consider.

The *Kampushi-sha* must go out. Perhaps not all this summer. It was possible that another season might see the end of the dry weather. But if it continued, in time all of them must go. They were quarrelsome when times were hard. They would not obey, he knew, if ordered to share their prize of hunting or farming with those whose luck was not as good. They were a people suited to foraging for themselves, and that was what they must do. Stillbirths . . . he shivered to think of them . . . must be ignored. Some living young were always born, though not nearly enough to keep the population stable, out there in the south.

In time, surely, the weather would return to normal. Then the depleted groups could return and heal themselves. Until then, it was the only hope for the survival of all. But they must be taught to return. They must be reminded of the old tradition. Help would come. The lights had failed them, it was true, but he could not believe that all the teachings of so many generations of *Haigun* had been false. Help would come from the sky. Those would come who would aid the suffering Gashta and bring them good food that would fulfill all their needs. They would bring caring and happiness and times of play and no worry. They must come!

His hands, while his eyes were fixed upon the stars, had arranged a pattern of twigs and pebbles upon the rock between his furry thighs. In the moonlight, he could see the Spiral centering it. The Home System. It was tied into the dream that had kept his people going for so long, and he refused to doubt any of it now.

There was a quiet sound at the base of his rock. Cord-Maker, who would one day be known as Stargazer in his turn, was a small shape of shadow, there in the moonlight. His fur, silvery by nature, was almost white in the brightness from Tansha.

"It is that this one may watch, too?" he asked shyly.

Stargazer grunted, careful not to show the gratification he felt at the eagerness of his pupil. He had tried many before finding one with the necessary intelligence and dedication for the task. Now he made room for him on the rock and resumed his watch of the sky.

"It is. . ." Cord-Maker sounded ill-at-ease . . . "that there is not so much snow on the Mountain as there was last summer. The stream—I think it runs lower in its banks. It seems to me a very bad thing."

The *Haigun* turned his head and looked into those big green eyes, so near to him. His heart surged with pride, for he had thought that none except himself had noted the things that were happening.

"True," he said. "It is a thing that is very bad. I sit here and watch the stars move, blue about white as I have taught you, and I wonder what will become of the

Gashta, if rain does not come. If snow does not fall in winter. If the stream does not run full, as it used to do."

Cord-Maker squirmed. His fur made a hissing sound against the rock. He reached with one tentative finger to touch the *Haigun* on his shoulder.

"There is a thing that I would say. Yet it is not my place to say it to you. It is that I overstep my position. . . ?"

Stargazer took the extended hand in his own. "Speak freely, my young *Haigun*-to-be. I must know what it is that you think."

"The *Kampushi-sha* must go out, back into the southern ways. Only the *Haigun-sha* can live, when the stream runs low and few gardens can flourish. Only we will share, at need, with our fellows. I think that if they stay here, all of the Gashta will die."

Stargazer felt peace, for the first time in many seasons.

"That is also my thought, though it pains me to hear it said aloud. That is what must be done, *Haigun-li*. And the time has come when we must tell the people.

"Tomorrow, we will wake them from their rest. Tonight, we shall sit together upon this ancient rock and plan what we must say."

ii.

From the last high spot on the ridge, the land stretched away southward in an amazing span. The line of Gashta stopped in their tracks to stare out over the place where they now must live. Only one of their number had ever gone out from the valley, and even he had some awe left

in him for that great expanse of copse-dotted meadow-
land.

"There is a great forest, further on," he said, turning
to Remembers-Things.

Remembers-Things nodded. "Others have said the
same. Let us hope, Climbs-Rocks, that there are as
many *zatku* as you and the others remember. Let us
hope that we are able to find much fruit and trees with
good seeds and vines filled with beans. There is a winter
to be considered, even though you say that it isn't nearly
as harsh as those we have known in the valley. I will not
be content to while away the warm weather in hunting
and play, then to find myself and my family growing
hungry when the seasons turn."

"We will not have to garden," the younger Gashta
said confidently. "I have spent many winters there in
the south. The rain falls and is warm. No snow comes.
Plants grow all the year. You will see. Life will be so
easy there that you will wonder why our kind has stayed
so rooted into that narrow valley in the north."

"If you do not understand that, you are a very dim-
witted Gashta indeed," grunted the elder. His face, a
dark tan amid the silver-streaked fur of his mane,
turned faintly darker as he looked at Climbs-Rocks.
"Those who keep the faith are still there, where we
could not now survive. They will send those who come
to aid us, when they arrive. And never forget that our
numbers will dwindle, here in these falsely easy lands.
Always, that has been true. This one knows, for I have
spoken with generations of those who have returned to
the valley. Only there did they begin to multiply again."

Sees-Far spoke for the first time since topping the last
pass. "I am torn in two ways, *Pa-ha-oko*. I see a wonderful place before my eyes, but my heart hurts for the
valley I have always known. Yet I was forced to leave it,
by those I love too well to disobey. You did not have to
come, Remembers-Things. Why is it that you are here?
Stargazer would not have forced you to go."

The old Gashta grunted again. He looked out over the
scene below, assessing the richness of the soil beneath

the head-high grasses he had been told of. After a long
moment, he turned his green-gold eyes toward Sees-Far.

"My family must go. You, the mate of my daughter,
must go. I am too old to take a new mate, to have more
little ones. Should I be left without a family in the years
of my əge? Besides, I have learned many things in my
long life. I remember much that is forgotten outside the
valley. Perhaps I may remind you of things that must be
remembered and teach you about things that you will
need to know. This is a very different life that we are
entering into. You will have no Stargazer to turn to for
advice. But you will have this one. It may be of help."

Climbs-Rocks had been fidgeting as the older one
spoke. "Look," he said, pointing. "Pulls-Weeds and
Runs-Fast are going ahead with the children. It is better
if all are together, for there are many *toshki-washa* here,
and soon we will leave the shelter of trees and bushes.
The *gotza* watch those meadows down there from the
tops of the mountains and from high trees. Hurry!"

The three moved quickly after the females and the
seven little ones. Now they were faced with a path that
dived over the edge of the mountain ridge like a stream
from a cliff. Small as they were, they were able to clam-
ber down the steepest spots using hands as well as feet,
letting their tools and weapons slide down behind them.

They arrived at the bottom of a deep cut amid a small
landslide of Gashta, tools, and dusty rocks. Remembers-Things found himself breathless, something that he
disliked about growing older. But he looked about,
nevertheless, with keen eyes, seeking out the cause of
any rustle in the abundant growth that lined the ravine
in which they now stood.

To his delight, he found that the greenery was laced
together by bean-vines. The intricate leaves were hard to
see in the shadowy light, but his vision was still keen,
despite his age.

"Come! Eat! We must rest for a time, now, for the
little ones are weary and frightened," he commanded.

Though the *Kampushi-sha* were resistant to com-
mands, as a rule, they never defied one that called upon

them to eat or to play. This seemed a fine time for both, and the group pulled armfuls of vines, piled them in a heap, and sat in a circle about the feast. As they stripped out handfuls of beans and stuffed them into their mouths, they chattered between bites. Some arranged the bean-hulls into patterns, and Remembers-Things smiled to see how many of those patterns were designed about the Spiral.

There came a shriek of excitement from the other side of the circle, and he looked up as one of the children, Petal, grabbed her miniature *zatku-hodda* and took off after a scuttling land-prawn. A crackling sound in the lower growth that supported the bean-vines gave notice that others of the *zatku* kind were moving there, and every Gashta in the circle forgot about the beans and caught up *zatku-hodda* for the hunt.

Petal, being young as yet and not having developed her own style of *zatku*-killing, gave her victim a brisk whack on the carapace to stun it, detached its head with messy enthusiasm, and turned it over to crush the under-shell. They left her blissfully picking out the meat with the creature's own claws.

Remembers-Things saw another moving through tall grass at the angle of ravine and slope. He darted toward it, hearing behind him the rest of his family, young and older, in loud and happy pursuit of the others.

This was a huge old *zatku,* its shell rusty and crusty with years. Much meat, he could tell. He fell into his killing-mode, dashing up behind the creature and using an overhand blow to addle its few wits. Once it was still, he pried it over with the shank of his *zatku-hodda* and positioned its head and body exactly. With one efficient blow of the thin-edged paddle of the weapon, he decapitated it. Then he contentedly crushed the under-shell and hunkered down to eat.

No such *zatku* had he tasted in years. Not since his youth, indeed, had one contained such flavor and juice. The drought over the range had evidently been as difficult for the *zatku* as for the Gashta, drying out their juices enough to change the taste.

He examined the shell of the creature. It was mottled with traces of reddish soil in the age-cracks. He had never seen such coloration before, and he called to Climbs-Rocks.

The young Gashta came, wiping his lips on the fur of his forearm.

"Look at this," Remembers-Things said, pointing to a line of dirt ingrained in the shell. "Have you seen such color in the soil before?"

Climbs-Rocks squatted beside him and looked thoughtfully at the now-empty shell. "Not here," he said. "Not even just south of here. But once my family-group went far-far down to a place where the ground is wet—like mud, only overgrown with grass and plants of all kinds. And that mud was red, like this. But it is a hand-of-moons journey from here. How could this *zatku* have traveled so far?"

Remembers-Things stood and wiped his own mouth and hands. "If *zatku* can thrive there, and if there is so much water there, then our kind should also do well. And we will be deeper into the warm country there. Perhaps we might move in that direction, slowly and without hurrying at all. It sounds like a *hoksu-mitto.* "

He was interrupted by a shriek of fear and another of agony. Forgetting his stiff joints, he grabbed his weapon and made for the bend in the ravine beyond which most of the others had chased their prey. Something huge and heavy flapped up through the heavy-hanging branches just as he thrust his head around the angle.

Gotza! And hanging from the fingerlike claws was one of the small ones!

The old Gashta flung his *zatku-hodda* as hard as his small arm could manage. Another whistled past his ear, as Climbs-Rocks also threw his own. They thumped into the burdened creature, which had been slowed by its need to avoid the thick growth through which it must make its way. It hooted with rage . . . but it dropped the tiny figure.

Pulls-Weeds dashed forward beneath the very shadow of the thing and caught up her child in her arms. Remembers-Things spared an instant to grieve for his daughter, as he caught up his fallen *zatku-hodda* and made off after the blundering *gotza*. It looked in vain for the thin spot through which it had spotted and stooped upon the child. Remembers-Things knew that if it should remember itself and forget its pain, he would become a short meal for it in even shorter order. But it must go away from the family, if he could manage it.

A furred body brushed past his elbow, and he glimpsed, for a moment, Pulls-Weeds's anguished face. The child was dead, as he had known that it would be. The mother would pursue the killer until it turned and devoured her.

Giving up the chase, Remembers-Things signalled to Climbs-Rocks, and between them they caught the maddened girl and brought her to a stop. It was hard to hold her, for her mind held only one desire—to sink her weapon into the killer of her child.

Now Remembers-Things felt old and more than weary. This was a bad place. The family must go farther south.

Pulls-Weeds was struggling in his grip. He looked past her furred shoulder at Climbs-Rocks, who was holding her other arm.

Her voice was shrilling almost above the hearing-range of the Gashta, but now her words were filled more with sorrow than with wrath. She began to shiver, and her father gathered her into his arms, holding her close as she rocked backward and forward with her agony. A step at a time, he guided her back to the spot where the bean-vines had been dumped.

Climbs-Rocks did not follow, and Remembers-Things knew that the younger Gashta was digging the grave-pit for little Feather. In a few moments, it would be time for the family to gather and place the tiny body there, and he wanted to calm Pulls-Weeds as much as possible before she saw her child buried.

There was a trickle of water dripping from a crack in the cliff. He pulled his daughter there and washed her face, her hands, talking all the while in the almost-forgotten deeper mode. The sound seemed to lull her. Her eyes lost their fixed glare and closed. She leaned against him, as he led her back toward the new grave-pit. Sees-Far came to meet them and touched her face with his own.

The pit was already dug. Such a small Gashta needed only a tiny grave-pit. There were many stones scattered about the base of the cliff, so there was no need to gather more for covering it.

Runs-Fast, tears streaming from her big gray-green eyes, held the bloodied infant. Tenderly, she laid it in the pit, which someone had lined with the springy ferns that grew against the cliff. With no word, all the Gashta, even the smallest, began piling stones into and over the grave. Pulls-Weeds, as if relieved to find use for her hands, brought more than any of the others, and when the task was done she stood for a long moment by the side of the little pile.

Now Remembers-Things remembered that this, his suffering daughter, was also the mate of Sees-Far. And he, too, had lost a child. The father stepped back and let Sees-Far take his daughter by the hand. They turned away, down the ravine that led into the broad lands that they had seen from the ridge above.

It was not a good beginning, Remembers-Things thought, as he followed his family along the deeply shaded way. And it seemed a good indication that now, freed of the dangers of the mountain tracks, they might do well to return to their old habits.

"There is a good feathertree ahead!" he shrilled to his family. "We should stop there and sleep until darkness comes. The *gotza* hunt rarely at night."

There was no protest, and soon all were relaxed on chosen branches, listening to the strange sounds of the creatures of this unfamiliar place. And, though all rested, only the children truly slept. Their elders were thinking deep thoughts about the terrors of being cast out of their familiar haunts, into alien and dangerous places.

iii.

It had been a terrible journey. The Gashta were unused to open country, and the wide sky had been a constant threat, even though the family had traveled by night. And the *gotza* had hunted by moonlight on two nights when both moons were high. It was strange that they had reached the cover along a stream without losing still another of their number.

Remembers-Things knew that there was still much danger, though the tree-cover along the stream's dwindling trickle gave an illusion of safety, after those days under the sky. *Toshki-washa* loved just such places. And those smaller, fiercer beasts that he had been told about lived near water, so those who had returned to the valley had said. Tiny creatures, not more than knee-high to a Gashta, they lived in burrows in damp ground and would dart out and sever a bite from anything edible and unsuspecting that might come within their range. A number of returnees had lacked fingers or toes or had had uneven spots hidden beneath their fur that marked the loss of a bite of flesh to a *kashi*.

Pulls-Weeds and Runs-Fast had the small ones moving in a close group led by Petal. Sees-Far came behind them, and Climbs-Rocks moved along at the outer edge of the line of trees, watching both the sky and the floor of the wooded space. Remembers-Things overlooked all, the memory of a limp body in a *gotza's* claws still a pain in his heart. If it could be managed, they would lose no more of their young through carelessness.

Now they must move along this channel, following it southward as far as its course could lead them. The lack of water had been dreadful, especially on the young, while they crossed the first open land. He shuddered to think what might happen if it became necessary to travel for many days without finding some stream. A shellful of water was so little, ration it as they might. The net bags were unsteady and caused constant drips and spills. No, it was better to stay beside the stream. There were enough adults to batter a *toshki-washa* into flight, if that became necessary.

They moved slowly. By day they climbed the best tree they could find. By night they went forward, always south-by-west, toward that well-watered land that Climbs-Rocks had described. The mountain range behind grew smaller so gradually that it seemed that they had not moved at all. But the ranges to east and west were visibly drawing apart. The size of the land into which they were traveling filled all except Climbs-Rocks with awe. The valley had been close, familiar, bounded on all sides by ridges or the Mountain. After that self-contained homeplace, these boundless stretches were frightening in themselves, even without all the threats that they held.

A time came when the adults had to carry the smallest four. Only Petal managed to trudge along on small bruised feet for most of the time. And when she flagged, she would climb onto her grandfather's back, leaving his hands free for axe or *zatku-hodda* in case of need.

Much later, there came a time when even the grown-ups could move no more. It was late in the year. Bean-vines had been stripped by birds and animals, as well as by those Gashta who had gone before them. *Zatku* were scarce, and even *hatta-zosa* were hard to find. They had gone as far as they could go on insects and round-fruit alone.

Remembers-Things knew that they must pause and hunt. Rest and food would give them new energy. If the children could walk even for part of each night, it would relieve their elders of their double burdens. Sees-Far agreed, as did the two females.

Turning to Climbs-Rocks, Remembers-Things said, "See where the sun stands in the sky. Now it is beginning to be cold, back in the valley. The cold winds will blow from the mountains soon. Will they send their breath so far as this?"

The younger Gashta, sitting at his elder's left in the circle, patted a pattern into the dampish soil of the streambank as he considered. The Spiral grew under his hands, as he answered, "I think it will not grow cold here for a time. Tansha will grow full once, Gozzo will wane and grow again and begin to wane yet again. This is a kinder country than that we left. Cold will come here, but only for a little space in the middle of the winter. And if we must remain here for a time, it will be safe to do it."

Remembers-Things looked about. Pulls-Weeds nodded, as did Runs-Fast. Sees-Far looked about them and hissed.

"See? There is no good tree for sleeping here. And we have passed none in some days. This one believes that we should go on for a bit, until we find a safe place to rest when the hunters are about."

Remembers-Things realized that the young Gashta was right. Unless they could rest with some security there would be no point in stopping. The others also came to that conclusion, for they gathered their bags and their weapons, marshaled the children, and set out again along the meandering bank of the stream.

Dawn had lightened the east when Remembers-Things saw the tree. At this point, the farther edge of the stream was a fair-sized cliff of rock, from which trickles of water flowed, from time to time, into the bed of the rivulet. The bank upon which they traveled was low, damp, and the soil was rich. Even so late in the year, fresh beanvines had sprouted, though their crop would surely be blighted by frost before it could come to ripeness. Up ahead, bright in the light of Gozzo, was an angled bend of the creekbed. A broken face of rock glowed there on the other side of the water, and from a deep cranny leaned the bole of a tremendous tree.

It was not a feathertree, or a *rogo*, or any of those species that had been a familiar part of their valley. Its bark was shaggy, and even in the dimness it glowed with pale-gray brightness. Its spokes of branches wheeled outward, and each limb was almost the diameter of an entire tree. The trunk curved away from the cliff that held its roots, almost touched the water at its lowest, and then soared upward after bridging the stream. The foliage was thick, black in the moonlight. It was a veritable fort of a tree, and Remembers-Things shrilled exultantly, bringing the rest of the family to a halt to stare at their new roosting-place.

The young would have darted forward in a body, but for the watchfulness of Pulls-Weeds. She swooped onto the group and held them with hands and voice. "Let the grandfather and Runs-Fast go first. There may be *hizzu* there, had you forgotten? Or *kashi*. Let them see. Then we will all go and climb up."

But there were no *hizzu* . . . at least none that the closest scrutiny could detect. The soil beneath the upward curve was unmarked by the burrows of *kashi*. The step from soil to trunk was made easy by a tumble of rock that had fallen from the cliff. It was, in the midst of this alien and hungry land, a true *hoksu-mitto*.

And, they found soon, there were sluggish shellfish in the stream just below them, though none such had been found at any point upstream. Fed full, they snuggled into broad nooks and slept deeply for the first time since leaving the home valley. Only Remembers-Things lay awake, remembering.

"The old tales say that good things will come to the Gashta. Help will come from the stars. A *hoksu-mitto* waits for us. Perhaps it may be true, after all, though I have not always found it easy to believe that. Perhaps, even before many-many seasons go by, we will find a place where we can be safe and not hungry."

Then he, too, slept.

THE SONG OF CAUTION

If we teased the *so-shi-fazzu,*
baited *toshki-washa,*
dared *gotza* to swoop upon us
   there would be no Gashta
     in this place.

We must be cautious, here,
walk small-small,
speak in voices the beasts
cannot hear:
   the fury in our hearts
     must burn low.

In our own place, long ago,
we were not dwarfed by everything;
this is another world,
huge and fierce and terrible:
we must walk small-small
   in this place.

iv

It was so hot. The night before had been suffocating, and Root-Grower had felt her face swell as she bent over her sharp-toothed bone rake. Even the light of Gozzo had seemed to burn upon the skin of her hands as they gripped the tool.

The soil, once loamy and sweet-turning under her hands and her sharp stick and her hoe, was now almost dust. The water that they rationed through the ditches seemed to do so little good. The hungry dirt drank it rapidly, and the next day's sun drew out the rest.

The worst aspect of this terrible summer was the dwindling of the stream. Even the least noticing of the Gashta had now realized that each winter saw less white fall on the peak of the Mountain.

It had been a dreadful thing, the sending-out of the *Kampushi-sha*. Though many of them had intended leaving soon, after months or a year of restoration in the home valley, a great many more had never left the place of their birth. They had never intended to go, though most of them had wandered, at times, over the mountain barriers to south and east and west of the level country bracketed by the ranges.

There had been sadness and outrage. Even-tempered though most of the Gashta had become, there had been much anger and rebellious talk. But the *Haigun* was the *Haigun*. For more generations than any of the Gashta could now count, he and his predecessors had guided affairs in this valley, and the less-than-settled ways of the *Kampushi-sha* had loosed their bonds to the home country.

Root-Grower yawned and sat up on the branch that she had chosen for sleeping. Most of her people had given up trying to sleep in the huts beneath the thorn-tree barrier. Open-work though they might be, the hot breeze made them unbearable. Individual families made it a habit to gather about their homes for a circle of talk, now and then, but until winter they slept in the tops of trees. That wasn't nearly as safe, but the bite of a *hizzu* or the swoop of a forest-venturing *gotza* was no worse than the stifling nights inside the wicker walls.

She listened. The normal day-sounds of the valley and the wood seemed to have been smothered beneath a blanket of dry heat. Not even the shriek of a hunting *gotza* interrupted the sleeptime quiet.

She settled herself again in her leafy spot and closed her eyes. The fur on her body trapped the heat close to her skin, she thought, though that from the outer air was hotter still. A dew of perspiration touched her smooth pale-pink face. She sighed and turned yet again.

She had thought of the *Kampushi-sha*, and now she

could not stop remembering. Those of her own family in whom the wanderer-blood was strong had been sent out. It had hurt her to lose them, though almost all of those of the *Haigun-sha* left in the valley were kindred as near as those departed ones had been.

The days of the out-going had been dreadful ones. Families had divided, for in the same group might be half who had the instincts of the ship-people and half who were driven by the needs of those who had been colonists. Mates had turned from each other, one to go out, one to stay within the disciplined ways of the valley. Her own mate had gone. Only their little Leaf was left with her to remind her of him.

She peered around the bole of the feathertree. Ah. The small one still slept, worn out with her night of following behind her mother, pulling ripe tubers from the dried soil. There had been a time, the oldest Gashta said, when the young could play in the forest by day, watched by a teacher, and their lives had been carefree. It seemed only a tale, now in these days of sparse food and dwindling *zatku*. Even the *hatta-zosa* had trundled their ratlike bodies away up the southward slopes. Fewer remained in the forests flanking the mountains with every passing season.

Leaf was so beautiful. Her fur was softest silver, a coloration that had become more common in recent generations. Root-Grower could remember her mother's talk of the things she had seen or had been taught in her own childhood. Pale fur had been a rarity, long ago.

"Inbreeding," Swift-Stone-Thrower had said. "The *Noho-washa* told us, when we were small, that when a few families are isolated for many generations, changes like this happen. She called it inbreeding. I did not believe her then, but now I am beginning to see things happen that must be caused by that."

But Root-Grower had been interested only in the idea of the Teacher. She had not remembered until many years later the term her mother had used. She smoothed her silver-gilt fur. Climbs-Swiftly, Leaf's father, had been a pale-golden Gashta. She could see in her own child the result of this inbreeding. She wondered what other matters about the Gashta might have changed that were less easy to see than color.

What had changed? Her mother had said that in long-ago times any Gashta who was wrong-headed enough to endanger his group had been killed. Now that was a thing that had changed, indeed, for only those as old as she who had heard the tales for themselves could believe that that could be so. No such Gashta had been born among the people in all the span of her life. Perhaps that was one thing that had changed. There would be others. Her quick intelligence sifted through the things she knew about her kind and their habits.

Talk. That had changed, she was sure. Her mother's tales had spoken of a time when there was another manner of talk than the high-pitched tones that the beasts couldn't hear. She wondered what it might sound like. Oh, there must be many-many things that had changed. She wondered if even the *Haigun* himself knew how many.

Leaf moaned softly in her sleep.

Her musings forgotten, Root-Grower slipped around the treetrunk and sat beside the sleeping child. Leaf had lived only four winters. In the time since her father had gone, two summers had parched the people and two winters had frozen them without hint of snow or rain. Only the mountaintop had received any snowfall at all, and that was much less than was its wont.

This land was becoming impossible for her kind. Sitting there in the feather-tree while most of the others slept, she saw that fact clearly and sharply for the first time.

She looked closely at Leaf. Two winters ago she had been a plump and carefree young one, quick to laugh and to talk and to help with the things she could manage. Now her tiny body was thinner. Too thin, very tiny. The fragile bones showed as her ribs moved with her breathing. Her face, amid the silvery mane, was less pale-pink than just pale. There were lines about her thin-lipped mouth . . . lines like those that came on the faces of the very old just before their time came to die.

A throb of fear shook the mother. She tried to remember the last time she had heard Leaf's shriek of laughter. When had the child last climbed a rockfall or a tree just for the fun of it? When had she and the circle of small ones last chattered their talk while they formed patterns with their nimble fingers?

Too long. Too long. The small ones were being made old by this life—this less-than-life—in the valley. The place that had been the haven and healing-place of the Gashta was becoming their grave-pit. A tiny and very old Gashta lay in the shape of her child. One without energy and without joy.

A terrible thing. The enduring characteristic of her kind had always been their ability to play, to have fun even while accomplishing the necessary tasks. Now that was being . . . indeed, had been . . . leached from them by the heat and the drought and the struggle to survive.

Root-Grower huddled on the branch beside the weary child. Her forehead furrowed with thought. Her fingers unconsciously traced the Spiral invisibly on the smooth bark of the treelimb.

Help would come. The ancient tradition of her people must be true. But if it came to find only dying or dead Gashta in this valley, what aid would that be, to Leaf or to her?

She had only the deepest respect for Stargazer. In the many years of his life as *Haigun* he had always been as wise as a living being can manage and far wiser than most ever achieve. He would stay, she knew, until he drew his last breath. It hurt to think of leaving him, for once she had been his mate for a time, and she knew the depth of his loneliness and the difficulty of his task.

Yet she could not stay here to see her little Leaf wither away, like a feather-plume in winter. There were *zatku* beyond the cross-range of mountains. There were *hatta-zosa*. There were round-fruit and beanvines and many more edible plants than existed in these colder places. So she had been told many times by those who came back to the valley.

If all her young, from this time forward, were born dead, then it must be so. It would be painful, for she adored her babies, but she could endure it.

This child . . . she looked at the sleeping Leaf in an agony of affection . . . this youngest child of hers would not die. She would make very sure of that.

v.

It was one thing to make a firm resolve in the safety of her own place. It was, Root-Grower found, another one to carry it out. All who could be sent from the valley had gone long before. There were no others who were willing to go out, unbidden, into those distant places where the *Kampushi-sha* now were trying to live.

Stargazer was entirely sympathetic. "This one knows that you are wise, Root-Grower," he had said when she approached him with her plan. "All can see that this valley is no longer a place in which our kind can flourish. The little Leaf is not growing well, and her eyes hold no laughter. All the small ones are the same. My heart weeps for them. It weeps for all of us; we know what waits for our kind out there in the ways beyond this valley.

"Yet I cannot say to any who now are here, 'You must go out with Root-Grower and Leaf, for they cannot go alone.' It is neither my right nor their duty."

She had looked into his weary eyes and had known that he would have gone with her gladly, if it had been in his power.

"This one would wish that you might give your duties to the *Haigun-li* and travel by my side," she had said shyly. "It is long since our paths ran together."

But both had known that the old *Haigun* was needed, more than ever before, by the *Haigun-sha*. To leave an untried leader to bring them through the terrible times that seemed inevitable was not right, and would not be the act of a Gashta.

So now Root-Grower stood, alone save for Leaf, beside a small cairn of stones at the foot of the mountain ridge that was the last barrier between the cross-range and the wide lands beyond it. It was such a tiny pile that it might have been natural. She knew that it wasn't. The stones were laid too carefully, and the place was much too far from the cliff for them to have fallen into such a heap. It was the grave-pit of a child. Like Leaf.

She shuddered and caught the small one's hand in her own. Leaf looked up, her wide green eyes wondering at the tightness of her mother's grasp. But everything was strange in this new place, and she stood quietly until Root-Grower was ready to move on.

That happened quickly. If one lay dead here, then something had killed it. Root-Grower handed her *zatku-hodda* to the child, cautioning her against rattling it against stones or bushes as they went. Then she took her flint axe into her hand and tied her cord-net bag of necessities about her waist. Whatever hunted here would not find her unready.

There was the scuttling of *zatku* beneath the rank vegetation that floored the ravine. There were still a few beans on the bean-vines. Leaf looked pleadingly at her mother, but Root-Grower went onward without pausing. Such plenty would tempt any Gashta to linger here. She had seen evidence that lingering in this spot was no healthy thing.

They caught convenient tendrils from the bean-vines as they passed them and munched as they walked, but not until the ravine widened into a saucer-shape, clear of trees and even of most bushes, did she stop. It had been a lush place, she could see. The dried remains of many edible plants showed that. But now it was dying—

dried by the same thing that must have caused the valley
to be so drought-ridden. Even the few feathertrees that
lined the edge to her left were looking thin and yellow.
The bushes that remained in the little valley were scanty
of leaf and sick-looking.

She looked back. The ravine was watered by many
small streams issuing from the rock of the mountain
itself. That accounted for the richness of its offerings.
Ahead lay harsh country for traveling. Water might be a
real problem, and food would be whatever they could
catch. To her relief, she could hear a few crickets ratch-
eting from the dried grasses, even now, well before
darkness fell.

She looked from west to east, north to south. No
wheeling *gotza* was on patrol, but she knew that one
might be sitting, invisible in some high place, watching
for movement in the flat country.

There was no going out into that wide-open space by
day. Her heart lurched. She knew that they must pass
the rest of the daylight hours back in the ravine, hidden
from searching *gotza*. And who knew what might hunt
there?

She hustled Leaf back, past the last bending of the
cut, to a spot where a huge feathertree leaned over the
space between the cliffs, which now were low and crumbling.

"Fusso, Pa-ha-uka?" asked a small voice from her
side. "This one is very hungry!"

She looked down at Leaf. If they must stop, then it
might as well be to eat as to rest.

"If you will climb into the tree and find a fine-fine
place to sleep, I will go back and find the beans.
Perhaps I may even find one of the *zatku*. But you must
wait here and be very still until I come back."

The little one scrambled up the smooth, slanting
trunk and settled into one of the spoked branch-
junctions. Her big eyes stared down at her mother
solemnly, and Root-Grower found time to hope that
one day she would see laughter return to her child's ex-

pression. Then she turned back up the ravine to find food.

There were more beans than she had thought. She filled her net-bag. Then she poked about in the ferns and bushes, hoping to frighten a prawn into motion. Instead, she caught a glimpse of ruffled golden fur. A hand rolled limply from her *zatku-hodda's* prodding. There was a Gashta lying in the concealment of the ferns.

She dropped to her knees and crawled under the overarching growth to kneel beside him. His face was smudged with soil and with green from its scrubbing against the ferns and the grass. Beneath the grime, it was terribly pale.

She caught the visible arm in both hands and tugged gently. Bit by bit, she pulled him out of the thick tangle into which he had evidently crawled after . . . what?

There was a dappling of blood on his side. On the left leg, too. She leaned over him, turned him as softly as she could, and gasped. His back and side were gashed and scored with deep claw-marks. Too small for those of a *toshki-washa*. Perhaps a very young one? She couldn't tell. But he had lost much blood, as the dark stain on the ground where he had lain attested. He was chilled, even on this late-summer day. He was, she had to admit to herself, all but dead.

Fire was a thing used only in the valley. It was too dangerous, too difficult to kindle, for those who wandered to use. Yet he must be warmed, and his wounds must be cleaned, or he would surely slip altogether into death.

Root-Grower backed out of the fern-growth and stood. Then she ran back toward the tree in which she had left Leaf. *"Bizzo*, Leaf! Hurry! One lies hurt, and you must help."

The child slipped down the tree. She was trembling with excitement at the call, but she moved swiftly after her mother, saying nothing. Root-Grower tugged at her small hand, urging her to greater speed.

Together, they crawled again into the brush and hunkered beside the strange Gashta. "He is cold-cold!" Root-Grower chattered, as her hands moved about the gashes, cleaning away the blood and dirt with handfuls of grass. Then, lacking any other means of cleaning the cuts, she licked them, one by one. Meanwhile, Leaf had cuddled close against the chest of their patient, trying to add her small warmth to whatever of his own he might have left.

When Root-Grower had done her best with the wounds and burrowed among the ferns to find a clump of low-growing *ko-so* to crush and spread over the hurt flesh, she, too, stretched against the Gashta, curving her arms about him. Together, they gave him their body-heat, knowing that at any moment the thing that had hurt him might return to complete the task.

The light faded. Their ferny shelter was dark, green-smelling, and filled with the living warmth of Root-Grower and Leaf. One moon sent a bit of filtered light through the tree-branches, the bushes, and the ferns to touch bits of fur here, a bare pink ear there, when the hurt one groaned.

The wisp of moonlight seemed bright to their sharp eyes. They pulled away and looked closely at him. As they watched, his own eyes opened, gazing up at them through a haze of pain.

Now was the time to go out, to cross this first valley's bare expanse without the threat of *gotza*. Root-Grower knew it, and she dreaded the thought of staying here in this dangerous spot, keeping Leaf away from whatever safety might be found in the thicker growth of vegetation in the wide lands she had seen from the ridge.

But they could not go away, now, and leave this one to die. He was looking at her. His lips were moving. She bent and put her hand across his mouth.

"Hhhhhh!" she breathed. "There is danger here. Talk into my ear!"

He blinked deliberately, and she knew that he understood. Then she put her ear close to his mouth, and he gasped into it one word. *"Fazzu!"*

She straightened and shook her head. "We stay with you," she said, "until you go with us. But you must go up into the tree. Tomorrow, when you are stronger. You must go up, or something will eat us all."

He breathed deeply. A grunt of protest came from him, but his eyes closed again, and soon she knew that he slept.

vi

It had been a day of toil and worry. Stands-Fast had toiled and worried more than any of his family, and he was more than glad to see the sun touch the edge of the western range.

At last, he had them all down from the ridge. Now, weeks after leaving the valley, his family stood upon the flatland toward which they had been making their much-interrupted way. Those who had gone before them seemed to have had no problems in crossing the mountains and were gone beyond the horizon. As far as he knew, there was no other family to come behind his, for he had brought his people out last of all. One of his mates had been on the point of giving birth, and they had waited to see the child born before leaving.

The infant had been the first to die. It had caught a chill on the ridge above their village, and nothing that its mother or he had done had helped the tiny thing. Its little grave-pit watched over the valley where it was born. And, as if the family were undergoing some bitter test the child's mother, Golden-Eyes, had been bitten by a *hizzu* the next day.

He shuddered at the memory. They had scaled the tremendous trees on the ridge, that second night away from home, to sleep above-ground in some safety. His

grandmother, Knows-Much; Net-Weaver, his other
mate; Hunts-Zeeto, his brother; and the two children
had gone high among the branches for their rest.

Below them had roosted his grandfather. Weaves-
Cords-Together (who was also Net-Weaver's father)
had taken his place with much grumbling. Something
had troubled the old Gashta, and he had talked at intervals far into the night.

He and Golden-Eyes had stopped even lower, for the
birth, the difficult journey, and the death of the baby
had drained her strength. He had not liked the spot they
chose, but she had been so weary and so sad that he had
said nothing. Both moons had ridden high all night, and
he had slept ill, itching to be moving forward in this
natural time for traveling.

Yet the night had gone well, for all that. It was only
with the first light that Golden-Eyes had cried out
sharply. He had scrambled to her side in time to see her
crush a *hizzu* with her right hand against her left forearm.

Few insects could penetrate the fur of the Gashta for
a deep sting or bite. But the *hizzu* was a giant among insects. It had finger-length pincers on its first set of legs
and sharp, vicious mandibles. It looked a bit like a tiny
zatku, but it held a poison within it that was dangerous
for Gashta. More than one, particularly among the very
young, had fallen victim to the tree-dwelling creature.

Even as he watched, her arm began to swell. He tore
away the crushed insect and flung it from the tree, his
nostrils wrinkling at the noxious stink of the thing. Then
he helped Golden-Eyes from the tree, half-carrying her
to a stream that ran among the tree-roots after issuing
from a split rock. Kneeling, he squeezed the punctures
with all his might. A bit of yellow stuff was mixed with
the blood that came out, and he redoubled his efforts.
When he had all of it that he could squeeze, he sucked
the wound hard, spitting the poison quickly each time.
Then they soaked the arm in the chilly water, hoping
that that would reduce the fever that was already burn-
ing in Golden-Eyes' flesh.

It had helped for a while. They had made her a nest of greenery beside the stream, for she thirsted, once the fever took her. The adults had taken turns sprinkling her skin and fur with the cool water. Stands-Fast had found *zatku* and brought bits of the meat to her, but she had been unable to eat.

Yet she had been strong and determined. Their other child, Sprout, was her heart, and she was determined to survive and see him through the journey they faced. But the fever raged past the power of cool water to soothe it. She cried aloud in a voice that most of the Gashta had forgotten, deeper than their high mode, almost a growl. She moved about until they had to hold her to keep her from running away into the forest.

And she died. It took many days and nights of suffering for them all, and at the end she was so wasted with the fever that her fur was stiff and dry, like the withered grasses of the valley they had left. A very small hole held her body, and none of them could grieve that her pain was finished.

To lose two so quickly had filled the rest of the family with dread. There had been talk of returning to the Valley. Yet they had all known that nothing remained there for them. What lay ahead could be no worse than what lay behind.

Then Weaves-Cords-Together had broken his shoulder. One of the many narrow ledges in the track leading over the steps of the ridge had crumbled under his foot. If he had been a step further on or behind, it would have shaken him mildly. As it was, he dropped, his foot found no purchase, and his shoulder smashed against a groin of stone that jutted into the path of his fall.

The tough old fellow had made little complaint, but he had been unable to move with his normal speed. That had slowed the group badly.

But now they stood at the end of the ravine that led out into the wide lands. Night was almost upon them, and they had rested a bit after their descent from the ridge. They might well find good cover before the sun rose again.

Stands-Fast heard a soft footfall as Net-Weaver stole up behind him with a handful of insects and a few bean-pods. "Eat," she said. "We must go fast tonight."

He munched as he waited for the darkness to cover the plain ahead. When it seemed dark enough, the line of Gashta passed him, heading for the southwest and a line of deeper darkness that marked trees or brush. He fell in behind Net-Weaver, his axe in hand, his *zatku-hodda* slung over the other shoulder. Those who had gone out before had warned of many beasts, in addition to their old enemies, that roamed these lands. All were big, all were fierce, and all loved the flesh of Gashta. He did not intend to be taken by surprise.

Tansha was at the full, that night. Gozzo, a half-fruit in the east, had just cleared the horizon. Something moved in that partial light, off to the left toward the floor of the wide plain.

The family was now well out into the open. There wasn't a tree within running-distance. Without a word, every member brought *zatku-hodda* or axes to the fore and dropped back into the semi-circle that was their old defensive pattern. And then the approaching beasts became visible.

Stands-Fast groaned aloud, and there were gasps from the others. The children, their tiny hands clasped around the hafts of their little weapons, began to hiccup sobs. For, thundering toward them with a half-ton each of concentrated power, came four *so-shi-fazzu*. The triple horns glinted in the moonlight, and the armored shapes were bulky and gray as they came.

"Fazzu!" cried Stands-Fast and Weaves-Nets, in one breath. The half-circle dissolved, as each of the Gashta darted for any bush or small stone that might offer a bit of shelter. The night was filled with noise and dust, and the stench of the big beasts swirled around them.

Stands-Fast had hurled little Sprout behind a rock and was turning to find the other child, when he knew that there was no more time. He whirled, axe in hand, to find one of the creatures looming over him. He hacked futilely at its impervious side as it dashed past, almost touching him. But, miraculously, he was unhurt.

The *so-shi-fazzu* did not pause in their stampede. Dust misted high in their track, and it was a moment before he could find his way about the small space where his people had taken over.

A whimper sounded from the rock where he had thrown Sprout. The little one was curled about the angular projection, but, once he was straightened out and examined, he seemed unhurt. The two of them wandered about the trampled spot, looking for the others.

The grandfather lay where one huge hoof had smashed him flat. Net-Weaver had died, her body flung over small Plum, but the child was also crushed. The grandmother had been gored straight through the body . . . evidently she had faced them upright and indignant, as always.

Except for Stands-Fast and his son, all were gone. The two, alone now, could not even bury their dead properly.

Without speaking, they turned toward the shelter of the ravine. If they were lucky, they might make it before sunrise. If not—neither was afraid anymore. Death was a thing so familiar to them now that it held no terror.

They reached the cut just as the first sunlight was lighting the sky. The slanting feathertree gave a place to rest, and both were too weary and distressed to want food, as yet. They slept, cuddled together at one of the spokelike junctions, until the sun was past nooning.

It was necessary to find food, then, and both dreaded coming out of their haven. Yet they did, *zatku-hodda* at the ready. Stands-Fast regretted his axe, which had shattered against the hide of the *so-shi-fazzu*, but he knew that he must do with what he had.

They found the beanvines again. They discovered a group of *zatku* that made its home, now, in that ravine where water was plentiful. And a *toshki-washa* found them.

It had Sprout before his father knew anything was amiss. The sharp shriek brought him around in time to see the little one disappear in one gulp. And then the beast turned its bright gaze upon him.

It was small, as such animals went, but even at that it was half again the height of the Gashta and three times his weight. He knew that he could not face it alone and hope to survive, so he turned and dashed desperately into the brush at the edge of the cut. The twining ferns hampered him. He dropped his *zatku-hodda* and struggled to force his way through to a small tree that grew in the tangle, though he could hear the padding of the thing's paws just behind him.

He did not turn. He had seen death, eye-to-eye, too many times already. It might take him if it willed. He was too weary, too lost, too bereaved to fight it.

The first blow against his back was almost welcome. He felt no pain, and that surprised him. Another blow sent him flat, and he scuttled away into the thickest of the tangle. Rooted into ferns and grasses, he lay, panting so that his breath whistled between his teeth, and heard the beast walk leisurely up and down before the thicket. He heard it turn away and pad down the ravine.

He was terribly astonished. He had been dead. He had accepted that; indeed, been grateful for it. And now he still lived.

Then the pain came. The world swirled in stars of anguish. The night rang with strange cries. The darkness fell upon him with terrible suddenness.

vii.

He was terribly feverish. Root-Grower sent Leaf back into the safety of the tree as soon as light touched the sky, but she stayed beside the injured Gashta, trickling water between his lips from her small shell, and setting her hand over his mouth when he groaned aloud. By day, the *toshki-washa* hunted in this ravine; she felt that with every instinct she possessed. He must not attract their notice.

In those shadowed depths, the heat of the late-summer sun, so much warmer than it would have seemed, now, back in the valley, did not add to his fever. She changed the ferns under his head often, as they warmed from his heat, and she inspected the wounds on his back regularly.

The shallower fan of cuts was healing already. The Gashta always overcame infection or injury very quickly —or not at all. The other, that ran around his side, all but baring his ribs, was another story. It radiated heat, and the edges, where the fur parted, were beginning to fester. Something must be done quickly, or the stranger would die.

Root-Grower felt herself trapped in an impossible situation. She knew that she must get Leaf across the plain, into the foothills of those distant mountains to the southwest. There would be other Gashta there, she felt certain. But not for generations had one of her kind been capable of leaving an injured Gashta to suffer and die alone. *She* could not, it was certain.

All day she tended the wounded one, her ears trained to catch any pad of paw or slither of scale against rock. He seemed not to realize his situation. Sometimes he muttered softly, and sometimes he raised his arms as if to ward off an attacker. She knew that whatever had happened to him, leaving him alone and hurt so badly, had been a terrible thing. It made her wonder, more and more, if she had been wise in bringing her child out of the Valley.

The sun rode across the sky, and she could see circling *gotza*, above the webwork of leaves and branches that roofed the ravine. More than once she detected the distinctive pad of *toshki-washa* paws among the grasses of the gorge, but always it was in the upper part, around the bends. None of the beasts came down toward the end of the cut.

Toward sundown, the strange Gashta opened his eyes again. This time his true self looked out of them. She could see memories swirl behind those green surfaces for a long moment, before he brought himself fully into the present.

"It is that you found me where I hid?"

"It is. This one hunted for *zatku* among the ferns, and there you were. It is a wonderful thing that the beast that hurt you did not follow after you and devour you. There was no thorn or other good barrier to hold him from your side."

The pinky-tan face amid the tumbled silver-gilt mane became a mask, for an instant. Then the eyes closed, and he said, "It had eaten my child. My last, my only child. There are others, now grown up long since, but I had three small ones. One died on the mountain above the valley. One was crushed out on the plain. And Sprout was eaten by a *toshki-washa*, in this treacherous and beautiful place. The thing was not hungry."

She caught her breath. So. She understood much, for the loss of one child was a terrible thing. To lose three in the space of a few weeks must be pain beyond bearing.

But there were other, more immediate things for their minds to consider. "The great scratch on your back—it must be opened. I am glad that you waked, for it will be easier if you can turn as I direct. I have sharpened my knife all day. It was that I knew you needed sleep . . . I did not like to wake you."

He struggled to sit, found that he could not, and sank back onto his side, facing her. "Best to do it now," he said quietly. "Before the sun goes down. And then I will try to join you in that feathertree where you must have left the little one—I remember seeing a small one? Or did I imagine that?"

"That is my little Leaf. And she is there, where every family that has come from the ridge must have rested for a time. We will do this thing. Then we will go there. You are ready?"

He nodded and turned onto his stomach. The wound oozed yellow pus, as she bent over the mauled back and

combed the fur out of her way with her fingers. Her
little flint knife had been sharpened to as fine an edge as
it could take, and she positioned it above the first of the
swellings that interrupted the line of the cut. Push!

Stinking ichor gushed out onto her hands, fouling
his pale-gold fur. She squeezed the spot until the flow
stopped. Then she lanced the other two. Neither was as
big or as badly infected as the first, and she cleansed all
with her knife, cutting away ragged bits of flesh and
skin, shaving what fur she could manage to remove, and
plastering the entire long wound with *ko-so* that she had
crushed into a wet pulp.

He had made no sound while she worked, but that did
not astonish her. The Gashta did not complain. Pain
had been their companion for too long. But now he
spoke, so softly that she had to bend to hear him.

"This one is called Stands-Fast. All my family
perished on the plain. Is it that I might go with you and
the little one? Even three is a group too small for safety,
and I am of little use now. Yet I ask it."

This did surprise her. She had been so busy that she
had forgotten to give him any greeting or to say her
name to him. Now she laid one cool hand on his hot
face and turned him back to lie on his side again.

"This one is Root-Grower," she said. "The *Haigun-
sha* are my own kind, but in my rashness I thought to
take my child to a better place than the valley has
become. Stargazer gave us his good will, or I would not
have dared this thing. Now I wonder at my ill judgment.
It will be good to have another to travel with us. And
perhaps my small Leaf will ease your heart for the loss
of your own babies."

He didn't answer, and she thought him asleep. But
when she looked down, in the last of the light, she saw a
great tear roll off his nose and drop into the ferns on
which he lay.

Once it was fully dark, and the stillness was broken
only by the shrilling of a few late-season insects, she
touched his shoulder.

"Is it that you can move now?" she hissed into his

ear. ''It is the time, if such is possible.''

Stands-Fast was not ill-named. With her strong arm
helping from the unhurt side, he managed to stand
among the ferns. His steps were unsteady, and she felt
him shaking against her, as she guided him out of the
tangle that had saved his life. Once they reached the
faint path down the middle of the cut, it was easier. She
could hold him against her side, steadying his body so
that it didn't wrench the cuts too badly. In this way,
they made their slow way to the feathertree.

One of his arms was almost useless, but the other he
managed to get around the bole of the tree. She boosted
him from behind, and Leaf pulled with all her small
might from above. They got him into the lowest wheel
of branches, where he collapsed, breathless with pain.

It was not high enough. They both knew that. But it
was infinitely better than the fern-bed in which he had
been lying. *Toshki-washa* did not climb well and usually
ignored prey above their eye-level. All in all, Root-
Grower was pleased. It had surprised her that he could
move at all.

Once Stands-Fast was settled, she and Leaf took their
zatku-hodda and moved up the way. They must all eat,
and *zatku* were plentiful in that place, though their
hunting was a dangerous business. They found four big
ones jostling about one of the little pools in a small
stream that trickled from the cliffside and ran away to
be drunk by the deep soil and the rampant vegetation.

They ate two where they lay, but Root-Grower took
the other two and carried them back to the great tree.
Stands-Fast must eat, and though it was less appetizing
to consume a *zatku* that another had killed, it was far
better than having none at all.

As he devoured the *zatku* one-handed, she sat on a
branch above and kept watch. The night was clear. The
moons gave much light. There was now another to share
her worries, and she had no doubt at all that he would
survive. Perhaps, in time, they might become mates,
being both unattached at the present.

For the first time in days, Root-Grower was content with her decision to come forth, out of the valley of her birth.

viii.

Leaf had never been so weary. Her feet were sore and bruised, for the floor of the plain was pebbled with small stones, but she limped on, following her mother and the new Gashta.

They had rested for a long while in the ravine, sheltering in the feathertree and hunting *zatku* or insects by night, until Stands-Fast was able to walk. They had not even thought to wait until he was entirely well, for the year was waning, and they knew that they must go southward before the cold and snow came to the mountains. Now they walked under the moons, making their way southwestward toward the line of vegetation her mother had seen from the ridge, many days ago.

They were all thirsty. The shells of water that hung in their net bags were so little that they knew they could drink only sparingly. Even little Leaf understood that, and she kept her small mouth closed, breathing through her nose as her mother had instructed her to do.

But it was frightening. The moons made her shadows lengthen out from her feet—one long-long ahead of her, the other strange and squat at her side. The noises here were not the noises she had heard all her life in the valley. They weren't even those she had become used to in crossing the mountains, or in the vine-tangled ravine. Strange hoots and screeches moved on the light breeze, and her fur ruffled upward to hear them.

She was so very small that the dried grasses stood higher than her shoulders. She couldn't see more than her own length in any direction, and she took some comfort in the taller shapes of her mother and the hurt one. They went together, ahead of her, trampling down the growth that would have been hard going for her short legs.

Stands-Fast was getting tired, too. She could tell it by the way his legs wavered under his weight, and she went forward and tugged at her mother's fur until Root-Grower looked down.

"That one is tired," the little one said. "Is it time to stop now?"

Root-Grower tried to smile, and the effort soothed Leaf's feelings. "Not yet. There is little time before the sun rises. We will go on . . . if you can?"

Leaf looked about her at the moon-spangled seas of grass. There was something in her throat, stopping her voice, but she nodded and dropped back again. But this time she saw that her mother made Stands-Fast put his good arm around her, so that he could lean against her when he began to stagger.

They stopped before the light was more than a smear in the eastern sky. The appearance of a fair-sized bush, large enough to shelter them from the gazes of *gotza*, persuaded Root-Grower that this was the best shelter that they would find here on this drought-ridden plain. Unable to climb such a small shrub, they grubbed out holes in the dusty soil at its foot and burrowed themselves into the spaces beneath the thin screen of half-dead leaves.

This was no place where any *toshki-washa* might hunt, Leaf knew. Those fierce creatures preferred well-watered spots where *hatta-zosa* and *zeeto* could be found for the taking. And it would be the most sharp-eyed of *gotza* that could spy their golden coats, covered with tan dust in the tan expanse of the plain. In this most unlikely of places, the child felt safe for the first time since leaving her home.

They slept well, for all were exhausted. Stands-Fast moaned once or twice, but Leaf fell asleep again instantly, each time. And when the sun went down again, they trudged onward, driven by their Gashta determination and toughness.

It was several sleeps later when they came to the trees along the stream. As they drank their fill, both adults looked down the shadowed channel. Leaf saw the lazy trickle of water in the stony bottom, the straggly trees that marched away toward the southwest.

"This one wants to go there!" she said firmly. No matter how much she drank, her mouth still felt dry.

Her mother smiled, and Stands-Fast grunted.

"We will go that way," Root-Grower said. "To those who do not know where they are going, one way is as good as another. And at the least, we will have water. There are insects, too, for the catching. But first we will rest."

The next days were harder than it had seemed they would be. Insects were few, *zatku* not to be found. A couple of small *zeeto* fell to Root-Grower's *zatku-hodda*, and the group kept going, but more slowly each day.

It seemed to Leaf that they had been traveling forever. The stream ran along to their right, the trees grew thicker or thinner, the *gotza* circled overhead by day, and the moons waxed or waned by night. Sometimes she thought that this dreamlike journey might go on and on, never ending, until she couldn't lift her feet to walk. Then she would lie down in the scurf of dead leaves . . . as she could remember curling into her father's arms when she was tiny . . . and sleep and sleep forever.

She had been walking in a daze. Then she realized that she was looking into a pair of green eyes that peered from the level of her ankles. She stopped and called out to Root-Grower, who turned, *zatku-hodda* in defensive position.

But it was only a little one like herself. A bit larger, she saw as the child climbed out of the creekbed and looked the newcomers over cautiously.

Stands-Fast had leaned against a treetrunk when he

was deprived of the support of his companion's shoulder. Now he turned, and his eyes grew large.

"Petal?" he asked, the question shrilling through the quietness of the place. "It is that you are Petal, the child of Runs-Fast and Climbs-Rocks?"

The child came forward, her wariness gone. "Stands-Fast!" she said with assurance. "You waited for a baby to come . . . where is Golden-Eyes? Where is Net-Weaver? And the grandfather and your brother, and all of them?"

The Gashta sank onto his haunches. There was a trace of blood on the fur of his side, again, and Leaf went to gather leaves and wipe it away.

As she worked, he said, "All are gone, Petal. Sickness and *so-shi-fazzu* and a *toshki-washa* combined to take away my family. Are yours still safe?"

"Come with me. We have found a true *hoksu-mitto*. There is food, there is a fine-fine tree for sleeping. Much water, stones to make *shokka-washa* with. We stay and stay, for every time Remembers-Things says to go, we all think of how hard it is, how hungry, in other places than this. And he does not urge us, for he is tired of traveling, still, though the rest of us are rested."

She tugged at his arm, and he heaved to his feet. Turning to Root-Grower, he said, "Did you know, back in the valley, the family of Remembers-Things? It was one of many children, and he is a wise Gashta. Perhaps they will let us go with them, when the time comes when we must move southward."

"Oh, yes!" Petal shrilled, pulling Leaf forward from the spot where she had shyly peered from behind a tree. "All must come together to my family! Remembers-Things has said that before Gozzo wanes we must go, for the cold times come, and Climbs-Rocks says that it never grows cold in the south. Come-come!"

And they hurried, as best they could, to follow the excited child as she danced along the streamside. Leaf knew, now, that her mother had been right. Things would be good again. There would be laps to cuddle into, arms to rock her, voices to comfort her when dreams were frightening. Losing her first timidity, she leaped down the path after Petal, and behind her she could hear her mother's laughter.

ix.

They saw the land before them, wide stretches of green sweeping away to meet the distant shape of the western range. Long before they arrived at their goal, they began finding streams that meandered from the higher lands, seeking the low ground of the swamp. But they were not, as Climbs-Rocks had remembered, deep with water. Most could be waded by Leaf or by Petal.

It was an ominous thing. If this rainless time continued, and if it covered all the places they could find, what would become of the Gashta then?

Remembers-Things had a bad feeling about this. Their journey, after leaving the great tree, had been hungry and weary and full of danger. Only the thought of the good place toward which they were traveling had kept the combined families moving southwestward. And now, from the top of a feathertree, the old Gashta could see that the lowland was no longer the bountifully-watered place that it had been in Climbs-Rocks's youth. There were yellowed patches amid the green. He could see dead and dying trees and shrubs. It was a better place, still, than that they had left. But if matters did not change, it would not sustain the young ones into adulthood. It was a dying land. Any Gashta could see that.

They sat in a circle that night, considering what they should do. Runs-Fast and Climbs-Rocks felt that they might find better conditions by keeping on their present route.

"There is a great water beyond the swamp. Wider

than the plain—wider than this whole land. Surely where there is so much moisture nearby, there will be enough to make the land good," Climbs-Rocks insisted.

Remembers-Things twined his fingers in his mane, brushing wisps away from his cheeks. "It may be so. Yet if this has changed, why might that not have changed, also? It seems to me that we might well turn east. You can see from any treetop that the forest is green there. The gorges that you remember will hold water, for water comes from the rock long after it ceases to fall from the sky. We have seen that in our own place. I would like to turn eastward."

Round and round it went, some leaning toward the trip to the seaward edge of the swamp, some longing for the forests to the east. The little ones sat, round-eyed and wondering, as the discussion wore into the night. At last, Stands-Fast spoke for the first time.

"We are a very large group of people. There are many little ones. Any place will be hard put to supply enough *zatku* or fruit or insects for all of us. We should part, now, going in different directions, taking with us equal numbers of little ones. Here where there are many trees there is less danger from beasts, so we need not so many weapons and hands to wield them. Some will find good places. Some will not. But if it is done in this way, then all cannot arrive in a place that will not support them."

Remembers-Things reached out to touch the hand of his daughter, on his right. He looked across the circle at the group of children. When one is old, it tears the heart to go away from those near to you, but he knew that this was a wise thing.

"I will go east," he said. "Who will go with me?"

Pulls-Weeds bent her head for a moment. Then she looked up, her eyes glinting greenly in the moonlight. "I will go, *Pa-ha-izza*. Will Sees-Far go with us?" She glanced aside at the one who had become her mate.

He shook his fur, folded his hands in his lap. Remembers-Things knew from the way he sat that he did not want to go east.

So did Pulls-Weeds. "Is it that you would like to go another way?" she asked, her voice thin in the stillness. "If that is so, then do not hesitate to say it."

He closed his eyes for a moment. Then he opened them and said, "The mountains westward look promising to my eyes . . . which are, you will admit, among the best of any Gashta. I would go there, if one or more will go with me."

Root-Grower looked up. "It was my thought, while we marched last night. The slopes seem very green. It is a good place. Leaf and I will go."

But the little one shook her head decisively. "Go with *Pa-ha-izza,*" she said firmly. "Go with the grandfather!"

It took a time to sort out the different groups. Leaf was totally determined not to be separated from Remembers-Things, and Root-Grower, being concerned for her child who had much need for her still, changed her plan. In the end, Remembers-Things set out eastward with Pulls-Weeds, Leaf, Root-Grower, and two small boys. Climbs-Rocks and Runs-Fast took Petal and one of their younger ones and set out toward the southwest. Stands-Fast and Sees-Far headed toward the western mountains with the remaining two middle-sized children, knowing that they would find other families as they went to provide mates for them.

Where they had sat in the circle, nothing remained except for the scuffed remnants of a few Patterns and many prints of small feet. They separated, as had so many groups before them, going into the forests and the gorges, the swamp, and the foothills.

It would not be long, Remembers-Things knew, before they had forgotten the things that he had tried to keep alive for them. The Valley. The promise of help from the stars. The very names they had called each other. Survival was a terribly hard thing and demanded a high price of those who succeeded at it.

He took the hand of little Leaf, as they walked across the last of the grassland toward a forested ridge that promised water and good hunting. The small ones were spaced singly behind Pulls-Weeds, and only they looked around, now and again, trying to see the last of the group to which they had belonged.

After a while, they looked only ahead and didn't turn again.

BOOK III.

The Hagga

~~~~~~~~~~~~~~~

The beasts grow very large,
    and we are small-small;
the *toshki-washa* hunts in our forests
    and he likes the meat of Gashta.

The *gotza* go over trees, above mountains,
    very near to the moon, it seems to us. . .
why do they not decide to nest there?
    To stay there?

Every bad thing eats Gashta!

i.

Leaf perched on a rock, her flint axe poised. A *zeeto* was munching grass-seed in the small patch of greenery beneath the overhang of the big boulder, and she was waiting for its narrow head to appear, as it emerged to follow the row of grasses that she had put there to attract one of its kind.

Her pink ears told her with perfect accuracy exactly where the creature was. Soundlessly, she rose to her knees, bent a bit to clear the edge, and severed the animal's spine, just behind the head. It would feed her, and her single little one, for a long while. She would bury it in the cool shadow beneath a stone in the stream. Surely, by the time it was too foul to eat, she could find another kill.

It had been hard since Remembers-Things had died. First, Root-Grower had been lost in a stream, then Pulls-Weeds had broken a leg, forcing the remaining members of the family to stop for a long while in the same location. Then their group had met another, and Pulls-Weeds had chosen another mate from that, leaving Leaf and her mate, Fast, quite alone. She could barely remember the two young ones who had accompanied her, on leaving the group she and her mother had joined so long before. And then Fast had not been fast enough, falling before a *so-shi-fazzu*. She had been left with the single infant she had borne alive.

She was lonely. Dimly, she remembered the time

when she and her mother, too, had been alone. She didn't like the sensation at all, but they had met no other Gashta in many-many weeks. Families might not be large, always, but she was used to having at least one other adult at her side.

She glanced toward the tree in which Whistle waited for her. For one so tiny, he obeyed well, she thought, seeing his silhouette against the sky, which was now touched with the first light of morning. They would eat well, today. And tomorrow—it must take care of itself.

She dismembered the *zeeto*, taking shoulders and haunches, and burying the guts and skin neatly before submerging the portions to be saved beneath a rock in the brook. The sun was rising. She hurried with her burden to the foot of the big *rogo*, placed the meat in her net-bag, and climbed the rough bole, shinnying up it by digging fingers and toes into crevices in the bark.

Whistle shrilled a greeting, though he was not yet old enough to talk plainly. She divided the meat between them, and they sat on the branch, knees almost touching, with the food between. *Zeeto* was not *zatku*. Not by any means. But it was good enough, for now, and perhaps they would find *zatku* in the forest that they were about to enter. That behind them had been full of insects, fruit, game of many kinds, but only the *zatku* seemed to satisfy the craving that she felt almost constantly. And the *zatku* were going southward.

The *rogo* was a very old one, and they were able to find a notch where one of the big branches had fallen to wind or lightning, some time in the past. Cuddled together in that space, the two Gashta slept, confident that not even the sharpest-eyed *gotza* could detect them there. They woke as the sun set, and both descended the tree to make a meal of the remaining parts of the *zeeto*. Then Leaf set out toward the south, her axe and *zatku-hodda* over one shoulder, her net-bag slung from the other, and her baby clinging to the fur of her shoulders, wedged between the weapons and her neck.

Gozzo was high, Tansha just clearing the treeline to the east, when they moved out of the gorge along which they had been traveling. The forest here was thick and heavily undergrown with vines and brush. Leaf was panting with exertion by the time she found a *zeeto*-track through the dense growth. It ran almost in the direction she had chosen, so she followed it thankfully. The weight of the baby, little as he was, told on her, burdened as she was with other things.

The tiny path ended abruptly. Leaf stopped, her head cocked on one side, and regarded the strange thing before her. The forest ended in a straight line—and so distant was she from her origins that she had to think for a bit in order to determine what it was about that wood-edge that was so alien to her forest-trained eye. But there was something even odder beyond the line. Something had roughed up the soil into billows that were more than waist-high to the little Gashta. The ground was loose, almost, as dust, but it was also moist. She hadn't seen such a thing—or had she?

She thought hard. There had been soil something like this. She could dimly remember it. It must have been in that valley that she was beginning to think was only a dream-memory. Gardens. Yes, her mother had made gardens, and she had walked behind, pulling . . . things . . . out of loose dirt much like this.

Her heart thumped with excitement. Could it be that there were Gashta gardens here? She had thought that none in these parts of the world used that way, now. And these ridges of soil were so huge—no Gashta could make such, she felt certain.

She retreated a little way into the wood and scurried up a small tree. It was a relief to set Whistle on a branch with a scrap of left-over meat from yesterday's kill. From that height, she could see a bit further into the cultivated land. No, this was no work of Gashta hands. As far as she could see, the ground was furrowed into regular billows. There seemed to be something like a small dark cloud rising beyond the roll of land that was at the edge of her vision. A tang touched the air, and she sniffed.

Again an old memory was triggered . . . smoke. In the

valley they had used fire. She had almost forgotten.

This was something that she had not expected. Her path lay across the stretch of troubled ground, but she knew that trying to walk across the loose stuff, burdened as she was, would be all but impossible. She must go around.

Standing as high as she could in the tree, she gazed left, then right, gauging the relative distances. The broken land went away to her left and out of sight. That to her right ended in another straight-edge of forest a short distance from her present position. That was obviously the way to go.

Rested from her short stay in the tree, she arranged her load and set out along the forest's rim toward the point at which the straight lines merged. As she went, her eyes searched the moon-spangled wood for any hint of motion that might mean danger. It was a bad thing to travel alone. Every kind of enemy she knew was so much bigger than she . . . a Gashta needed many-many eyes in order to look for them all.

By dawn, she was far down the arm of wood that edged the empty space on the west. The plume of smoke had dwindled in the night, but with sunrise it rose again, and she began to hear odd sounds. Short barks of sound with almost the patterns of speech. There came a shrill hum that pierced her sensitive ears with painful intensity, and she saw a . . . thing . . . come out into the early-morning mists and begin moving along those rows of troubled soil.

There had never been a beast like that! It glinted more brightly than *so-shi-fazzu* armor. Its voice didn't vary from that piercing hum. Behind it, the dirt was changed, showing fresh moisture, and straight-line dimples followed a turning thing.

It had been a long time since Remembers-Things had told tales that made Leaf's mind work hard. The stress of hunting and running and caring for Whistle had made her forget, almost, how to think to a purpose other than survival. Now, resting in the new day, she looked across the rows of soil and thought. Really thought, with that quick Gashta wit that had been submerged for so many generations of exile.

Whatever was out there, she concluded, was not a creature. It was a thing.

She watched closely. It was, she could see, putting something into the ground. The way her mother had done, when she was tinier than Whistle. To make it grow into food. Yes! She felt that she had it in her hand, now.

That was a thing-that-makes-gardens. She admired it intensely. How much easier that was than digging with stones and sticks and bending to set each seed or shoot into place by hand. A *hoksu-etto!* Wonderful, wonderful thought, indeed!

This decided, she almost settled herself to sleep. Then another startling thing came into her mind.

Things must be made. Hands and minds were required for making things, as her kind seemed to have known for always. What kind of creature would it be that could make something like *that?*

Her big green eyes opened wide, sleep forgotten.

It would be a big creature—like almost every other on this world, she felt sure. Nothing else could or would make a tool so large. It would have hands. She could see from her perch parts that fitted onto other parts in a manner that cried out for the use of hands. The only thing she knew that had hands suitable for such work was her own kind, so she made a mind-picture of an oversized Gashta.

To think of something so convenient, it would be very smart. That thought shook her, for she knew on an instinctive level that only the fact that the Gashta were wise far beyond their size had allowed them to survive the predations of the animals here. A very large creature that was extremely intelligent might well be a terrible threat to her, as well as to Whistle.

She shivered. Then she turned and caught Whistle in her arms and composed herself to sleep.

She woke to moonlight. It was early yet, she could tell from the fact that Tansha was still low in the east. She stretched, her fur glinting silver in the moonlight. The rustling in the undergrowth told her that both insects and *zeeto* must be plentiful. Perhaps even a *zatku* might be stirring here. She took her *zatku-hodda* from the branch where it had rested beneath her net-bag.

"Stay here!" she cautioned Whistle. Then she slipped down the tree and set off through moon-dappled glades to look for something to feed her child.

There were *zatku* here! She heard their distinctive scrabble-lurch-crunch in the leaf-mold of the forest floor long before she saw the first. He was a young one, his shell still almost translucent in the moonlight. She circled him, poised her weapon, and brought it down neatly upon his carapace. It was the work of a moment to sever his head and to turn to the next.

The Gashta were never wasteful. One apiece was all they would kill, even of *zatku*. She knew that she could eat all of one and whatever Whistle didn't use of the other. She caught the first by a claw and dragged it back through the trees toward the spot where Whistle waited.

She heard him cry out before she was through the thick-branched brush to a point from which she could see his tree. There was the small dark dot that was Whistle, on the limb where she had told him to wait. But there was a big black thing bulking large against the treetrunk. And it was moving toward her child!

She dropped the *zatku* in the track she was following and hurtled forward, shrilling her cry of rage. The thing in the tree seemed not to hear her. Like the beasts of the forest? But she had no time to think of that, now.

Whistle's shriek sent her up the tree more quickly than she had ever climbed in her life. As she came near the place where the big, slow thing was moving upward, she could smell a peculiar reek—something in it of smoke, something of animal, and something else, very strange, very alien.

Tansha was high, now, and Gozzo was still up. She could see the thing. It was something like a Gashta—very remotely like, in that it had arms and legs and head positioned as her people did. But it was covered with something that was not fur. And on the huge foot that she was approaching there was a covering that seemed to be made of the hide of a *toshki-washa*. That familiar smell had not been obliterated by all the other odd stinks that this creature was surrounded with.

It had its hands on Whistle, now. The small one was crying out to her, its few words desperate. She scrambled a few inches further, leaned forward, and set her teeth into the leg above the *toshki-washa*-hide thing.

There came a bellow from above, almost deafening her, but she clung hard with hands and toes and teeth, feeling the hide of the thing give, tasting sweet-salt. Blood. She hung on, as the leg moved, began to thrash frantically. It tore her grip loose from the tree, but her teeth were set, and she was ready to die with them buried in that alien flesh.

She swung dizzily over the space below her. The thing she was biting moved up, and she banged her side against the bole of the tree. Then something the size of her head came down at her, knocking her loose from the leg, making the world spin even more madly than her drop into the undergrowth would have done. She lay stunned, breathless, and watched the intruder climb down the tree with her struggling little one in its hand.

As it set its feet on the ground, she struggled to rise. That made the dark sky come down and wrap her mind up in its arms. The last thing she heard was Whistle's despairing cry, as he was borne away through the trees.

ii.

August Mirabeau was a woods-rambler. Always had been, to his father's disgust. To give some legitimacy to his nightly prowls, he set a few traps along animal-runs.

He never told his father, however, that he was careful to spring them before leaving them to do their work. Lemaitre would have hit the roof.

No, August hadn't the least desire to find some mangled little beast in his old-fashioned snares. He wanted to scent the wind, feel the mulch give beneath his bush-goblin-hide boots, feel the trees around him in the darkness. He carried a rifle, for it would have been purest folly not to, what with the assortment of sharp-toothed predators that roamed Beta Continent. But he never used it except to defend himself. That was where he had gotten the hide to make his boots.

His mother had been much like him, but she had died so long ago that her memory was taking on the haziness of a dream. And, though his father had been devoted to his mother, he found her traits inconvenient in a twenty-year-old son whom he depended on for help in grubbing out the farm.

August often wondered what it was about his father that made old Lem take the hardest road, no matter what others were available. This farm, for instance. Beta wasn't really open for farming, as yet. Might never be, if the Company decided to keep it closed. But nothing would do but to clear their acreage right here in the middle of the woods of southern Beta. The title he had bribed a Company employee to fake for him wouldn't hold up a minute, under inquiry, August knew. But as long as they kept a low profile, they might get away with it. For a time, anyway.

He was strolling along, his quick eyes flicking from moon-dusted bush to tree-bole, to moonlit sky. One of the big trees raised its wheels of branches against the star-flecked darkness overhead, one of the moons streaking it with cool light. On a branch, not too high from the ground, was a small animal unlike any he had seen in his year on Beta.

He stopped, peering upward. Its fur shone pale-gold in the moonlight. And it was so small—less than a handful of fur. It had to be a baby whatever-it-was. Alone in the woods at night!

He leaned his rifle against a nearby bush and stretched. He could just reach the lowest branches. As he pulled himself into the tree, the tiny thing above him began to go "YEEK! YEEK!" in a voice so shrill that it made goose-pimples rise on him.

"All right, little fellow. I'm going to get you and take you back home. You'll be nice and comfy, and I'll find something you can eat. Pa can't find too much wrong with a critter as little as you are. Just take it easy, now. I'm almost there."

He heard a rustle below him, as if something else were climbing the tree. He had come just in time—something was after that baby. It probably wouldn't have survived the night, without him! He reached for the creature, and at the same time a set of terribly sharp teeth sank into his leg.

"By the Great Ghu's Grandfather, what's that?" he yelled, kicking wildly. He pulled himself onto the next set of branches and leaned down. Something furry was fastened to his leg, just above the boot-top. His fist knocked it away into the under-growth.

He turned back and caught the squirming young one, tucking it tightly to his side as he slid down the tree.

"Just lucky, Tiny. If I hadn't been there, you'd be something's supper, right now. We'll go on back to the house, right now. Pa'll take to you. I just know he will."

His voice was more hopeful than confident, but he caught up his rifle and headed back toward the house and his waiting father.

Lem wasn't a bit pleased . . . at first.

"You haven't enough crazy things you want to do. Anything to take you away from our real work! Now you bring in this pitiful little whatsit and it'll need all kinds of special attention. I swear, Gus, you're just exactly like your Mama, and no mistake. I never could understand what the two of you saw in roaming around the country, picking up every lame or lost beast you came across. Looks as if you'll never outgrow that."

"Well, Mama never did, that's for sure. The week she

died, she caught a sick kitten—you remember? It was almost well when she took sick herself. We kept it a long time—I guess we just gave it away to come here, didn't we?"

Lem's face softened, his scowl easing into a faint, reminiscent grin. August had found long ago that he could avoid most chewing-out if he could bring his mother into the discussion.

"Sarah was something, that's for certain. That crazy cat! It took on, when she died, as if it knew what had happened. Do you remember . . ." he had been standing beside the box into which Tiny had been put. His fingers were drumming on its edge. Now the little creature stood up in the box and touched those fingers with its own. Lem stopped, astonished.

"Damn if that's not the tamest wild thing you've ever brought in. Most of 'em scramble around and around until they're worn out. And even then they shake when you come near them. Look at the little dingus! He's putting his hand up against mine to see the difference in size . . . And look at that hand. If you forget that it's ninety sizes too small, it might be a real baby's. Where did you say you found this little critter, Gus?"

August told the story again, this time putting in everything he could think of to prove that his intervention was the only thing that saved the little one from certain death. When he was done, Lem stroked his jaw—with his left hand. He left the other in the grip of Tiny, who was examining the oversized fingers with much attention.

"Ever think that that might have been its Mama? Did you get a good look at it?"

Gus blinked. *"Not really. It was just fuzzy and not very big, and it bit like hell. I knocked it off into the brush. Didn't see it when I got down with Tiny, here. You don't think . . ."* his voice trailed off, as the enormity of the thing he might have done hit him. *"You think I'd better go look for it? See for sure?"*

Lem shook his head. *"No. It's been a while. If it came to, it's gone. If not, it's probably dead. No, the only thing we can do is to take care of this young one, if we can figure out how to. Look how human it is, when you get up close. Little face is just like any child's. Hands, too. It's just the fur that makes you think it's an animal.''*

Tiny looked up and yeeked imperatively.

"I'd say it's hungry,'' Lem observed. *"Probably its Mama had gone off to hunt. Like a cat does. See what we've got that it could eat. Mash up some of that stew we had for supper, Boy, and I'll see if it's thirsty.''*

While Gus warmed the bit of stew, Lem dipped a bottle-capful of water and set it beside the infant. He had expected it to lap up the liquid, but it looked at it, leaned over and sniffed. Then it cupped its hands and drank daintily from them, filling them several times.

"By the Great Ghu! See that? Now that's not like any animal I've ever seen or heard of! See if it wants any of that stew, Gus.''

August set a saucer of mashed-up stew beside Tiny. The baby scuttered over to it and sniffed deeply. It yeeked politely and dug in with both hands. But it managed its food tidily, not wasting a speck as it ate. When it was through, it rinsed its gravy-stained hands in the rest of the capful of water.

The two men looked down at it. Then they gazed at each other, their eyes full of wonder.

"I never heard of any animal that washed its hands after it ate,'' said Lem, at last. *"There's one on Terra that washes its food. I saw one once in a traveling exhibition. But it's just an animal, and nobody would ever think any different. This little critter—it's almost human! I'll bet there's somebody with the Company that would get a kick out of this. They've got a big lab at headquarters. Lots of scientist-types.''*

"I'd just as soon they didn't get their hands on Tiny,'' said Gus, lifting the little creature and cupping it in his hand. *"They'd get so busy measuring and testing and examining that they'd forget he's just a baby. Look at him, Pa! He's full, now, and he wants to go to sleep. See him curl up in my hand!''*

Tiny was, indeed, very sleepy. He had, after all, been kidnapped by a giant, removed from his tree and his mother, and introduced to a universe of strange sights, sounds, tastes, and sensations. The warmth of Gus's hand soothed him.

They tucked him away in his box and covered him with a pair of worn-out drawers. Before going to bed, they stood watching him for a long, long time. There was something so helpless and appealing about the little creature—both felt the tug of its dependence. Neither looked toward the window, where a little face peered in at the scene.

iii.

Leaf came to amid the ferns and vines. For a bit she was confused . . . what had happened to put her here? But something inside remembered that a dreadful thing had happened. Whistle? Whistle! A giant animal had taken him away!

She sat up, and the world spun madly for a moment. When it steadied, she stood, very carefully, and moved toward the tree where she had left her small one. Empty, as she had known it would be. But her axe was still on the lower branch where she had left it. And her *zatku-hodda*—ah, it was lying in a beam of moonlight, beside the *zatku* that she had been bringing for Whistle.

There was no hunger in her, now, but she crouched beside the prawn, cracked its under-shell, and ate it. She knew that she might not be able to hunt for a long time. At least until she found and rescued Whistle. Then she shouldered her weapons, secured her net-bag, and set off southward. That alien stink was still strong in the aromatic air of the wood, and her sharp Gashta nose led her with as much certainty as if she had seen the creature walk through the forest.

It was a long way, but she covered ground more quickly than ever before. Any predator that might have met her on the path turned aside on scenting her, for all wild things knew that it was more than dangerous to get between a female and its young.

Ahead, at last, she saw a light. Not a moon. Not a star. Not even a fire, which she remembered vaguely from her infancy in the valley. A white light, low to the ground.

She avoided the beam that the light threw across the grass, sidled into the bushes, and crept to the opening through which the brilliance came.

Her big green eyes widened in disbelief. A big bright space was inside that hole. And two of the huge creatures were there, looking down at something in a . . . a kind of nest. On a thing that stood up, square, between them. The brightness nearly blinded her, and she dropped back onto her haunches and covered her eyes with her hands. After a time, whirls of light stopped moving behind her eyelids, and she risked another peep. Just in time to hear her child's voice.

"Josso fusso?" asked Whistle. "Is there anything to eat? I'm hungry!"

In the midst of her worry, she was proud of him. It was the longest sentence, and the best-pronounced, that he had achieved. But the things that bent over him didn't seem to understand. Then one made a deep booming, barking noise, and the two moved about, clattering things.

To her relief, she watched them feed Whistle. The baby seemed to be completely at ease in its new surroundings, and Leaf relaxed a bit. Small Gashta were reliable indicators of the intentions of other animals. They seemed to have an instinct even more acute than their elders for anything that posed a threat. Of course, a creature six inches tall had to have some compensating factor to allow it to survive.

With much satisfaction, she saw the baby finish its

meal and wash its hands in a little thing more cupped
than a shell. Whistle might be the only one of her
children to live, but he was so bright and so brave that
she could feel nothing but pride in herself as a mother.

Her heart jumped, as one of the huge hands moved
down to lift the baby from the odd nest. But Whistle
said nothing. She could see his furry shape curl up in the
big palm.

The things . . . she had begun to think of them as
people, albeit out-sized ones . . . were making their
noises again, and she realized that this was talk. Real
talk. These were definitely not animals. They were
makers-of-things, as she could see when she gazed about
the room. And they were carers-for-little-ones. She
could see for herself, as they put something down over
Whistle and stood watching him sleep.

When the light went out, she curled down into a patch
of shrubbery and closed her eyes. A circuit of the big
thing in which her child was sleeping had assured her
that there was not even a Gashta-sized opening that
wasn't covered with something hard and clear that she
could see through. That was interesting. So was the
light. Everything she had seen in that brightly-lit place
had intrigued her.

Tomorrow, they would come out. They were day-
creatures, she felt sure. And the thing-that-makes-
gardens probably was theirs. She could hardly wait.

First light found her crouching beside the biggest
opening she could locate. Tracks on the dusty wood
before it told her that those big feet came this way
frequently. Inside, she could hear them stirring, their
deep-toned talk vibrating the air. And she heard
Whistle's chirp of greeting.

She was tempted to go back and look through that
other hole to see what they were doing with him, but she
suppressed the desire. Whistle trusted them. She felt
that they were not dangerous to him. If she was to get
inside, she must stay here until this big slab of wood
moved aside, as she saw from the marks on the wood
below her feet that it must do.

After a long time, there came the heavy thud! thud! of approaching feet. She drew back, clear of the slab, tense and waiting. There was a clicking, and the thing swung outward. Leaf sprang forward, almost tangling with the legs coming out, and was inside the room, blinking in the harsh light.

"Uka! Uka! Bizzo! Aki pokko!" cried Whistle, dancing up and down in his box. He was talking better than he ever had before.

"Mother is here," she answered, avoiding the grabbing hands of the other big one. "You can show me in a minute. I must talk to these—these Hagga, these big ones, right now. If I can make them hear."

The baby subsided, only his big bright eyes showing over the edge of his box. Leaf backed slowly to the thing that held her child, watching the two Hagga, who were, in turn, watching her with much interest. They made no more moves toward catching her. That reassured the little Gashta.

"This one is my little one," she said, her voice shrilling in the confining space. "It is that you care for him, but he also needs my milk!"

One of them hunkered down, almost on an eye-level with her. Its big voice boomed, but she didn't understand the words. She lifted her hands to her ears politely, trying to show that she couldn't comprehend what he was saying. Then she turned and swarmed up the table-leg to the box. It was a snug fit for her, but she managed to get into it and take Whistle in her arms.

They stood staring at her with their tiny dark eyes. The big faces turned toward each other. Their shoulders moved, and their hands. Then they went out, leaving the mother to greet her child properly.

iv.

Lem had never seen anything like it. The little furry creature had swished past his leg so fast that he had hardly had time to glimpse it. Then it had been dodging like a dancer through Gus's hands. But it hadn't scurried around the room, terrified, as any other animal would have done. It backed up to the table. It watched them exactly as if it were sizing them up.

The baby had yeeked at it, and it had yeeked back. After that, the little one had settled down to observe what happened, just as if she had reassured it. And that this was the mother of the thing in the box he had not a doubt in the world. But their shrill voices were purest torture. Something like feedback shrilled through his hearing-aid, making his head ring, and he turned, after a moment, and followed Gus outside.

"Looks like we've a family of them, now," he said. For once he didn't sound irritated, even to himself. "I wish we knew what they are. Never heard any description of things like those, even from the prospectors. Pretty little things, aren't they?"

August nodded. "I'm glad I didn't hurt her, when I hit her. Did you see the lump on her little head? That must be where my fist hit her. I wish I could tell her I didn't mean it. I thought she was something after the young one."

Lem laughed. "Wouldn't surprise me a bit if you could explain that, one of these days. That is one smart critter. And she understands enough to know that if we didn't hurt her baby, we won't hurt her. Think about that for a minute. There're a lot of people who can't figure that logically."

"You think they're intelligent?" Gus sounded doubtful.

"Intelligent? I know for damn sure that they're intelligent. Look at that baby! It sized us up, figures us out, and settled down as happy as could be. Its mama is do-

ing the same thing, right now. There may be some who have to have some damned expert tell them something before they'll trust their own judgment, but I'm not one of them. If those little fuzzy people aren't intelligent, then neither are we. And that . . . whoo-boy!" His laugh shattered the morning. "Can you guess what sort of cold sweat Grego and the Company boys would be in if they knew that Zarathustra has a native species that is sapient? They'd mess their pants, Son. Then they'd set out to kill off every one they could find before anybody else could discover them."

August turned pale, as the implications hit him. "You're right, Pa. The Company isn't about to give up title to this planet. It's a gold mine to them, what with the farming and the veldbeeste herding, and the sunstone trade. We'd better keep this mighty quiet. But I hate sending them back into the woods. You can see that they're too small to have to cope with things as big and tough as bush-goblins and damnthings. They need somebody to take care of them."

"Well, they've got us, haven't they?"

Without waiting for an answer, Lem went to the toolshed and got out a saw and a couple of hinges. "Make 'em a door," he said, seeing his son watching him questioningly. "They've got to have the run of the place. You don't shut up people and keep them prisoners."

The saw burred at the tough wood, cutting out a neat rectangle. When the wood came away and fell onto the floor, a small face peered through from the other side.

"Yeek?" asked Mama.

"Just a minute. You'll see when I get the hinges on. One door coming up!"

And the minute the oblong of wood was hung, she pushed through onto the porch. Then she pushed back. With a squeak, Tiny joined her, and for a while a frantic game of make-the-door-swing kept the Mirabeaus in stitches.

"Time to eat breakfast," said Lem at last, wiping tears of laughter away with the back of his sleeve. "This is better than a circus, Gus."

They followed the little ones into the house and set about making breakfast, working around both of the visitors. And they were into everything. Their curiosity was accompanied by emphatic yeeks that almost blasted Lem's head off. At last, he fiddled with the modulator of his hearing aid, trying for a level that would let him hear August, yet wouldn't transmit those ultrasonic yeeks directly into his brain.

He sat at the table, manipulating the complex instrument. Tiny sat facing him, short legs spread apart to let his plump stomach rest on his thighs. Every move the man made was echoed by the baby, who squinched his minute face when Lem frowned, twitched his fingers when Lem moved his own, and generally followed his motions like a mirror-image.

Lem laid the thing down and straightened to unkink his shoulders. Tiny made a faster-than-sight dive and came up with it in his hands. By the time Lem got it away from him, it had been through enough to destroy its usefulness forever, but he clipped it onto his ear, hoping that something still worked. Being almost deaf was a nuisance.

The infant turned to look down at its mother, on the floor beside August's feet.

"Uka, posse-waji? Fusso? Ja'aki fessi!" he said, quite plainly.

"Gus! August Mirabeau, did you hear that?" Lem shouted.

Gus looked up from the stove. "Just their usual yeeking, Pa. What's the matter?"

"Give me that skillet, and you put this in your ear. Listen!"

When the device was clipped to Gus's ear, Lem leaned down and put a saucer of fruit, bread, and plume-bird eggs beside his small guest. "Ready for breakfast, Ma'am?" he asked.

"Fusso!" she said, happily. "Pa-ha-li, bizzo!"

The boy's eyes widened. He didn't understand what it was that she had said, but he could hear the words quite plainly. He took the aid from his ear and held it up to the light. Nothing looked different, but something definitely had changed. The shrill yeeks that had been audible to human ears were evidently only the lower range of the sounds of the furred creatures' language.

Tiny had skittered down from the table to sit beside his mother, digging into the saucer's contents with neatness and enthusiasm. As they ate, they chattered, by turns, as if commenting on the quality of the cuisine. Lem was leaning on the edge of the cookstove, his face red with suppressed laughter.

"You're right, Pa. They are sure enough, bona fide sapients. You think we ought to notify the Navy? They've got all sorts of experts on Xerxes."

Lem straightened, sobering. "You want to get us kicked back to Mallorysport? With all those drifters and bums? By the Great Ghu, August, sometimes I think you never use your head for anything but storing fluff!" He stirred the eggs in the pan, his back bristling. "We've found them. They're happy, it seems as if. As long as we all get along fine together, there's no need to tell anybody anything. We just go along with our farming. If anybody comes nosing around, we get the little ones to hide out in the woods until they're gone. But nobody has ever come this far into the woods, and there's no reason why they should. Not for years, yet. If ever. The sunstones are further north, and what else is there to bring people onto Beta?"

They sat at the table to eat their own breakfast. The two Gashta, having finished their meal and washed their hands, climbed up and sat on one end of the table to keep them company.

Lem could see that they were itching to look into all the strange things in the room. It was a bit of a worry, for who knew what they might take apart with those clever hands of theirs. He puzzled all through breakfast. When he pushed back his chair, he went into his bedroom and rummaged in the big chest that hadn't been opened since Sarah died. In one corner he found what he had been looking for.

He went back into the kitchen-sitting-room with it in his hand, and Gus looked astonished.

"Mama's Chinese puzzles? You're going to let them play with those?"

"Can't hurt them. They're solid wood—some Terran stuff like mahogany or such. And they're small, just right to fit in those hands. I'll bet this keeps them busy all the time we're in the fields. Out of mischief. You wouldn't want to come back and find the communicator taken apart, would you? We'd never know what was going on in the rest of the world, if that happened. I . . . couldn't seem to stand to get these out, before now. But these little people—it's not like having some human play with them."

They left Tiny and his mother sitting on the table, busy with the intricately-interlocked squares. The two were so fascinated with their new toys that they had made only the briefest of excursions outside, after breakfast, to relieve themselves, returning immediately to the tabletop and their new toys.

Lem felt that he had handled that situation very well, indeed. At noon, he and Gus came into the sitting-room to find the puzzles entirely apart, and two puzzled Fuzzies busy trying to figure out the way to get them back together.

"You know, that's interesting, August. I never thought about it before, but who'd think, just seeing those things with no explanation, that the point was to get them apart and then reassemble them? An animal wouldn't. I've seen a lot of so-called intelligent beings that it never would occur to. These little guys are an awful lot like us, you know that?"

Gus had put the stew on and was getting the bowls out of the cupboard. Tiny, feeling a bit tired of his puzzle, scrambled down from his perch, dashed across the short expanse of floor, and went hand-over-hand up Gus's pants leg. Arriving at the top, he surveyed the situation from a convenient shoulder, then he ducked inside the boy's shirt collar. The big green eyes peered, sideways, out of the slit between the top two buttons.

Lem sat to watch the other Fuzzy manipulate the puzzle parts.

"We've got to name them," he said suddenly. "Can't go around calling them hey you and whatsit. He's Tiny, already, but what'll we call her?"

Gus glanced over, raised his eyebrows, and said, "Well, she's got eyes as green as grass. How about Grass?"

Lem shook his head. "Not pretty enough. She's a beautiful little lady. As beautiful, almost, as your mother was. Hmm. Gus, would it bother you if I called her after Sarah? I never thought I'd want to do that, after she died, but somehow this feels right."

Gus was so utterly surprised that he could only nod. He would never have believed that his father could change as rapidly as he seemed to be doing, in the one day since the small creatures had come to live with them. His mother's name. He looked at the small furred person, and she gazed back at him with composure. There was a hint of impishness deep in those big green eyes that reminded him of his mother, indeed.

"A fine name," he said.

They left for the afternoon's work with easy minds. Nobody could have behaved better than their two Fuzzies, that morning. They expected the same for the afternoon.

Lem felt something that he had almost forgotten, as he stepped onto the porch, that evening. Anticipation. He had thought it had died with Sarah. Only a few times had he shared the sensation with August, after her death. But his throat held a lump, as he opened the door, and something suspiciously like warmth filled his heart.

He stopped, just inside, staring around in amazement.

The amount of chaos possible to one Fuzzy seemed to be in inverse ratio to its size. Double the number of Fuzzies, and something like disorder to the tenth power resulted.

The house looked as if twin tornadoes had passed through it. Nothing was torn up, he found when he looked carefully, but everything was upside down, inside out, or dumped, as in the case of wastebaskets, firewood-box, stationery tray, and nut-and-bolt-bucket.

"By Ghash and Garnets, they've stirred the place with a stick!" he choked, as Gus came in behind him.

Two pairs of eyes regarded them soberly over the edge of Tiny's box.

The Gashta are a tidy people, and they know disorder when they see it—or create—it. Leaf suspected that her afternoon's fun might have repercussions . . . and she wasn't wrong in the least.

Lem sat at the table and looked at the two fiercely. His graying brows met over his black eyes. His voice was a boom, as he said, "Now look here, kids. This just isn't going to do. We keep a neat place here, the best we can without help. And if you're going to live with us, then you've got to pitch in and clean up this mess. Come on! Down on the floor. We're going to get this place spotlessly CLEAN!"

"Ke-en?" asked Leaf. She looked about, wondering what he was getting at.

Lem shook his head. Then he grinned. "Got to get you a hearing aid, Gus. You think my old one would do, if we turned it over to Tiny for a minute? Anyway, she just said 'clean,' or I'm not sitting here. Now to show her just what the word means."

It didn't take long. Once Tiny and Sarah understood that all the things they had had such fun doing all afternoon must now be undone, they pitched in and had as much pleasure from the cleaning-up as they had from the messing-up. Lem had intended to sit and supervise, but neither he nor Gus could stay out of the game that the two Fuzzies made of restoring order.

Supper was served at the table—for all four. The fact that the two Fuzzies had to sit on rather than at the board subtracted nothing from the festivity of the meal. And, when the stew-pot was put in the middle of the table, Lem found the two puzzles, side by side. Back

*just as they had been when he took them from the
trunk.*

*All through supper, he stared from one to the other of
his guests. They were so furry, so cute, so cuddly. But
under those pale-gold manes, behind those innocent,
snub-nosed faces were minds at least the equals of his
own. He knew it as surely as it was possible to know
anything. It made him a bit uneasy.*

*But that unease vanished, after the supper bowls were
cleaned and put away. Gus built up a low fire in the
stove they had made from a steel drum, for the evening
was cool for so early in the fall. Then Tiny climbed up
Gus and burrowed into his lap. Sarah did the same to
Lem, leaning back into his arms so trustingly that he
began, almost unconsciously, to stroke her fur.*

*The room was quiet. He and Gus seldom talked
much, except about things of immediate importance.
But this was a different silence, somehow. Filled with
warmth. With contentment. With . . . but he stopped his
thinking right there.*

*His wife had been all the love he needed in his life. He
had determined never to let anyone or anything take her
place.*

*Yet a tiny voice in his heart persisted in whispering,
"With love."*

V.

Life had never been so easy . . . or so much fun. For the
first time, it occurred to Leaf that the old tale of a wonderful place for all the Gashta might be a true thing. The
tale had said that those who came to aid would come
from the stars, true, but in observing the strange devices
that her new family used and controlled she came to the
shrewd conclusion that they might well have traveled to

this world from another. Why not, when they could set the machine in motion to plow up or to cultivate their fields and never dirty their hands?

She spent many an hour enjoying the ride in the closed cab of the cultivator. While the thing moved up and down, measuring out seed or fertilizer, thinning plants or tilling in weeds, she watched the steady lights of the meters and gauges, saw how Gus or Lem programmed into it the task that it was to do that day, and thought very deeply about the people who could make this most wonderful of things.

Tiny was too fidgety to spend a half-day riding across the fields. He usually tagged after whichever of the Mirabeaus was designated to cut wood for the heater or to tighten the fences about the pen where they kept their stock of plume-birds. But she loved the hum of the mechanism, the quiet rolling of the soil outside the window. And most of all she loved the lessons in talking that she was given in those long hours of sweeping back and forth over the land.

Gus had begun it. "Meter," he would say, pointing to the seed-density control.

"Mee-to," she would echo, bending to see exactly what kinds of marks were on the face of the thing and where the knob was positioned.

"Lever," he continued, and she nodded and said, "Lee-va."

They went over every item in the cab. They named everything they could see from its windows, all the parts of Gus's clothing, her own fingers and toes and face and fur. As the weeks went by, and the winter crop was put into the ground, the little Gashta built up an amazing store of words.

Lem realized it first. "You know, we're talking to the kids almost as if they were human?" he asked his son one evening. "Don't often hear them say something in their own language, anymore. And that Tiny! He does out-do any young one I ever saw. You'd think he'd been born right here with us, the way he's beginning to rattle on. And have you noticed how much help he is when you're fixing fence or mending the out-buildings? You hardly have to think about needing a nail or a wire-cutter, when there he is with it. The little cuss understands what we're doing, that's all there is to it.''

They were sitting before their heater, enjoying the glow of warmth from its rounded sides. The field work was finished with, for the time being, and they knew that a winter of chess and reading and boredom lay before them. But this winter looked as if it might be far different from the last. Instant fun and games lay in their laps in furry bundles, listening to the talk and beginning to doze.

August tickled Tiny under the ear, and the little one wriggled luxuriously and closed his eyes again. ''They're almost too bright,'' he admitted. ''I've come to see that you're right about not telling anybody about them, but Pa, what if there's more out in the woods? The fact that nobody has reported them doesn't mean that the woods may not be swarming with them. They'd be dead sure to stay away from any place where a prospector was placing his shots. And from the air they'd hardly show up at all, even if you knew to look for them. What about them? I hate to think of the little guys toughing it out in the chill, running from bush-goblins and getting eaten by damnthings. Makes me sort of sad.''

Lem nodded agreement, but he had nothing to suggest. Leaf, in his lap, had understood quite a lot of what had been said, however. And, being Gashta, she understood that life is an uncertain thing, requiring that what you intend you must do immediately. She didn't stir, for she knew that an attempt to go outside into the darkness would distress both the Hagga. She waited quietly for bedtime.

Whistle had adapted almost entirely to the new sleep-by-night schedule. It had been harder for her, and it was no problem to remain awake after both the Hagga were breathing heavily in their bedrooms. Then she slipped from the blankets that she shared with Whistle, found her *zatku-hodda* in the corner where she kept it, and crept softly out through the swinging door.

She had not been out in full dark since finding her new people. Now, in early winter, beneath two chilly-looking moons, she breathed the night-smells of the forest and stepped out briskly. The winters in this part of the land were mild, with no snow. The air was crisp and tangy, and the leaves of many generations of trees scrunched softly under her furry feet. It felt fine, being alone in the forest again . . . fine, and free. But it was not a thing that she wanted very much of for very long. Not any longer. Now she knew that there was a good life for her kind, and she had no idea of turning her back upon it. Or of sharing it, indeed. The Gashta were loving, but they were shrewd and attentive to their own needs.

Knowing the way she must go, she traveled swiftly and soon found herself back near the gorge she had left so many-many weeks ago. It was the logical place for any migrating Gashta to come out into this side of the stream. She found a high rock and sat on it, gazing through the shadows with the ease allowed by her fine night-vision. She knew that some of her people would be coming in this direction, for the *zatku* had moved here in numbers. They had led her after them, and others would come, too. Tonight. Or tomorrow. In time.

For all her spacefaring ancestry, Leaf was the product of generations of nature-oriented people. Nothing could be rushed, she knew. One decided what to do, and then one waited for an opportunity. Patience was such an inborn trait, by now, that it hadn't even a name. It was a fact of being.

So now she waited on her rock, her *zatku-hodda* by her side, just in case a restless *zatku* came into her view. Her nose found no scent of *toshki-washa*. The land was too steep here for *so-shi-fazzu*, and the *gotza* were asleep for the night. There were other, less frightful, things in the forest, but she relied upon her sharp ears and her sensitive nose to warn her if any such were on the move.

But no Gashta came that night. It was, indeed, many

nights afterward when her musings were interrupted by the familiar sound of the talk of her own kind. She had been napping, trusting that very thing to warn her if anyone came along the game-trail beside her rock. It was impossible to nap by day—there were too many fascinating things to see and to do about the farm for that, so she had combined watching and dozing in a cautious mixture.

She roused at once, however, and crawled to the edge of her rock. "This one is here," she shrilled. "Is it that there are Gashta nearby?"

"Ja'aki bizzo mitto," came the reply. "Others are with me. Who is there on the rock?"

She scrambled down to the path, which at this point was covered with tall ferns that had not yet been touched by frost. "It is that I come to tell you. Help has come for the Gashta."

"From the stars?" came the quick question. A male with dark-golden fur stepped out into the moonlight to look at her closely.

"It may be so. They have many-many powerful things. *Hoksu-washa*, indeed. And fine places for us to live. Fine food to eat. I have seen them. I think, if you go on to the east, that you will find them, too. They are Hagga. . . . very big people, HUGE people. They look very strange, very frightening. But they are not dangerous. Not like the beasts of this place."

"It is that you have found such Hagga?" came the quiet voice.

She wriggled uncomfortably. Her family, she knew, had just enough room for her and for Whistle-Tiny. There were—she counted a hand of adults, as well as a baby in this group—too many here for her *hoksu-mitto* to hold.

But she was no liar. None of the Gashta were, that having been one of the unbalanced traits that had been excised from her race.

"This one has found such. My small one is there now. But it is not so big for so many-many people. My Hagga say that other Hagga live to the east. It is there you must go and find your own. Tell others, if you see them. They have no fur, and they are tall-tall. More than *so-shi-fazzu.*"

He grunted softly. Then he put out his hands and took both hers. "These ones are grateful to you. We will go east. We will tell others, if we see them. It is time . . ." he looked about at his family, standing patiently in the moonlight . . . "that help came to the Gashta. It has been promised in the old stories, but I thought those to be dreams. We grow fewer and fewer. We will soon be gone, without some help, from the stars or from some other place."

He took the baby that his mate had handed him. It climbed onto his head and sat there surveying this strange female with big, glimmering eyes. There was a hissing of shrill conversation among the group. Then they hugged Leaf and went on along the path. Before they had gone ten paces, the big ferns swung behind them, hiding them from her sight.

Leaf looked about at the night. The smells, the sounds; the feel of the forest was familiar. It was not comforting. She had a better place than this, now. She turned and hurried back toward shelter and safety and her new family.

vi.

The family moved eastward, as the strange female had suggested. But they went slowly, for as they forged through the forest and threaded their way up and down streams in order to find possible crossing-places, they found more and more *zatku*. Evidently, the prawns had migrated here in great numbers.

They grew fat. *Lo-Shta* (Dark-Fur) and his mate congratulated themselves often on finding such rich hunting-ground. Whether or not the Hagga they had heard about lived here, it was a good place for Gashta.

Baby grew too heavy to sit on the heads of any of the adults in the family. He was cross about it, but every shoulder was his to perch on at any time. He sat there with bad grace, for it had always been a peculiarity of the little Gashta that he preferred head-sitting to anything else. However, that was the worst drawback to this new territory that any of his family could find.

One afternoon, as they rested in the tops of two adjoining feathertrees, something big crossed the sky above them. It was NOT a *gotza*. Generations of experience had made *gotza*-recognition a matter of certainty among their kind. It was quiet, it had no wings, and it moved in a straight line.

Dark-Fur looked after it, once it had passed out of sight. His forest-bred eyes noted individual trees beneath the line of its flight, and his mind was busy.

"The one we met said that those Hagga have wonderful things. That was a thing, for there has never been a flying-beast like that in our skies before. And a flying thing is a *hoksu-washa*, indeed. It is that it might be going back to its nest for the night, as the *gotza* do."

"We are in a new place," his mate said. "It might be that other things fly in these places. Things not-like *gotza*."

"No Gashta we have ever met has mentioned such things. No, that is a Hagga-thing. I will follow it to its place. Will any go with me?"

They talked among themselves, but none wanted to go on such a chancy errand. There was no discussion, once the decision was made. He detached the baby's hands from the fur of his mane, touched his cheek to that of his mate, and trudged away with his *zatku-hodda* at the ready.

It was not safe, going through the forest by day. He hurried, but he was cautious. The thing he followed was long out of sight and hearing, but his unerring sense of direction kept him to his course, even when the light failed him. He toiled through the darkness, his ears pricked to identify every sound from trees and under-growth, and he lost little time in his journey.

He knew that he was going straight, as that flying thing had gone. He hoped that it did not roost very far away, for he hated leaving the family for long at a time. It was a great relief when, just before sunrise, he found himself standing at the edge of a clearing, in the middle of which were several very large and totally unfamiliar humps or hummocks. There was also light there. No sunlight, or even that given by one of the moons. The Hagga was evidently at home.

Dark-Fur didn't dare explore too closely while the alien creature was there, so he climbed a small feather-tree to wait for developments. After a time, a huge creature came out of the big place and climbed into the smaller place—the flying-thing, *Lo-Shta* saw, once he looked closely. It rose from the ground and went back the way it had come.

Here was the chance he had waited for. He scurried across the grass and peeped into a small place like a burrow, if burrows stood above the ground. Many bright things lay on a flat space just above his eye-level. He could see glints, as the sunlight struck through cracks around the opening. He climbed up and inside.

A wealth of tools and weapons lay there. He couldn't decipher the uses of most, but one stole his heart. It was long, and one end was sharp, just right for digging. It was also tapered enough to be used for killing *zatku*. And it had a wooden handle, just right for his grip. He looked about, took the thing from the platform, and slipped down onto the floor again. With such a weapon-tool, he had no need for an ordinary *zatku-hodda*, and he left it lying where he had dropped it.

Now he had ample time to sleep, and he lost no time in finding a safe spot and curling up for a long nap. When he woke, the sun was low over the trees, and he nosed about the place, looking for a way to get into the big-big place. But there was no opening that he could find that he could fit through.

The Hagga returned just before sundown, and Dark-

Fur retired to the forest. It was a long time before the strange light went out, and he bounced restlessly from tree to ground to bush to shed to window, as he waited. But the night brought no better luck than the day had— less, for he had not looked for any more new tools. One was all that any Gashta could ask for, two was a bit of a burden.

Though the Hagga busied itself about the place for a time, it left at last. And it didn't close the barrier to its burrow quite tightly. Not nearly tightly enough to keep out a determined Gashta.

Dark-Fur moved cautiously about for a bit, but it was unfamiliar and a bit frightening inside the Hagga-place. And he could smell strange odors that confused his sharp nose. He resumed his prowlings outside for most of the day.

He had returned to peep into the Hagga-place again when he heard the hum of the flying thing as it returned. He slid into a shrub, as the big creature tramped past. It turned almost immediately and went back to the flying-thing, but now the strange light was inside its burrow. Dark-Fur couldn't resist taking a look at this wonder.

He stood in the square space. Other door-holes opened from it in bewildering array. He was trying to make up his mind what to do when he heard the sound of footsteps—forbiddingly heavy ones. He darted into an opening, through another space, into another, smaller space that was much darker than the rest. Inside it, in turn, was a chilly place with something hanging around it to conceal it, like vines about a nest. He slipped into the concealment and peeped out through a narrow slit in the stuff that hid him.

The big feet clumped about for a short while. There were anonymous clicks and thumps and squeaks that he didn't try to identify in such an alien place. Then the sounds came toward the place where he had taken refuge. He crouched into a tiny ball, but his eye was still at the crack.

Suddenly the place was filled with that dazzling light. In spite of himself, Dark-Fur cried out. His startled leap had pulled aside the stuff, and he was looking up—and up—and up at the biggest creature he had ever seen.

It was not so heavy as a *so-shi-fazzu*, but it stood much taller. Its head was covered with coarse whitish fur, and its face, too, had a straggle of fur across its middle. But its body! There was no fur at all, there. Instead, it was covered with something so strange that the Gashta had no word at all for it.

The thing hunkered down to face Dark-Fur. It made booming noises at him, but there was no threat in them. And it didn't make any quick motions that showed menace.

Dark-Fur looked up at it, his big green-amber eyes solemn. "You are Hagga?" he asked, but the thing didn't understand his words. He had not really expected it to, for he couldn't make out anything it was saying, though its big voice continued to talk to him. This was nothing that could understand Gashta, that was certain.

It reached out a hand, very slowly. Dark-Fur almost drew back, but the motion was so tentative, so obviously non-threatening, that he stood still and let the thing touch his fur. Then, his curiosity overcoming his caution, the Gashta reached out a hand and felt of the stuff that covered the Hagga's body.

It was amazing. Not fur. Something like the stuff he had hidden behind but softer, not so slick.

While he was thinking this over, the creature began to stroke the Gashta's fur. Very gently the big warm hand smoothed over the little body of the person before him. Dark-Fur found, to his surprise, that he was being lifted into the Hagga's lap.

Not since he had been a small one had he been lifted so. There was something infinitely comforting in the feeling it gave him. The huge body of the thing radiated warmth, and its burring voice was soothing. When it stood, holding Dark-Fur in its arms, he didn't protest. Something inside him breathed a sigh of relief.

For the time being, he didn't have to worry about anything. Not about predators. Not about shelter. Not about food, even, for had not the stranger said that the

Hagga had wonderful things to eat? And something deep inside him was responding to the physical presence of the big creature. As if some lost part of him had been found.

They sat in the other big place, on something soft that fitted the Hagga comfortably. It talked softly all the while, and in a bit it indicated that it wanted to examine Dark-Fur's teeth. This startled the Gashta for a moment, until he realized that the Hagga wouldn't have any idea what sort of food he could eat until he saw the kind of teeth he had. Very logical. Evidently the Hagga were not only clever at making things. They also had good logical minds.

Once the creature had looked into his mouth, it carried him into still another space and set him on the floor. The Hagga moved about doing inexplicable things with its hands, and at last it handed down a bit of something brownish.

Dark-Fur sniffed it. "*Hoksu-fusso*, indeed!" he cried, and stuffed it into his mouth, overcome by the craving that its scent evoked. That gnawing hunger that no plant or creature on this world had ever quite satisfied found itself damped to nothing by this strange food.

If the Hagga didn't understand his words, at least it did his actions. It put a large piece down beside him on a flat thing something like a shell. Dark-Fur took it in both hands and began eating with gusto. After a bit the Hagga put down a little container beside a big shell of water. The *hoksu-fusso* was delicious, but dry. The Gashta scooped up a shellful of water and sipped gratefully.

The Hagga was evidently hungry, itself. It moved about, getting things out of a cold-place, mixing them up in another thing not-like-a-shell, and setting them on a high white thing that made heat. While it was waiting to eat its food, it sat down beside another high place and put something in its mouth. And it made fire!

That was enough to make Dark-Fur think furiously, but even stranger was the fact that smoke like a forest fire poured out of the creature's mouth when it took the dark thing out. Only when the dark thing was put aside so the Hagga could eat did the Gashta think to finish his own meal.

Then he thought of the tool he had found. He had forgotten it, in his excitement, but no Gashta was ever fully at ease without his weapon at hand. He ran into the big-space where he had left it to hide from the Hagga and brought it back into the eating-place. Once it was beside him, he set out to finish his food.

The Hagga looked down. Then he spoke and came to squat beside Dark-Fur. He looked at the tool, then at the Gashta, and spoke softly. Dark-Fur moved aside so the Hagga could see his treasure. He picked it up and looked at it closely. Then he returned it to its place and began doing something with water at still another high-place.

While he watched, *Lo-Shta* mulled over the things he was seeing. And the things he was hearing, as well. The Hagga repeated the same sounds often. Those directed at himself sounded like "Fuh-zee." He marked it in his memory as the thing he was to be called by the Hagga. Then he set about examining the place where he now found himself.

There was so much to explore, so many strange things to handle and set aside that *Lo-Shta* became a bit excited. Pots and pans rattled, waste-bins were peeped into (and immediately shunned, because of the odor). The Hagga, all in all, seemed to be a patient person, for he seldom scolded, though there were many things that he took away from the Gashta before he had time to look at them closely. There were lovely, long, sharp knives that he coveted . . . until he realized that they would be here, and he would be here. For that was his intention.

They went, after a time, into the big room that the Hagga (the sounds he always made when pointing toward himself were "Pa-pi-Jak," so the Gashta began to think of him so) used for resting. There was a huge thing like a hollow stump. It held all kinds of things, and Dark-Fur immediately turned it upside down. Out fell a lot of very white stuff that crinkled in his hands. He bit a piece of it, but it tasted sharp and a bit bitter. Then he found that he could make it smooth, with his hands. He played with the stuff for a time, discovering all its properties.

When he tired of that, he found a lot of dark-colored, thin, and shiny stuff that he could pull out long, drape about himself, and make rustle like a *zatku* in dead leaves. It was interesting, but eventually he got tired of that, too, and started for another opening to find new wonders.

Pappy Jack picked him up and took him back to stand beside the mess he had made. Dark-Fur suspected the problem, and the Hagga confirmed it with a few words and gestures. It was the sort of thing that you did with small ones, to teach them. He was rather irritated at being treated so, and he questioned the whole proceeding, but Pappy Jack was firm. With as good grace as he could manage, the Gashta returned everything to the stump, except for two items that looked interesting enough to keep.

One was square, bright-colored. The other was really strange—transparent but solid, it had something hard and bright on the top that he couldn't get off. He held them out toward the Hagga and asked if he could keep them.

The big creature mumbled something and knelt beside him. He slid something on the little box, and it was magically open. Wonderful for putting things into. Then he took the other thing and twisted the top round and round. Dark-Fur watched intently, seeing that the top moved up, then off. The thing was now open! Before he could say anything, Pappy Jack twisted the top back the other way, and the thing was closed. Then he handed the bottle to the Gashta.

Dark-Fur took a good grip and twisted. Nothing happened. He tried harder, but the top wouldn't move.

"What is this one doing wrong?" he asked, but of

course the Hagga couldn't understand. He didn't move to help, either.

The Gashta looked closely at the bottle. Ah. If one direction wouldn't work, then the other might. He twisted in the opposite way, and the thing was moving in his hands. It was obviously coming off.

"Yes! Yes! This one sees the way to do it!" he said.

Pappy Jack patted him, stroked his fur as one does for small ones when they do well. Dark-Fur was beginning to understand that to one of the Hagga's size, he must seem very like a small one, himself, so he didn't resent that. Instead, he felt inside the top, then around the neck of the bottle. He held each up to the light and saw how the threads ran. Obvious, once you knew the trick. It was a new thing . . . yet something inside him recognized a whole set of principles that had been lost to his people for generations.

The Hagga seemed excited. He moved to one side of the space and began pushing at small lumps. A wide space on the wall began to glow. Then there was something—it looked a bit like the stuff in the wastebasket—there, with marks on it.

Pappy Jack spoke to the bright thing. Then he pushed something else, and it died. Dark-Fur looked up at him inquiringly, and the Hagga lifted him and took him over to the sitting-place and put him on his lap. There was another of those glowing things there, for he leaned forward and pushed something, and it, too, began to glimmer.

The Gashta gave a cry of alarm and burrowed into the front of the Hagga. There were fires there! Great, raging fires, the like of those that sometimes pursued the Gashta through the forests after a storm. And sometimes caught them, too.

Pappy Jack smoothed his fur and made comforting noises. Dark-Fur, a bit ashamed of his outburst, straightened and turned to look again, but this time there was something truly wonderful on the panel before him. Many times he had seen the sun go down in brightness, true, but this was from a very high place. And in the space between that place and the sunset was a *hoksu-mitto*, indeed. Tall shapes that loomed black against the bright sky stood in regular patterns. Wonderful!

When he had looked his fill, Pappy Jack made more pictures come. Most were of made-things and of places that the Hagga had evidently changed to suit their own purposes. But there was one very strange picture, one that stayed with him for a long time afterward.

It was looking at a round thing that hung in darkness. Part of it was bright, part so dark that it almost blended with the background. There were glimmers and glints from it that reminded him of the sparkle of mica in the rocks of the gorges. It was totally unfamiliar, yet something inside him said, "This is a thing that the Gashta have known."

Then a lot of strange sounds came from the screen, coming from many Hagga holding all kinds of odd things. And one stood up before them and waved his arms as if warning of entire flights of *gotza*. It was puzzling—and tiring. He wiggled.

Then he smelled something. Something familiar and delicious. Though he was still overly full of his meal, habit sent him to find his new *zatku-hodda*.

A *zatku* had found its way into the room. Dark-Fur swung his weapon back, dashed after the *zatku*, and chopped the thing's head off with neat precision. Flipping it over, he cracked the undershell and crouched over the thing to eat it. Even on a full stomach, it was very good, indeed.

When he had finished, he cleaned up his hands and started back toward the warm lap he had left.

"NO!" said Pappy Jack. That sound had been the first to take on clear meaning, for it had been used a good many times already, that night. "Wastebasket." That one, too, was becoming familiar.

Dark-Fur sighed. It was troublesome to have so many-many things, to be rooted to one spot that must be kept neat. But he hunted out all the shell-fragments and put them into the hollow stump—*wastebasket,* he thought. *If that is its name, then it is the thing to call it.*

Once that was done, the lap was open to him again, and he curled into it and watched the bright images come and go on the glowing thing. He fell asleep there. He woke as he was carried into another space, the one he hadn't seen yet.

Pappy Jack took a big soft thing from a box in the wall and folded it into a heap on the floor. The Gashta inspected it carefully, finding no *hizzu* or other insects in it. Then he thought of his treasures. He placed them carefully beside his bed.

He looked at the door. The Hagga didn't take the hint, so he stood beside it and said, "I've got to go into the bushes, for goodness sake!"

That got results, and he went out, dug a hole with his new, all-purpose tool, and covered the result neatly. Then it was time for sleep, night though it was. It had been a day of much excitement and interest, and it had worn him out. He burrowed into the blanket, laid his cheek against the soft-soft warmth of it, and drifted into sleep, while the light from the other room lit a dim glimmer on the walls.

vii.

He woke when the light from outside crept through the room. For an instant, he wondered frantically where he might be, for the feel of the sleeping-place, the smells of the room, the sound of the Hagga's breathing were altogether alien to anything he had ever known before. But it took only a moment, and then he remembered the entire sequence of events that had brought him here.

He rose from his blanket and went to the side of the Hagga's sleeping-place. It was big, as it would have to

be for such a large creature. The edge came just below
his chin, as he gazed at the long shape lying there.
Dark-Fur thought of the warm lap, the food, the wonderful pictures. A bubble of pure joy seemed to be rising
through his whole being, and he bounced onto the bed
in one leap and began to dig his new friend out from
under its coverings.

Pappy Jack woke, laughing. They had a fine, though
short, tussle, there in the dawn light. Then Dark-Fur indicated clearly that he wanted to go outside again, and
that brought the Hagga up to open the door. He had
something in his hand that whirred intriguingly, but the
Gashta was too concerned with his own business to investigate it. And by the time he had finished and come
back into the house, it had been put away. But he forgot
his disappointment in the interest of breakfast.

As they ate, Pappy Jack made marks on a piece of the
white stuff. Then, without any pause at all, he went out
into the place where the fine tool had been and did wonderful things with wood and things that buzzed and
whirred and rasped and screeched. When all was said
and done, there was a perfect Gashta-sized door set into
the big Hagga one.

Lo-Shta was touched. The big creature both knew
and cared for his comfort and convenience. The small
person popped in and out of his personal door a good
many times before he realized that Pappy Jack had gone
back into the workshop.

He hurried in to watch the fascinating things that
went on there. There was a fire there, and Pappy Jack
was putting the end of a long rod of something into it,
getting it hot-hot, and beating on it with a big thing that
clanged loudly at every stroke. It changed shape with
every operation, and soon the Gashta realized that
something very useful was coming into being, right
there before his eyes. When the wide end was completed, Pappy Jack did something that sputtered and
hissed and made an acrid smell, with the result that a
ball was securely attached to the handle end of what
could only be a really superior kind of *zatku-hodda*.

He bounced as he waited for the thing to be finished.

It was for him—just the right size, not too heavy, he could see from its thickness. Good for digging, good for chopping off *zatku*-heads, good for hurting *toshki-washa*, if there was need of that. Such a weapon had not been dreamed of among his people before, as far as he knew.

When Pappy Jack handed it to him, he caught it up and ran outside. It dug marvelous holes. He made two or three before he stopped. Then he looked for *zatku*. It would be a *hoksu-washa* for killing them.

He found one in short order. It took only one brisk chop to remove the head. Two slaps with the flat of the blade broke the shell open. With this very hard tool, the work of *zatku*-killing had been made very easy.

Behind him, he could hear the whirring of Pappy Jack's strange machine, but he was too excited with his new weapon to pay it any attention. Once he had finished the *zatku*, he rummaged about in the shrubbery near the house, killing imaginary *toshki-washa* and putting to flight many *gotza*.

He had ventured out into the open and was digging another hole when something made him look up. An all-too-real *gotza* circled low, watching him from above the screen of feathertrees.

Imaginary *gotza* were all very well, and his new weapon scattered them satisfactorily. This was another thing altogether. He streaked for the house, shouting for help all the way. If there were any creature capable of putting *gotza* to rout, Pappy Jack was it, he felt sure.

The Hagga rose to meet him, making its deep talk. *Lo-Shta* bounced up and down with the force of his words, and Pappy Jack seemed to understand that something was very wrong. He went to a place like branches and took from it a long tube with a wooden end. He made it click sharply, and the Gashta knew that it, whatever it was, would be a satisfactory weapon against *gotza*. He followed as the Hagga went to the big door and looked out. It had risen from its first swoop and was coming around for another. There was a terrific boom! of noise, and the *gotza* tumbled backward in a way Dark-Fur hadn't dreamed that one could do. It fell straight down out of the sky and hit with a thump at the edge of the grass.

It was dead. Even from that distance, the Gashta could tell that. What a weapon! A *hoksu-washa*, indeed. He saw something sparkle in the grass near Pappy Jack's feet and darted over to pick it up.

"May this one have this thing?" he asked, holding it toward the Hagga. The answer was clear, and he took it into his bedroom and put it with his treasures. But when he came out, Pappy Jack picked him up and took him outside, into the other house-place where the flying thing was kept. They went up into a place at the top, and Pappy Jack put him down into a small sitting-place.

There was something making a noise, like a huge heart beating. They went out of the building, and then they went up into the air. Never in all his life had the Gashta dreamed of flying like a *gotza*, yet here he was in this wonderful thing, going up into the air as if he, too, had wings. He was a bit nervous, at first, but when they swooped low over the *gotza* and caught it with the flying thing's claw, he felt more at ease. Once they had the *gotza* firmly in their clutches, they went up and up until the Gashta could see out across the forest from above. He looked toward the spot where he had left his family. Even with his sharp Gashta vision, he couldn't hope to see them as they rested in the trees, but he thought of them with longing.

They took the dead creature away and dropped it into a gorge, which made sense to Dark-Fur. If you are rooted to one spot, then you certainly don't want *gotza* rotting around your door. Then they zoomed away over the mountains, which didn't look nearly as big and forbidding from the air as they did when you were scrambling among their stones and streams, looking out for *gotza* and *toshki-washa*.

When they got back home, he ate a big lunch with Pappy Jack. Then he lay down on the soft thing that the Hagga called a couch and drifted off to sleep. The Hagga was gone when he woke, and the flying thing was gone too. Dark-Fur knew that both would be back by nightfall, so he went out *zatku*-hunting again. There were many things around the house that he found interesting, and he had only just finished eating when Pappy returned for the night.

He didn't scorn to eat supper again. He had spent too many hungry times in his life to forego food when it was offered. When they went into the big room, Pappy Jack dug around in one of the big things there and brought out a thing that he handed to the Gashta.

Dark-Fur looked at the thing carefully. A made-thing. And there were threads on the straight thing. The round thing fitted closely, but it was obviously not a part of the little rod. Did it have threads on its inside, as the bottle-top did? He gave a twist. Then he ran into the bedroom and brought out his bottle, removed the top, put it on again, and then turned to the nut and bolt. They worked the same way.

"The same principle, exactly," he said, holding up the parted items. "Very interesting, and I can see that it would be useful, too, if a person made a lot of things as you Hagga do."

He unscrewed the bottle-cap and put the nut and bolt into the container, then put the cap on. "There are things on that flying thing, I remember, that must be twisted-on. And in the food-place, many things like that. Wonderful!"

Pappy Jack had, after making some of his talk, wandered away into the sleeping place. He had left his smoking-thing beside the chair, and Dark-Fur climbed up and took it into his hand. He put the stem into his mouth and puffed, as he had seen the Hagga do.

The bitter smoke tickled his eyes and his nose and his throat, but there was something soothing about it, nevertheless. He puffed again. Not a bad thing, indeed. He thought he would like it a great deal, in time.

Pappy Jack, returning to the room, seemed upset and took the pipe from him. But he brought another fine thing, so Dark-Fur was not too much disturbed at having his smoking interrupted.

This was a big thing, as high as the top of a Gashta's

leg. It, too, had a top that twisted on and off, and Little
Fuzzy had it off at once. The other side of the top was
shiny—he could see someone there, and it shook him
for a moment to think that he was looking at another
Gashta. But it moved only when he did. It squinched its
eyes when he squinched his, moved its lips when he
spoke. It was himself, as he had seen sometimes in the
still pools of streams. He set the lid aside.

When he looked into the thing, he became excited, indeed. It was full of things like rocks, but they were of all
colors, clean and many-shaped. He dumped it onto the
floor and rummaged through the contents.

There were many shades of many colors, and he
sorted them to suit his eye's needs. Once they were
arranged in order, he began to make a pattern. Never
before had he seen such a dazzling array of pebbles
for making beautiful things with, and he was soon
absorbed. He made a number of them, stretching them
across the floor of the big space. There were all sorts,
but when he looked back at his handiwork, he realized
that the Spiral was predominant.

MAKING PRETTY THINGS

Set bright stones carefully;
make a beautiful thing that is
    pleasing to the eye,
comforting to the heart.

Fingers shape leaves
    and blossoms,
pebbles, shells, and sand
    into many patterns,
centered with Spirals,

That shape lives inside us,
its nature forgotten,
but it creeps out secretly
from our fingertips.

He looked over at Pappy Jack, who was pretending to smoke and watch the screen and pay no heed to the Gashta. He glanced back down at the nearest Spiral. It would be interesting to discuss this tendency with the Hagga, if he could ever make sense of that deep-toned language. There was something about the Gashta that clung to that pattern through the generations. He could remember the oldest ones he had ever known; they, too, made that shape . . . with pebbles or leaves or simply by patting it into dust or mud. It meant something to his people, he felt.

The very old tale that had comforted generations of Gashta . . . could it be true even past the finding of the Hagga? Might there be Gashta who walked among the stars and had made-things of a cleverness to rival even those of Pappy Jack?

Little Fuzzy yawned. It had been long-long since he had thought so hard and so deeply. It was time for sleep. Remembering the wastebasket, he picked up the stones and placed them back in their container. It and his new *zatku-hodda* went into the bedroom with him and were the last things his sleepy eyes rested upon before he went to sleep.

viii.

He woke late, the next morning. For a moment he lay listening for Pappy Jack's heavy breathing, but everything was quiet inside the house, though he could hear a lot of noise from the birds and little animals that haunted the feathertrees outside. The Hagga had gone in his flying thing to do whatever it was that he did in the daytime hours.

Lo-Shta stretched luxuriously. Never had he slept so well or so safely. He was full-fed, comfortable. This was, indeed, as the stranger had said, a *hoksu-mitto* of the finest sort. He knew that he must take this opportunity to go after his family. They must share in this wonderful thing, too.

He went into the kitchen and found a lot of the *hoksu-fusso* in his bowl. He ate only a little, for he was still stuffed from the night before. He would take some for the others, wrapped in leaves. With his new weapon, it wouldn't be too dangerous to carry something in his hands.

He stopped beside his bed and looked about. The Hagga might be worried about him, if he took a long while to return. He would leave a message that the big one might understand. If not . . . well it was the best thing he could think of. He pulled the rumpled blanket smooth and laid the older fine weapon on top, corner-to-corner. There! That was something that wouldn't happen accidentally, he felt sure.

But it wasn't enough. The big Hagga was clever, but as yet the Gashta didn't know how much he really understood. Ah! A pattern! He had seen the sidewise glances that Pappy Jack had slanted at his designs, the night before. Perhaps if he left a really wonderful pretty thing, it would tell the big one that his new friend had not left him permanently.

He used almost all of the stones. The pattern was so beautiful that he hated to leave off looking at it, but after a short while he took his new weapon and went back to the kitchen. He found a thing something like a net-bag that was even better than leaves for carrying the *hoksu-fusso* to his family. That, if nothing else, would persuade them to come with him, he felt sure. Then he went through the living room and pushed through his private doorway.

The forest seemed even bigger, after the security of four walls and a roof. He could hear *kashi* scuttling under the leaf-layer, and he shivered. If only he could avoid an encounter with one of the really big beasts on this journey, he felt that he would bring back his family in only a short time. It had taken him less than a night, after all, to reach this place. If he took no time for sleeping, his family might be here, safe and well fed; he could have them back by the next morning, he felt.

He sped through the wood, his ears cocked, his eyes busy. It was a perilous time for his kind to travel, as he knew quite well, but the new *zatku-hodda* gave him confidence. He was persuaded that it might even allow him to make himself felt in a brush with *so-shi-fazzu*. Not that he could stand one off. That was absurd. But the feel of the weapon was firm and cool in his hand, and he traveled less anxiously than he would have without it.

Afternoon found him nearing the spot where he had left his people. He stopped before he reached the clearing around the big trees and gave a wordless call. Four voices and Baby's excited squeal answered him. He rushed forward, swarmed up into the branches, and hugged them all around. Baby clambered up him, pulling his fur severely, and sat squarely on his head, obscuring his vision entirely. He reached up and pulled the small one into his arms. *"Vov, Pa-ha-li!"* he said sternly. "No more on the head. You will break my neck!"

Then he thought how much he sounded like Pappy Jack, on the night he had found the wonderful place and been discovered there. Perhaps he was, in a true fashion, a small one when it came to the world of the Hagga. He understood so little of their ways and their things. He hugged the baby and tucked him onto his shoulder, while he told the rest of them his tale.

"And this so-wonderful-place, it is not so far? And there is food there?" his mate asked.

That reminded him. He pulled the bag forward from its sling over his shoulder. "Here!" he said, breaking off pieces and handing them around to the eagerly waiting hands. "This is a *hoksu-fusso* of the finest kind. Taste it!"

They sniffed, a bit dubiously. Delighted expressions dawned on their faces. The stuff disappeared with great speed, though quite a lot of the Baby's crumbled down his father's neck and mixed with his mane. When Baby had finished what was in his hands, he climbed down and clung to his parent with one hand while picking out crumbs with the other.

That was the only argument necessary. Once they had tasted, they were ready to find the place that held this wonderful food. Their bodies relaxed, warmed, and they felt ready to start at once.

They didn't make the return journey as quickly as Little Fuzzy had done. Baby saw to that, with his frequent requests to change carriers or his needs to go into the bushes, or his cries after round-fruit. But they made good time, for all that, and Gozzo was not high when they came into the clearing and saw the thing that Dark-Fur called a house standing up from the ground. It was strange in the moonlight, and they hesitated when he urged them toward his small door.

He held it open and said, "There's nothing there to fear. This one has slept there in safety. Go in. Go in, for the light is shining and Pappy Jack is awake."

Pappy Jack's voice boomed from inside, "Little Fuzzy?"

"See? He is calling this one! Go in like Gashta!"

This time they went through, one by one, trailing their *zatku-hodda* and carrying Baby. They stopped in a bunch and stared at the huge space and the very strange light. Their eyes were wide, their mouths a bit open, and *Lo-Shta* felt a triumphant glow all through himself.

He put his weapon on the floor and flew toward Pappy Jack, who stooped and caught him in his arms. They sank together onto the floor. The Hagga was talking all the while, and there was no mistaking the pleasure in his voice. It spoke more than any words could have done, even if the Gashta could have understood him.

The family put their weapons and net-bags down beside Little Fuzzy's fine-fine *zatku-hodda*. The scene on the floor drew them, albeit slowly, toward the two who were hugging and talking (each in his own language) and making much of each other.

Talking to them. Oh, surely, the Hagga was welcoming them? The youngest male, greatly daring, moved near enough to touch the not-fur that covered the big creature. Dark-Fur watched with delight as he reached up and tugged at the fur that made a bar across Pappy Jack's face. Pappy Jack roared with laughter, and soon the entire family was piled up with the two. And, sure enough, as soon as Baby had looked the situation over, he decided that this was, indeed, one large enough to accommodate his habits. With a squeal, he climbed up the huge person and sat on his head!

ix.

Noho-Etto, whom the Hagga called Mama Fuzzy, was the sober questioner of the family. All knew that, and they respected her skeptical view of everything from the possibility of avoiding *gotza* to the safety of sliding down boulders into a stream. More than once, her sound good sense had saved one or the other of her family from disaster.

Now she was bewildered. All her life she had lived in the forest and the edges of the mountains. Things that lived or grew in those places were totally familiar to her, and she could judge accurately the potential for danger. This, however, was something completely outside her experience. A place unlike any she had ever seen, a creature alien to all that she knew. It shook her, and it made her wary.

Yet she was unable to resist joining her mate and the Hagga, as they hugged and tussled and played on the floor of this big place. It had been so long since she had dared to forget herself and really do a thing-that-was-fun that she was pulled into the tumble before she knew it. But she stopped immediately when she saw her only surviving infant sitting on the thing's head as if that were the only thing it had been made for.

Before she could decide what to do, the big creature placed Baby on the floor and said something in its rumbling voice. Her mate said, "*Hoksu-fusso!* When Pappy Jack says dinner, he means food-to-eat. *Bizzo! Bizzo! Ja'aki fessi.*"

They hurried after the Hagga into a place that was strange and interesting. But the food that he put down in two big-big containers interested them more, after their long trek. *Noho-Etto* ate sparingly, saw her infant well supplied, and looked around for the Hagga. He was not there.

Something jumped in her chest. They had left all their tools and weapons in the other space. They were things that had been made with painstaking labor, either by themselves or their people before them. If they should be lost—survival was hard, with them. It would be far harder without. She hurried into the place where the things had been piled.

The creature was looking at their possessions. She saw him lift an axe and look at it closely. But he was careful, she had to admit that. He fingered the *zatku-hodda*, and the saw that she had notched from a bit of flint with a straight edge. The knives and their drinking shells were examined and replaced. When he stood, she came through the doorway and stood beside the pile, anxiously checking that everything was there, undamaged.

Baby, who had been eating a fruit on her shoulder, now finished it off in a terribly untidy way and scrambled over to the Hagga, up his long shape, and onto his head. That decided her. Anything that would let a fatling like Baby sit on his head couldn't be all bad. She climbed into the offered lap and relaxed, totally and without reservation. This was, indeed, a wonderful place. It had been so long since she had been small enough to sit in a lap and be petted that she had almost forgotten how warm and comforting it could be.

She had almost slipped into a doze when the rest came pelting in from the kitchen, ready for a frolic. Something had loosened inside her, in that short time of relaxation. The wariness and suspicion that she had found so useful in the forest, she now realized, was not needed here. She shrugged it aside and bounced off Pappy Jack's lap to join in the game going on all around her. Not in years had she allowed herself to play so. She felt Baby land on her back and scramble around to join in, too. She squealed and laughed and pushed and tickled and lay in a tangle with the others until she was all but breathless. It took a while to wear out, but they were tired from their journey, and they settled at last, yawning, their eyes heavy.

The beds he made for them were so comfortable that *Noho-Etto* kept waking up in the darkness to feel the softness. Baby, beside her, and *Lo-Shta*, on her other side, slept without moving, but she could hear odd sounds, clicks and whirs and little squeaks unlike the things she was used to hearing in the forest at night. When she settled into sleep, at last, she knew that she would have to get used to all these new things, wonderful as they were.

The morning brought something so exciting that she lost all her doubts. Pappy Jack made those fine-hard weapons for all of them. When he offered to trade them for the wooden and bone and flint things they had brought with them, not one of them hesitated. These chilly things would neither splinter nor chip nor crack. They took the place of both axe and *zatku-hodda*. And, feeling quite certain that they would not have to forge into the forest again, she knew that they would no longer need knives or saws.

It was great fun, trying out the new things. There were many *zatku* about, and the family killed and ate the ugly things until they could hardly carry their full bellies. Lunch was nice, but not necessary, and afterward the whole family went outside again to play off their fullness.

It was late. The sun was almost down behind the trees of the clearing. She was sitting lazily, watching Baby, when something moved in the edge of the forest. A lifetime of training had her on her feet, shouting lustily, before she knew that she had moved. With Baby in her arms, she followed her mate into the house, with all the others close behind.

Her mate was shouting, "*So-shi-fazzu!*" as emphatically as possible, as he went into the eating-room to look for Pappy Jack. She peered through the door, as he and her young brother attempted to make the Hagga understand. Their words, she was beginning to believe, were not heard by the big creature—at least, not as words. Perhaps as noise. She suspected that it, like the large creatures of this world, lacked the sharp hearing of the Gashta.

Now Dark-Fur was making horns of his fingers, turning himself into as good a counterfeit of a *so-shi-fazzu* as could be done with Gashta equipment. One arm straightened.

"Boom! Boom!" he said.

The Hagga looked at him, puzzled.

He went through the entire pantomime again. His mate didn't know what to make of the ending part, but she recognized a *so-shi-fazzu* when she saw it mimicked, and this time the Hagga did, too. He seemed, in fact, to be seriously concerned that all of them had escaped into the house. He looked over the whole family. Then he nodded.

Then she realized what *Lo-Shta* had been doing with the straight arm and the sharp sounds. The Hagga took down a long thing that shone with a wicked gleam. It clicked satisfyingly as he examined it. When he went outside, she and the rest, except for her mate, stayed inside. Nobody but a fool went looking for a *so-shi-fazzu*—a fool or, of course, a Hagga.

She did, however, go around, looking from the windows as Pappy Jack moved around the house. She shrieked as the animal dashed toward the Hagga's back, but her mate had seen, too. He sprang past Pappy Jack, turned, and pointed back.

Then everything happened terribly quickly. No

sooner had the Hagga turned than there was a terrific sound, then another. But more astonishing than the noise was its effect on the beast. It not only stopped in its tracks, it was pushed back as easily as a Gashta could hurl a round-fruit. Amazing! It was indubitably dead.

The excitement over, she found that Baby was clinging to her fur, shaking all over, and making whimpering sounds. It took a bit of time to comfort the small one, and only her brother's call moved her to the window in the big room, just in time to see the flying thing that her mate had followed to begin with rise into the air. It swooped down over the *so-shi-fazzu*, and carried it away as easily as a *gotza* carries a young Gashta!

The Hagga were, she decided, very useful people indeed.

X.

Lo-Shta had realized that Hagga needed much petting and a great deal of fun and games. As these were things that the Gashta dearly loved and had had little opportunity to indulge for as long as he could remember, that made life with Pappy Jack doubly delightful. While they were eating their evening meal, he explained his observations to his family.

"It makes him happy when we play with him. He has been alone here, we know. Possibly for a long-long time, and he was lonely before we came. He feeds us and gives us things and keeps us safe from predators, so it is only fair that we make him as happy as possible. Remember—this place is where we all must stay. We can't go away to a fresh one when it is untidy. So we must all take care to be neat with our things. You can see that he likes a clean place for living, and we can help with that. But this one believes that the best thing we can do for him is to love him. See how he enjoys it!"

Mama Fuzzy widened her big green eyes. "True. He even seems to find it delightful when Baby sits on his head. Even the time Baby wet on him before he could get down and go outside! We must be very good to him, for one lonely enough to put up with that must have been very unhappy. It is good that we have come to take care of him."

When they went outside, Pappy Jack stood and watched for a long time before he went back into the house. The light was almost gone when the family followed him, but there were so many-many things to show them inside that Little Fuzzy was hard put to know where to begin.

At last he went to his bottle that contained the nut and bolt. This made for much interest and excitement among the group. Even Baby managed, after a bit of coaching, to unscrew the nut from the bolt, though the bottle-cap was too large for his tiny hands. The older family members found it easy to grasp the principle, which he explained to them fully, holding up the threaded parts to the light so that they could see how they fitted together.

They were interrupted by a terrible sound. Not a *gotza*—its scream was raw and shrill, not an earbursting hoot like this. For a moment they sat motionless. Then, without a word, they dashed for the gun-rack, expecting their Hagga to take down the weapon and go out to kill whatever dangerous beast might be making the noise.

To Dark-Fur's astonishment, he didn't even approach the gun rack. Instead, he went to the big door and opened it.

Well. If Pappy Jack wasn't afraid of the thing that hooted, *Lo-Shta* couldn't allow himself to cower under any gun-rack. He crept to the door and looked out. Something was settling onto the moonlit grass. It wasn't really like Pappy Jack's flying thing, yet it must use the same principle, for it sounded much the same, and it moved up and down in the air in the same way.

He felt his heart give a thump when two more Hagga got out of the thing and came toward the house. He tugged at Pappy Jack's not-fur, and the big creature picked him up and put him on his shoulder. That assured the other Gashta that there was nothing to fear, and they came and peeped out.

One of the Hagga stopped and boomed something at Pappy Jack. He answered, and they continued talking as they went into the house. Once they were inside, it seemed safe to assume that they were the kind of Hagga that Pappy Jack was. The Gashta began getting acquainted at once, though one of the Hagga seemed a little shy.

The other got down onto the floor immediately, with the Gashta he had picked up cuddled in his arms. In a bit the other one sat down, too, and Dark-Fur was delighted to see *Noho-Etto* go close and hold up Baby for him to see. Baby, fearless and excited, jumped over to him and tried to climb onto his head. He bumbled at Pappy Jack for a little. Then he lifted Baby off his head and handed him back to his mother.

Pappy Jack went off to the eating room and left the two newcomers to Gashta hospitality. The shy one took something out of his not-fur and handed it to Dark-Fur. It was bright-shiny, not like the weapon. It rattled, and it had a long hole at one side of it. Finding nothing else coming into his mind to do with it, he put the hole to his mouth. The rattling got louder when he breathed out.

Ahh! He blew heartily, and a satisfying shriek filled the air. Even a *gotza* would be taken aback by such a noise, he felt certain. His family looked at him mischievously, and he dashed for the kitchen with his new toy. Pappy Jack was equal to the situation. He opened a container of the fine-fine food.

"I'll bet you're all ready for some Extee-Three," he said, setting the bowl down within reach.

"Esteefee?" asked Dark-Fur, as he reached for the treat. Then he called loudly to his family, "Come, the *hoksu-fusso* is ready. It is called Esteefee!"

The shrilling from the big room stopped as if by magic. All thought of noise-making was banished by the appearance of the wonderful food.

That consumed neatly but with gusto, he sat with his family and watched the antics of the Hagga. They talked a great deal—almost as much as the Gashta, indeed. And they seemed to admire the collection of tools and weapons that Pappy Jack had saved after trading the fine new weapons for them. But he became bored, after a while.

"That thing on the wall," he said to the others, "Gets very bright, and pictures come on it. Very interesting. Things you've never seen or heard of. It would be nice if Pappy Jack made it work for us."

They had finished their food, so they all looked at the wall he indicated. Pappy Jack glanced toward them, saw the direction of their gazes, but seemed not to want to make it shine for them.

"He pushed on that and turned the thing next to it," Dark-Fur said, jumping onto a chair and stretching to reach the controls. He went through the motions he remembered seeing, and the screen turned bright immediately. But it only showed a long stretch of moonlight on grassland, and they had all seen that with their own eyes too many times to count. He turned the knob again.

Instant excitement! A lot of Hagga were running and pushing and fighting over a round thing much larger than a fruit. Now and then the screen showed a sea of shouting Hagga-faces, and the noise was like nothing they had ever heard. They were all absorbed at once in watching the Hagga play like Gashta.

> Who has the round fruit?
> He!
> She!
> I!

Round and round
run the Gashta.
Small ones,
big ones,
golden ones,
and the pale-furred ones.

They laugh
and push,
tripping,
and scrambling
after the round-fruit
that is too mashed
to eat.

After a long time, the picture changed, and they lost
interest. The new Hagga were getting out of their chairs,
obviously making ready to leave.

Dark-Fur, feeling himself, at least in part, to be their
host, hugged them both. That brought the rest of the
family to say goodbye, also, and their new friends left
in their flying thing, leaving a good feeling for them
among the Gashta.

"The stranger we met was right," he said, as the
vehicle moved out of sight to the east. Of course, Pappy
Jack didn't understand. That was too bad—the Gashta
must find a way to communicate with these big people.
It was too inconvenient this way.

But it was late, and the day had been an active one.
This was not the time for thinking hard, though *Noho-
Etto* did say to him as they went to bed, "They don't
hear us. You can see that. They would recognize words,
if they heard them. They are like the *toshki-washa* and
the *so-shi-fazzu* and the other big animals. Their ears
are different."

It made sense. Sometimes he said things that brought

no response at all from the big creature. Well, there would be time to work at the problem. Now he must sleep.

xi.

The next few days were full of quiet interest, but there was no time for trying to improvise a means of communication with Pappy Jack. He left in his flying thing early and returned late. They missed him, but there were plenty of *zatku* to kill and eat, and none of his family ever tired of sorting through the contents of the wastebasket or of making pretty things with his tin of stones.

Except for a circling *gotza*, there was nothing to disturb the happy Gashta, and Pappy Jack returned in time to do away with that problem. All in all, life had never been as safe or as fascinating as it now became.

And one day they had a visitor, all to themselves. Pappy Jack was still away in his flying thing when another, something like the one the first pair of Hagga had come in, landed on the grass.

They all felt a bit shy at first, but Dark-Fur, or Little Fuzzy, as he was beginning to think of himself, soon overcame that and went to greet the Hagga who got out of it. And this was a truly interesting specimen! He had red fur on his face, though not all over it. It was strange that his kind grew fur on their faces when that was the only large space on any Gashta where fur did not grow. They were like Gashta-in-reverse in that respect. It was truly a pity that there was no way in which he could ask this new Hagga about that difference, for he seemed an unusually receptive and intelligent member of that species.

As soon as the family saw the newcomer sit on the

doorstep and let *Lo-Shta* climb onto his lap, they swarmed out of the shrubbery and came to sit or stand beside him, jostling and tickling and jockeying for position. It was great fun, and he seemed to appreciate that as much as they all did.

Once *Noho-Etto* checked him out and decided that he was just as nice as Pappy Jack, she loosed her grip on Baby, and the small one climbed the red-furred one as if he had been a tree. Once safely ensconced on top of the new Hagga, Baby proceeded to cling with both hands to the reddish fur there, as the rest of them had a free-for-all with their new friend.

In the midst of their fun and games, the flying thing returned, and Pappy Jack climbed out, his grin interrupting the flow of his face-fur. The family ran to meet him, explaining every move of the game and commenting favorably on this particular friend of his . . . though, of course, he couldn't understand a word they said. It just seemed impossible to keep from talking to the big creature. He seemed so very like a Gashta, once one forgot his size.

It was easy to understand what Pappy Jack was doing when he pointed to each of them and talked about them to this delightful stranger. In the process, they discovered with delight that they all had fine new names. In the past few generations, names had slipped badly among their kind, they knew. Such small groups all knew each other, anyway, and they thought of each other in mental pictures or short sharp sounds. Now they found, as Dark-Fur had earlier, that they had become Ma-ma Fuh-zee and Ba-bee Fuh-zee, Mike, and Mit-zee, and Ko-Ko. All Fuzzies, which was a sound with a nice buzz to it. They found it charming.

When Pappy Jack went into the eating-place to make food, the newcomer looked at their old tools and weapons, which their host had put away as carefully as if they were useful to him. The Hagga were strange, there was no doubting that, but they were indubitably nice. They watched politely as this one felt their handiwork, looked closely at the knife and saw strokes on the wood

of the *zatku-hodda*, and shook his head. That seemed to
mean amazement among the Hagga, too, and Little
Fuzzy wondered what he found so unusual about such
ordinary work and implements. The Hagga had such
fine things—much better made and more durable than
the things his own people had been able to craft from
what they could find.

When Pappy Jack had dinner on its way to being
done, he returned to the big room and talked for a long
time with his friend, who seemed to be called Ben.
Un-ca-Ben. A good, smooth name, to be sure. While
they talked, he turned the screen on again, thinking that
that would keep the younger ones and Baby quiet while
the men were busy with their own concerns. The huge
fires that had frightened him so, the first time he had
seen them, were a huge success with the family. They
had been told that nothing there could come out of the
wall and hurt them, and the thought of watching such a
dangerous conflagration from complete safety thrilled
them all.

But the ting of the bell on the cooking thing in the
kitchen brought them to attention. Ko-Ko turned off
the screen, and Dark-Fur led the way toward the
kitchen. There was much conversation while they all
ate. It was frustrating that so much of it wasn't understandable to all the parties involved, the Gashta
thought, but they were too busy with their food to let
that bother them too much.

Afterward, the two Hagga talked again, while Dark-
Fur and the family quietly digested their big meal. But
then came an exciting thing, indeed. Un-ca-Ben turned
on the other screen and put Little Fuzzy, his mate, and
Baby on the table before it. Then he took Mike and
Mitzi and Ko-Ko into his lap and punched a lot of
things. When that was done, he put Baby on his head,
and Dark-Fur watched nervously. He wanted no repeti-
tion of Baby's accident, for he felt that something
important was about to happen.

The screen blinked, and still another Hagga-face

looked out at them. He started to say something. Then his voice went queer, and he looked very different. He was looking back at Un-ca-Ben and the Gashta family, *Lo-Shta* realized, after a moment. And he was as surprised to see the Gashta as they were to see him.

A wonderful thing! Evidently, this Hagga was very far away, but his own Pappy Jack's screen could make-see-and-talk in two directions.

There was a lot of Hagga-talk, then, but it was interesting to watch the other one's antics. In a bit he did something that made a shrill sound, something like a *gotza*-cry. It made Little Fuzzy jump, but he saw at once that it was something that the Hagga was doing with his own things at his end of the conversation. Then nothing happened for a long time, so he and his family got down and wandered over to the other screen again. In a bit, the screen they had left went dark, and they decided that that game was over. They settled to watch the fires again.

But after a long while they were taken back to look into the communication screen again. They were sleepy, by then, and ready for bed, but Pappy Jack got esteefee, and that woke them sufficiently for another bout of watching the distant Hagga. This time there was another one. Not-like the first, or like Pappy Jack or Un-ca-Ben. A female Hagga! It must be—there was a firm indication of mammaries beneath her not-fur.

She seemed very excited about something. They enjoyed looking at her, as the three Hagga made a lot more talk. She had a lot more fur on her head than the males they had seen, but she had none at all on her face. Another interesting thing to note. And her voice was higher. Not nearly as high as the Gashta's, of course, but several tones higher than those of the males.

Little Fuzzy was making mental notes of all the things he was learning about the Hagga species. Things were beginning to fit together, somewhat. It would help so very much if he could talk with them, but until he could find a way to make them hear him, it seemed hopeless.

He sighed, and it was a relief when the screen went dark and the Gashta were sent off to bed. But he didn't sleep for a long time. There was too much to think about.

xii.

It had been a long and lonely journey down from the north. *Fe'h-Shta* (Golden-Fur) and her sister had met few other families, and those had been firmly settled for a time, not needing new mates or more members. But now they had come into a forest full of *zatku*. Never had they seen so many . . . and there was plenty of round-fruit, too. They were now so far south that no trace of the winter they had left behind had followed them, and the undergrowth teemed with edible insects and beans and berries.

Though they needed at least one male to make their family complete, they were not unhappy with their new location. The thread of sadness that the lack of small ones wove through their lives had become so familiar that they hardly noticed it, anymore. They had each had mates, before now. They had borne babies, but none of them had lived.

The two had been ambling through the forest. It was past the time when they should have climbed a tree for their day's rest, but neither was sleepy, and they were in good cover. No *gotza*, however sharp its eyes, could spot them as they moved. And there was neither sound nor smell of *toshki-washa* in the air. Feeling quite safe, for the moment, they peeped out into a glade that opened in the circling feathertrees.

"There are things there," said Golden-Fur, her voice timid. "*Bizzo!* See?"

Her sister looked over her shoulder. There were,

indeed, things on the grass. Big-big things like boulders, but regular in shape. And big animals—or people—that were sitting beside something flat that stood on legs. The things they sat on had legs, too, and held their bottoms off the ground. Convenient!

And there were Gashta on the grass! A hand of them —and a baby! Their hearts yearned toward the small one, which was beside its mother, digging for something in the grass. Without thinking, they started forward, out of the cover of the wood.

The female gave a shrill cry and ran for one of the hummocks, driving the baby before her. And the thing she used to bump him along—how wonderful! It shone in the sunlight, brighter than mica in a streambed.

One of the huge creatures was on its feet, now, heading for the biggest of the strange-things. Another held up something dark in his hands and proceeded to stand up on the big-flat-thing. The third looked straight at them and spoke in a deep voice.

Golden-Fur and her sister stopped where they were, uncertain whether to stand their ground or to retreat into the forest. This was a situation unlike any they had ever found before. Then they moved forward, into the clearing. There was no feel of danger here, no matter how strange the entire matter seemed.

Then the first of the Hagga came out of a hole in the strange-thing with something in its hands. He came toward them, his deep voice somehow soothing and attractive. He stopped, just before they both lost their nerve and retreated into the trees.

He took something from his hand and put it into his mouth. That interested them both at once. Food? Ah! Yes, food. And he was offering them some. How polite of him! When he held out a bit of the food to each of them, they almost went forward to take it. But not quite. That would be foolish, until they understood more of the creature and its companions.

Behind him, they could see the other Gashta lined up, glittering things that were like *zatku-hodda*, yet were not quite like them, either, held ready to challenge them. This must be a fine-fine place, if these were ready to drive away intruding Gashta to hold it for themselves! That seldom happened among their kind.

Then the Hagga tossed the bits toward them. The delightful odor rose to their nostrils. Ahh! Something more than fine! *Hoksu-fusso* of the best sort, from the scent. Golden-Fur swooped down on the fragments, tossed one to her sister, and retreated to stand beside her as they tasted this new food. It smelled wonderful, and it tasted even better. How delightful! They edged forward toward the huge creature. It handed them more bits of the *hoksu-fusso*, and they were so entranced with the stuff that they hardly realized how near they were to this strange thing.

It moved, in a bit, and took something out of its . . . fur? . . . no. But there were two of the shining implements in its hand, just the sort that the female had prodded her small one with. It held them out, pointed to their worn *zatku-hodda*, and made signs with its hands.

Ah! It wanted to trade. The Gashta often traded things they didn't need for tools or weapons they did, so Golden-Fur understood swiftly what it was the Hagga wanted. But that seemed to anger the stranger-Gashta.

"This is our Hagga!" cried Dark-Fur as he came near. "I found him and he belongs to my family. Go and find your own Hagga. There are more—all these others came from other places in flying things. And one is a female, so there are probably even young ones somewhere. Hunt for your own *hoksu-mitto!*"

Those with him echoed his words, but the big creature offered them some of the fine food to distract them. They paid no attention to him but continued to threaten her and her sister with their gleaming weapons. She understood their feelings, true, but this was a place so wonderful that she had no desire to leave it. She was about to go into fighting stance when one of the two young males stepped out of line, dragging his weapon behind him.

She sighed and relaxed. This was a family that was obviously short of females. She watched him approach, lay his weapon on the ground, and set his foot on top of it. Wonderful!

She stroked his fur, patted his head and tickled his ears. Her sister was doing the same, and the young male was making noises of contentment.

Their objections allayed by the formal ritual, the other Gashta family thrust their *zatku-hodda* into the ground and ran to greet the newcomers. There was much hugging and stroking, as they absorbed the textures of fur, the body-scents of the strangers. Even in darkness, Golden-Fur would know each of them now, as they would know her.

Her male sat, suddenly, and they all dropped into a circle to talk over their new relationship. "These ones could go back into the forest?" he asked tentatively.

"It is so," *Lo-Shta* agreed. "There would be not-so-many for Pappy Jack to take care of."

Noho-Etto clasped her hands about Baby as if the thought of having one of her family go away made her unhappy. "There is much *hoksu-fusso* here," she said. "Much space for all of us . . ." But she did not insist.

Golden-Fur, now that her family had been completed by the presence of a male, was ready to go in either direction. She had come out of a forest filled with food. She was ready to return, and her sister agreed with her. So when Ko-Ko nodded and picked up his bright *zatku-hodda*, she followed him toward the wood, quite content with the turn of events.

But before they reached the trees, Ko-Ko thrust his weapon into the dirt and ran back toward the big Hagga. He hugged him as if he were Gashta, and cried, "I don't want to leave you, Pappy Jack. I want to sit in your lap and watch the pictures move and eat esteefee with you!"

The big creature bent and smoothed his fur, and Golden-Fur could see that there was real affection between the two. That made it very different. She took up the *zatku-hodda* and followed her sister back toward the Hagga.

The other family followed them.

"It is that you might stay," said Dark-Fur, as if the thought had just occurred to him. "Pappy Jack is a fine-fine Hagga. He is alone, when these others are not visiting. Two more Gashta could not make a great difference to him."

Golden-Fur turned and hugged him, and then the entire group was hugging and talking with much excitement. In a moment, *Noho-Etto* caught her hand and pulled her toward the strange-thing, which the older Gashta said was a house.

That was a wonderful place, indeed, and the tour of inspection was interrupted only by a call from the Hagga. That meant, she learned quickly, that food was ready to eat in a room set aside for such things. And after eating, the whole group went into another big place and watched pictures move until they were all very sleepy.

That was a wonderful afternoon, for after a nap she had a frolic with all her new family and the Hagga as well. It was becoming clear that these new-found people were the best thing that had ever happened to Gashta. After she had played herself out, she sat with Mama Fuzzy, who told her the tale of the coming of her family to this place.

"These others," she said, gesturing toward the female and the biggest male, "talked on the big screen to Pappy Jack and Un-ca-Ben. Then they got into their flying thing and came here to see us. The Hagga are very fond of Gashta, and we love them very much. They need love and attention and games and petting, as you can see.

"And they are very good at names. Have you learned your Hagga-name? They call you Gol-di-loks. Your sister is Cin-da-rella. Pretty names. It is as well to humor the Hagga in this thing, as they cannot hear or know our own."

She was interrupted by a strange sound that sent the others flying toward the house-door, where they climbed up on a high-place, all together, and waited to see what would happen.

Two more Hagga climbed out of the flying thing that now landed on the grass, which was getting very crowded with the contraptions. They were as much fun as the others of their kind, and the Gashta began playing with them at once. Goldilocks decided that a world full of Hagga might be noisy, but it was far more interesting than the world she had known all her life. And in the midst of this new frolic, came still *another* of the flying-things. And there was Unca-Ben, with the other Hagga that Mama Fuzzy said had come with the female and the big male. Such excitement and activity was about to become exhausting, she felt.

When a big-big flying thing came, Pappy Jack didn't let it put down in the crowded space by the house. He went over the stream and made the Hagga inside stop it there. And there were three Hagga getting out of it! Truly, Little Fuzzy hadn't been mistaken when he said that there were many-many Hagga. Here in the space of less than a day, she had met two hands of them, after a lifetime of never dreaming they existed. Amazing!

It was a confusing time, even when they ate. So many Hagga talking in their booming way made Gashta heads hurt, but none of the small people indicated this to be so. It would not be polite, for they were eating Pappy Jack's food and living in his house. These others were his guests and must be treated properly.

But after dinner, while the big people talked, Little Fuzzy brought out a wonderful thing. "Those-three brought us presents," he said, nodding toward the one called Ruth and the big one and the one who came with Unca-Ben. "This thing is all made of sticks and balls— see? They fit together and make *shokka-washa*, when you put them together." He proceeded to demonstrate, and after a little Goldilocks and Cinderella began to help. Lovely!

Before they had time to tire of making new designs with the sticks and balls, Pappy Jack pulled down still another kind of screen (Goldilocks began to wonder exactly how many screens there could possibly be) and made a thing go "Whirr!" And there was Little Fuzzy, digging a hole and using it. The thing he used to dig was not his new tool, which he called a chopper-digger. It was a long, straight thing, shiny on one end but dull on the other. And there he was after *zatku!* There were all kinds of pictures of him, doing different things, and then came another—one that brought Goldilocks to her feet, amazed. There was her sister! And beside her was another. Could it be herself? It must be, for there was all the ritual of the afternoon, from the time the Hagga had stood up on the table to the point at which Mama Fuzzy had taken them into the house to show them around.

It was a strange evening, all in all, and Goldilocks found herself ready to go to sleep when it was over. She and Cinderella made themselves a bed and put Ko-Ko in the middle of it. It was very good to have a male of their own again!

The next day brought much activity among the Hagga, but she was learning all about her new home and paid little attention to it. When Pappy Jack finally returned, she and the others had already finished their evening meal and were ready for a quiet time of play and pattern making with the sticks and balls. She felt that she had not had a chance to get to know the big Hagga, so she invited him to help her make designs with the colorful pieces. He sat on the floor companionably and they worked together for a long time.

After a while, Unca-Ben left, and the family had a good-night tussle with their own Hagga before going to bed.

The days were full of interest and excitement. The goings and comings of the Hagga kept anyone from becoming bored, and Goldilocks began to feel that she had always lived among the big creatures. The female—An-te-Ruth she called herself—was particularly nice, and Goldilocks loved sitting in her soft lap. And she adored the bright thing that hung around her neck, making little tinkling sounds.

She shook it, now, listening to the music it made. Then, daringly, she held it toward An-te-Ruth's face and asked, "Is it that this one might have this pretty thing?"

The soft-voiced Hagga smiled and lifted the chain off over her head. The thing she said must be a gift-speech, and Goldilocks quivered with delight. Now this beautiful thing was her own. When it was safely around her neck, she moved her head to make it sing quietly. Oh, how lovely!

She showed it to the family. She tried to show it to Pappy Jack and Unca-Ben, but they were so busy talking that she crept away without disturbing them. All day, she moved about to the music of the pretty thing, and in the afternoon she thought of the newcomers over the stream. Their big flying-thing, where they lived, was in plain view. She would go and show it to them!

There was a Hagga-thing across the stream. Very convenient, as most of their constructions were. You didn't have to wet your fur to get across to the other side. Beyond it she could see two of the new Hagga talking in loud voices. They sounded a bit angry, but she would show them her lovely new ornament. That should make them happy again.

She crossed the stream toward them. Behind her, she could hear hurrying steps, as if one of the big people she had left behind were going to join her. Fine-fine!

There was one of the big ones, just ahead. She padded up to his side and pulled at his not-fur, holding up her charm so that he could see. The big face turned down toward her. She smiled and jingled it for him. His big foot swung, caught her in the side, and knocked her flat before she realized what was happening.

She looked up at him, her big green-amber eyes puzzled. The foot moved again, and she shrieked as it crunched into her small body.

She covered her face with her arms, as the foot moved for another attack. This time it crushed her into darkness forever.

xiii.

Little Fuzzy, being highly adaptable as were most of his people, didn't object to change. The adoption of the two new females had been a pleasant family-change of the sort he had known all his life. The intrusion of all the strange Hagga into the quiet life he had expected to live with Pappy Jack was another thing, but interesting. Yet it had all been exhausting and, in a strange manner, upsetting.

He was beginning to understand quite a lot of the Hagga-words, and those that were passing between Pappy Jack and Unca-Ben had been unsettling. They were concerned about something. Not a Hagga-thing, indeed, but a thing that concerned his own family closely. He had not quite figured it out, but he was feeling a bit apprehensive by the time the big air-boat (he had learned already to distinguish between the different types of flying-things) was settled on the other bank of the stream.

Though he had come to believe that the Hagga were, indeed, the promised "help from the stars" of the old myths, there were a couple of the new ones who filled him with strange feelings. Almost the feeling he had always had when he knew a *toshki-washa* was prowling, or a *gotza* was circling overhead. Danger. But he tried to persuade himself that that was not a thing that he should feel for any Hagga. All of that kind had been almost Gashta-like in their affection for his people.

Still, there were so very many new things to observe and to learn that he spent little time in worrying about his odd reactions to the newest-comers. An-te-Ruth and Unca-Gerd and the dark-furred Hagga who came with them spent a lot of their time playing with him and his family. They seemed to be observing the Gashta closely, also. This amused Little Fuzzy mightily, for his people were also noting everything they could detect about the Hagga. He wished that he could explain the joke to Pappy Jack, but until he learned to make himself heard he could think of no way to do that. If he had only known the way to make-marks-to-talk, as the Hagga did, that might solve the problem, but that seemed a thing that would take much learning and practice.

In the midst of talking and playing with the Hagga on his side of the stream, he had been keeping a cautious eye on his family members. He had seen An-te-Ruth give her ornament to Goldilocks with some jealousy. It was a thing that he would have liked, himself. But he got over it quickly, and threw himself again into the current game. The day passed into evening, and he and Mama Fuzzy were sitting quietly, for once, at the table with An-te-Ruth when he saw Goldilocks trudging across the bridge toward the airboat. Something inside him gave a big THUMP!

At the same moment, Pappy Jack saw, too, and cried out loudly. Then he ran after Goldilocks. Little Fuzzy realized that Pappy Jack had felt something ominous about those other Hagga. He, also, was afraid for the young female.

But now Goldilocks was out of the sight of Pappy Jack—Little Fuzzy could tell, because one of the air-jeeps was between him and his quarry. And she was going up to the big, smooth-faced Hagga called Kell-Og and tugging at his not-fur, holding up her charm.

Little Fuzzy found his hands clenched on Mama Fuzzy's hand. The huge creature kicked the small gold-furred Gashta, and she fell onto the grass. Before she could rise again, the big foot swung—again and again! Goldilocks screamed, and the Gashta found himself running, along with the entire family and An-te-Ruth, toward the spot where Goldilocks was lying. But even as he ran, he remembered with fierce joy how Pappy Jack, on seeing what lay beyond that air-jeep, had flung his fist into the Hagga's face and made blood run. And then—only now did Little Fuzzy realize that he had heard a loud noise, something like that the big-bang-weapon made. And another of the three newcomers had fallen onto the grass.

The one they called Mallin was now loud-talking to

Pappy Jack, but Little Fuzzy followed An-te-Ruth to
the side of Goldilocks. Her fur was bloody, as if she had
been caught by a *toshki-washa*. She didn't move, and he
knelt beside her, with Mama Fuzzy on the other side,
and they tried to lift her. There was no flutter of life
beneath their hands. She did not see, though her eyes
were open.

"*Hudda*," he said, and Mama Fuzzy agreed, "She is
surely dead."

They laid her down. The family made a circle around
her still shape. She had not been one of them for long,
but she was Gashta, nevertheless. She must be tended
carefully.

> This was our sister!
>   *T'ho! T'ho!*
> She was Gashta, our sister,
> She was brave, our sister,
> She was loving, our sister.
> There was only one *Fe'h-Shta*.

Through all the sudden uproar, Baby Fuzzy had clung
to his mother's fur, on her back so as to be out of the
way. Now he crept around into her arms, as if for comfort. She swayed from side to side, as she sang, and the
rest of them took up the chant, their circle moving
rhythmically. It seemed to make the baby feel better, for
he loosed his frantic grip on his mother's fur and tried
to sing, too, though he didn't know all the words to the
song.

> It is that Death walks always beside Gashta.
> Terrible beasts, poisonous insects,
> great birds of prey
> are always nearby, always ready.
>   *T'ho! T'ho!*

With a detached part of himself, Little Fuzzy knew
that things were happening among the big people. An-
te-Ruth had moved away from them, toward the knot of

Hagga who were still talking, and toward Unca-Ben, who had come in his air-car. But that was Hagga business. Now there was Gashta-business to attend to. He sang more loudly, and the shrilling of the combined voices rang through the air.

> This was our sister Gashta.
> She walked in danger all of her life,
> but she lived happily
> in spite of fear or hunger.
> Yes! Yes!
> Now she is safe
> with Death.

When the chant was done, it was time to make the grave-pit and bury their sister. The group stood and slipped the shafts of their chopper-diggers beneath her and lifted carefully. They moved as one toward a distant corner of the clearing and laid her again onto the grass. Cinderella took her own chopper-digger and began to dig. Mike and Mitzi joined in, and the others went to look for rocks to cover the grave.

When the grave-pit was dug, everyone began to lay stones over the body that Mama Fuzzy had wrapped carefully with grass. They put them in gently, and when the grave was covered they stood beside it for a long moment. Then they took their weapons and moved in a sad procession toward the house.

Only Baby Fuzzy looked back. "What happened?" he shrilled. "What is dead?" He burrowed his face into his mother's fur. *"Pa-ha-ouka*, I'm afraid!" he said, the words muffled. But nobody had the heart to explain to him.

There was a lot of confusion. Two more Hagga had come before Goldilocks was buried. One of them was the one who had given his family whistles. And that one stood, silent and respectful, while the ceremony was completed. He took off the thing that covered his head-fur, too, standing with his back very straight and his head bowed. Little Fuzzy felt much affection for the big creature. He, too, mourned the loss of Goldilocks.

Then he took Pappy Jack and the sick Hagga away.
Little Fuzzy was frantic for a time, but Unca-Ben took
the family back into the house and fed them esteefee
and talked to them a long time. And for the first time,
something of his meaning really came through.

"Your people are intelligent, you know very well,"
the Hagga said to him. "And the men who came in the
airboat didn't want you to be. They work for the Company that thought it owned this world. Once you are
proved sapient, they won't own it anymore. So they
want to make everyone think that you are animals. They
are angry. But now Pappy Jack has said that the man
who kicked Goldilocks is guilty of murder. And that
one has said that Jack is guilty of murder for shooting
the one who pulled his gun on him. There will be a trial"
. . . Gashta, listening intently, visualized something like
their own talk-circle . . . "to find whether each one is
guilty. It will be a very important thing for you and your
people. I wish you understood what I'm trying to tell
you . . ." Unca-Ben sighed.

Little Fuzzy, who had understood much more than
anyone would have expected, tried his best to make
Unca-Ben hear, but it was of no use. He simply smiled
down at the Gashta and offered them more esteefee.

Little Fuzzy didn't know what a Company was. He
had only the faintest idea of what murder might be, for
there was no tradition of it in his people for uncounted
generations. But he knew death, and he remembered the
tradition, unused for so long that it, too, was almost a
myth, that unfit Gashta were killed. He felt a twinge of
fear.

Surely Pappy Jack would not be killed for trying to
protect poor Goldilocks?

He discussed it with the family for a long time. Mama
Fuzzy reassured him, at last. "Of all the Hagga we have
seen, only those in the airboat were bad-Hagga. The
others will do what is good. We can only wait."

And he had to settle for that, though he couldn't help
but worry quietly, on the inside where she couldn't see.

xiv.

Baby Fuzzy was frightened and sad and confused. He had not understood what had happened to Goldilocks. Nobody had explained anything to him. Pappy Jack had disappeared for a long time. His world seemed to be coming apart around his ears.

But this new Hagga who had come back with Pappy Jack was making the little white-furred baby Gashta forget his troubles. From the first, he had not minded any amount of head-sitting or face-fur-pulling. He was so very large that entire games could be played on the front of him and even on the back of his neck and shoulders. Unlike the other big people, he had fur on most of his face—nice curling fur that was partly dark and partly as white, as Baby Fuzzy's own.

While this new one—Unca-Gus—and Pappy Jack and Unca-Ben and Unca-Gerd talked, he invented entirely new concepts in hide-and-seek and peep-out-and-hide-again. Best of all was the fact that Unca-Gus's beard went around the sides of his face. Baby Fuzzy could conceal himself beneath its fullness at the front, in the warm neck-space, and then he could creep, unseen, around to the back without any of his family being aware that he had moved.

His father was sitting on Unca-Gus's lap, along with Mama Fuzzy. Baby peered out of the face-fur with interest, as Little Fuzzy took the pipe that this new unca offered him and put the stem in his mouth. Beautiful billows of smoke came out between his lips. Wonderful!

When that palled, he went back to his scamperings about the person of his Hagga. The sound of hooting brought him to a halt, hidden in beard. It would be great fun to spring out and surprise Pappy Jack's friends in the blue not-fur, when they came in. He had enjoyed their other visits, even the last when Goldilocks had been killed. Pappy Jack had hidden the whistles, but Baby remembered their shrill voices with much fondness.

Pappy Jack opened the door. The big Hagga in blue
was outside, with almost a hand of others. Two were in
blue, like himself. Two others were not. Baby parted the
curly strands and peeped out, as the two others came in,
followed by the three in blue. They all looked stiff and
uncomfortable. Pappy Jack was suddenly radiating
wariness, as if a *toshki-washa* were inside the room with
him.

There was a lot of talk. Baby could catch a few
words, now, but this made no sense to him. He didn't
know what a Court Order might be. Impound Fuzzies
sounded threatening to his tiny ears. When the two
strangers took sacks and began running around the
room, chasing his family, the little fellow made a con-
vulsive movement, but Unca-Gus put his hand to his
beard and calmed him. Something in the touch told the
tiny Gashta that he might well retreat behind this solid
mountain of flesh. He had just seen his parents stuffed
into sacks, and if those *toshki* strangers could do that,
how could a mere infant resist? He snuggled behind Gus
and watched over his shoulder, shielded by his screen of
face-fur.

More than a hand of sacks now wiggled on the floor.
The two strangers were talking very loudly, making
their marks-that-talk on paper, putting their thumbs
into something black and messy, and pressing them,
too, onto the paper.

Why didn't Pappy Jack take down the gun and shoot
those bad strangers? They were almost as dangerous-
feeling as that bad one that he had shot when Goldilocks was killed. Nothing was as it should be. He could
feel Pappy Jack's anger and sadness. It filled the room
with its scent and its vibrations, but the man did
nothing.

Then the entire group was gone, the bags still
wriggling frantically as those bad Hagga carried them
away. For a moment the men left in the room said
nothing.

Unca-Gus broke the silence. "Have they gone,
Jack?" he asked.

Pappy Jack nodded. Then the big man leaned forward and lifted Baby Fuzzy out of his hiding place. Baby caught his face-fur in both hands and said, "What happened? Where have they taken my family? Why didn't Pappy Jack shoot them? Tell me something." But, of course, the big Hagga didn't understand his words.

He was, indeed, talking quickly with the others. And in a very short time they were all in the flying-thing that Unca-Ben used, shooting through the sky at amazing speed. Baby was fascinated. And when they zoomed out over a wide expanse of flat stuff that changed from gray to blue to green, moment by moment, shifting around as if it might be water, he was stunned. Was this the Big Water that he had heard about from far-wandering Gashta?

When the other continent loomed up on the horizon, the little one was even more surprised. This was another land entirely, he could see. There were huge houses on it, and a wide-wide place all covered with smooth stuff where all sorts of flying-things sat about or scuttled like bugs beneath his interested eyes.

He had no doubt that this was the place where those bad Hagga had brought his people. And Pappy Jack and his other friends were coming to get them back. He snuggled into Unca-Gus's arms and sighed, relaxed for the first time since his family had disappeared into the sacks. He should never have doubted his own Hagga.

They would make things come right again. He knew it.

BOOK IV.

Toshki-Hagga

·········

It is sad
for away-from-home people.

The gardens we planted,
the houses we wove
beneath the thornbushes,
the stream that came from the mountain
are all behind us.

The mountains were high and cold,
the wide lands strange and full of danger.

Yes! Yes!
It is sad
for away-from-home people!

i.

From Ernst Mallin's private diary:

I have never been so angry in my life. It is bad enough that a mere nobody—a prospector, *indeed!— has discovered a new species almost upon my very doorstep. An amateur! And he has made it quite clear to any thinking being that they are probably sapient. But that professional insult has been compounded by Leonard Kellogg's incredible stupidity. The loss of temper and self-control that allowed him to kick that unfortunate . . . animal . . . to death was inexcusable. And now the entire mess has been dumped into my lap!*

To this point in my career, nobody has been able to challenge me in my own field. My competence is unquestioned, and my word is respected among my professional peers, though it is not inaccurate to say that there are few who can be called such. Never has any assistant of mine given me cause to think that he might disagree with me. Until now!

I am faced with a most terrible responsibility. And my own people are giving evidence of being at odds with my purposes. Van Riebeek resigned on the spot! Ruth Ortheris is not at all happy with things as they stand, though she has said nothing, so far. Yet the fate of the Chartered Zarathustra Company rests in my hands, mine alone. It is a most uncomfortable position in which to be placed.

If only Kellogg had controlled himself when that little

. . . *creature . . . touched him! Now, if the Company loses its Charter and the ownership and control of this planet, it is directly attributable to that idiotic act. I wish Jack Holloway had shot the fool, along with that incompetent gunman Kurt Borch. A scientist doesn't take along a gunman when he goes to examine a new species.*

If Holloway had shot them both, it would have removed any excuse for a murder trial—two, actually, if you count that one accusing Kellogg of murder in kicking Goldilocks to death—that would hinge on the sapience or non-sapience of the Fuzzies. And Pendarvis! Judge Frederic Pendarvis is hearing the case himself.

There mustn't be the least shadow of a doubt in the case I must make proving these creatures to be animals. Clever, but only animals! Even with all my assistants cooperating to the fullest, it wouldn't have been easy. Now Van Riebeek is gone, and Ortheris has already refused to lie to protect Kellogg.

Not that I can blame her. If anyone should have been kicked to death, it was Kellogg himself.

But now Victor Grego has dumped the entire mess into my hands. I'm the wonder-worker of the Company, and sometimes the reputation is a burden. But when the President of the Company gives me a direct order, I must comply, however it galls me.

Not that I have been overly sensitive in the past, I must admit. I have done some things for my Company that don't rest lightly in my memory. Probably—I can be quite honest within the confines of this diary—I will do more. I am, after all, a Company man. This organization has given me much of my education, my position, unlimited funding for research, equipment, laboratory space, and manpower. But I have paid off for them. The new strain of veldbeest for the off-planet market, for instance. The fruit and grain adaptations I've made for the on-planet farms. Kellogg was never anything but a figurehead. I have always been the mind behind the Division of Scientific Study and Research.

Now I am at the head of that arm of the Company.

Given these circumstances, I might be happier with my old position.

I do not delude myself. If the Company is forced into a Class IV situation, subject to a civilian government that must protect a native population proven to be sapient, it will mean a loss of billions, both here and off-planet. And how can it be justified? Certainly not simply on the basis of a few pretty little animals, however bright they may be.

The sunstone trade alone . . . those gems are worth a fortune apiece on the interplanetary market. And they are found on Beta Continent, the one spot where these creatures have been found. The Company's monopoly in sunstones, buying from prospectors and selling on the gem markets of the galaxy, will be lost.

This trial is going to be a pivotal thing for the Chartered Zarathustra Company. Augustus Brannhard is a lawyer of great skill, drink as much as he will. He and Holloway and that naturalist Ben Rainsford are going to be a tough combination to beat. Leslie Coombes is a fine attorney. The Company wouldn't retain him otherwise, but when it all comes down to the wire, the entire burden of proof is going to rest directly on my shoulders.

I have seen the tapes. Those creatures frighten me. They are (I admit this only privately) quite likely to be sapient. If I could produce a group of them that was demonstrably irrational? . . . Hmmm.

I thought about the notion for along time before calling Grego. When his face appeared, I said, "I may have an idea. But I'll need some Fuzzies. Several, preferably in the wild state. Can we manage that?"

Grego thought for a moment. Then his eyes lit up. He is sharp, that one. "I think we can manage that," he said.

We shall see what happens when I try to drive them insane.

ii.

It was hot in the sack, and the air was thick and stifling. Little Fuzzy wriggled about until he found a tolerable position against what he was sure was another of his family. Pitching his voice as high as possible, he identified himself.

Ko-Ko answered, then Mama Fuzzy, Mike and Mitzi and Cinderella. Little Fuzzy felt his heart thump with one hard thud.

"Where is Baby?" he asked. He felt Ko-Ko shift uneasily against his shoulder.

But Mama Fuzzy's voice came from beyond Ko-Ko. "He was hiding in Unca-Gus's face-fur. Unca-Gus stayed very still, while those *toshki-Hagga* ran after us, and I knew that Baby had been playing all over him. He is a very bright Hagga. Baby is still with Papa Jack."

Little Fuzzy's breathing eased. He fingered the small knife that he had slid into his hand when he pretended to be trying to hide in his bed from those bad men. He had curled himself up into a ball, whimpering as if he were terrified, and they hadn't thought to look at him to see if he was hiding something. He knew that he could cut them all loose, but they were in a flying-thing. He recognized the hum of its engines, and the initial lift off the ground had been unmistakable. There was no escape, here. He must wait until they landed.

It was a very long ride. He worried over Pappy Jack's behavior almost more than his own predicament. It had been so unlike the Hagga he knew and loved. Pappy Jack wasn't afraid of anything at all. He had the guns. There must be some very good reason, incomprehensible as it seemed, why he had let the men take his family away.

After a very long time, the flying-thing went down and touched ground again. Differently. Little Fuzzy had never been in an air car that set down on anything but soil or grass. This came down with a grating and an echoing that told the Gashta's sensitive ears that the surface under it must be very hard and smooth. He made a mental note of that. It might possibly be of use later.

He was bundled roughly up into hard arms and carried away to a bumpy vehicle of some kind. All was confusion for a long time, then, and he was carried this way and that, up and down, until even his inborn sense of direction was sadly confused.

But at last he was taken from the sack and put into a small square thing with a top on it. There were a lot more of them, and he saw the rest of his family put into those, and the lids were secured—with a bolt that shot through two loops and was secured with a nut. Ha! Wonderful! He knew that he could have them out in short order, once he had a chance to cut the mesh (it resembled the stuff the Gashta made net-bags out of, but it was harder and shinier) that walled him in.

The dark-furred Hagga who had come to visit Pappy Jack was there. So was An-te-Ruth. She looked at him so sorrowfully that he knew she didn't like what was happening, though he saw that she seemed to be working with the other Hagga in the room. For a moment, the face of the Hagga called Mallin—who had been with that-one-who-had-kicked-Goldilocks—appeared above his cage. Dislike shook Little Fuzzy to his furry toes. Then he was gone again. Soon afterward the rest of the Hagga left, too, and the door closed behind them.

The Gashta waited until there was no longer any sound from the other side of that door. Then he took the spring-steel knife that Pappy Jack had made for him and began patiently cutting at the wire in an upper corner of his cage. It wasn't as hard as he had thought, and it parted fairly easily. He bent it back in a neat triangle and folded it out of the way. He wanted no cuts and dripping blood to make tracking him easy.

It took only a short while for him to remove the nuts from the securing bolts. His people were freed very quickly. But where should he lead them? He reached up very far and took hold of the door handle. It wasn't too different from the one in Pappy Jack's house, and he opened it with only a little trouble.

There was a long narrow space, with doors on either side. He looked into one and it reeked of that dark-furred one who had put him into the cage. He led the small group inside and looked about for something the others might use as weapons. On the table lay a long piece of metal—not sharp and not well-weighted, but good enough for now. He handed that to Mama Fuzzy, who took it with a grimace. The others were rummaging, too. They found some bent-wire-things that might be useful, along with a couple of the metal things that Pappy Jack used to make his marks-that-talk. Not too bad for weapons, at a pinch.

All the searching had made a grand mess of the room. Little Fuzzy cocked his head on one side. What might he do to tell the betrayer of Pappy Jack just what he thought of him? Then he knew. He dumped the waste-basket in the middle of the floor. The Hagga hated that above all things, he had found. It was the ultimate insult, and he left it as a message to any who might come.

It was dark in the hallways, but the Gashta, used to moving at night, found that to be no hardship. When they came to the end of the passage they were following, however, there seemed no way to go. Double doors stood there, with a line of buttons beside them. Little Fuzzy had touched enough buttons to know that surprising and sometimes frightening things could happen when you pushed unfamiliar Hagga buttons. He wanted none of those. But Mitzi gave a squeak to catch his attention.

"This-one sees a door . . . over there!" she said.

There was a big picture on the wall, all straight lines and angles. It ran straight across the little door, making it hard to see. But there it was, and it had a metal bar across it, instead of a handle.

By now, Little Fuzzy and his family were used to figuring out Hagga principles. This was no latch that you worked with your hand. It wasn't anything that could be screwed. It could go, as far as Little Fuzzy

could see, in only two directions, up or down. He put
both hands under the bar and lifted. It didn't give a bit.
Then he caught it from above and pulled downward.
And that did it. The thing swung open, and beyond it
was a narrow dark place leading down. The floor was a
lot of little floors, each just lower than the first. A long
step for Gashta legs, but he went forward into the
darkness.

They went down and down. At times the slant turned
into a flat place, and a faint outline of light showed that
another door opened into it. At the first, he stopped and
felt, and there was one of the bars on the inside. Good.
They could always get out.

Now he was following his instinct. It led him, at last,
to open one of the doors in a flat place and to go out
into another hall. He raised his head and sniffed. An-te-
Ruth's scent was strong in this place. He followed his
nose to a door, but it wouldn't open, no matter what he
tried. Another, just down the hall, did yield to his insis-
tent hands, and he was glad to find it opening into a
small nook that held long-handled things and buckets
(the family loved buckets—they made lovely drums!)
and unidentifiable Hagga-things. Just right for hiding.

"When An-te-Ruth comes, we will make her hear!"
he said.

Mama Fuzzy put her small warm hand on his. "She
seemed to belong to this Hagga family," she said doubt-
fully. "She might take us back *there* and shut us in
again. Do you think?"

"An-te-Ruth cried when Goldilocks died. She looked
so sad at me when they locked us in those things. She
will hide us. You will see!" He nodded emphatically in
the darkness.

They managed to sleep a bit, though the air was close
and full of strange smells. It seemed a very long time
until there was a stir of life outside their door. Feet
clumped down the hallway, but always the wrong feet.
Once a set of quick, light steps sounded, and Little
Fuzzy had his hand on the door handle when he realized

that, though they were very like, they were not the steps of the one he was waiting for.

But at last she came. He knew it by sound and by scent, even before he peeped through the slight crack he opened and made certain with his eyes. And the passage was empty! He burst through the door and caught her around the knees, from the back.

"An-te-Ruth! Hide us! We got away, but this-place is too big. We can't find our way!" he pleaded.

She looked down at him, and he could tell that he had startled her for a moment. But she looked past him at the others, nodded decisively, and opened the door of her office. "Inside, Kids," she said. "Until we can do better."

She looked at them. Little Fuzzy knew that she was thinking hard, for her eyes went narrow as Hagga-eyes did when their minds worked hard. Then she put her head out of the door and looked.

"Come on, Fuzzies. The way is clear!" she said, and they followed her down the hall and into a big place that was full of boxes and strange Hagga machines.

"I think you'll all fit into this one," she said, pulling forward a thing-on-wheels that held a huge box.

She lifted them, one by one, and set them gently into the thing, giving each a hug before she let go. Then she brought some strange stuff with hard, shiny cases like beetles and set them into the middle of the box. Over the lot, Gashta and all, she put a layer of loose stuff like dry grass.

"I think you can breathe all right—I've punched some holes where they don't show for air. Be quiet, Kids. I'll have you out of here in no time!" she said.

The box went dark, as she put something over the top. Little Fuzzy could hear her fastening it down tightly.

"You see? Now we are caught again!" said Mama Fuzzy at his elbow.

But Little Fuzzy didn't believe that at all. If she had intended to put them back into the cages, she wouldn't have hugged them so tightly when she picked them all up. No, she was going to get them away from this big-big place. He knew it.

Her steps went away for a little. Then they came back, followed by a pair of big feet that thumped on the floor enough to shake the box and its carriage.

"Load that onto the van, will you, Rog? It's got to go to Henry Stenson's lab, this morning. For repairs, I think. Anyway, I was told to deliver it first thing, so I'd better be on my way."

Now what was a van? Little Fuzzy wondered. And what were repairs? And what might a hen-ri-stin-son be? For every word he knew, there were several that he couldn't define satisfactorily. But he decided that it was too late to worry now.

Either his family could trust An-te-Ruth, or it was back to the cages. And he hadn't any doubt that she was going to get them away from here and back to Pappy Jack.

iii.

Silver-Fur had liked this camping-place better than any his family had found in many nights. There were big trees for sleeping in during the day, and *zatku* lurked under every bush and fern-patch. As the drought had crept southward from the north, his group had stayed just ahead of the worst of it, and they had been traveling intermittently for a long time. It seemed forever since he had left the valley of his youth. None of his companions had been born then, and he had begun to feel an ache in his bones after a long night of walking or hunting.

"It is good here," he had said to Bud, once they had had time to settle into the new terrain. "This one would like to stay for a time. What do the others say?''

She, being the only female in the group, was consulted carefully on anything that might affect her happiness. Not that she was mated with any of them. Not now, after losing four babies, one after the other. She had drawn apart from them in that way, but she was still cheerful and cooperative in all family business or play.

She looked up at the old male, her amber eyes shining in the starlight. "This one would also like to stay for a time," she said. "This one is weary. The *toshki-washa* that chased us from the last place wore us all to weariness, I think. They will agree. We have spoken, as we hunted and played. This is a good place."

They did not, of course, remain in the same precise spot. That would invite unwelcome attention from any predator that hunted the area. But they worked out a sort of circuit, covering the same ground over a period of several nights of ambling. It was much easier than breaking new ground, for they knew how the land lay and where there was water. They all rested more easily in those huge trees, too.

So while Gozzo waned and went dark and came new again in the east, while Tansha moved lazily from new to full, they moved about their chosen territory. There seemed to be no *toshki-washa* there, and the brush was too thick, the trees too closely-set for this to be *so-shi-fazzu* country. Even *hizzu* were rare. They became comfortable with this new place. Even a bit careless.

Of course, there were always *gotza* circling above the trees, but the branches were thick, and by day, when they might have been seen, they took care to choose concealed spots for sleeping. Yet there was a strange kind of *gotza* in the sky. It didn't shriek, it made a humming sound. And it didn't circle. Its path was straight as that of an insect. They had all seen it, over the past day or so, and it had become a concern to every Gashta.

Silver-Fur had almost decided that it was time to change their hunting ground, because of that unusual predator. It was difficult enough to deal with huge and fierce-fanged beasts whose habits you understood. It was insanely risky to chance meeting one whose reactions and intelligence you didn't know.

He had discussed it with the family in the Circle, just before climbing the trees for the day. Now he opened sleepy eyes, watching for any trace of the strange thing. They were agreed that if it showed itself today, they would move southward once again.

Almost at nightfall, when he was stretching the sleep out of his bones and muscles, it hummed overhead, high above the tallest of the trees. He sighed. He had hoped that it would be possible to rest here for at least another turning of Gozzo, but that was not to be. Tonight they must strike out again.

Though, like most of the *Kampushi-sha*, they hunted independently, they traveled in a cautious and rational manner. Ku, the strongest of the younger males, forged ahead, his eyes, nose, and ears sharpened to their utmost acuteness. Ik, his older brother, ranged to the right, Bud to the left, and Silver-Fur kept a measured distance to the rear. No prowling *toshki-washa* would catch them unaware.

They moved, almost invisible, through the moon-spangled forest, skirting pools of light and avoiding animal paths. Generations of survival had taught them things that their ancestors had not known when they came to this world.

Silver-Fur watched and listened, all attention, but in one portion of his mind he was thinking, *If only the old tales were true. Help from the stars? They cannot even give light, on those nights when both moons hide their faces.* His ears twitched forward and back, his eyes saw every motion of every leaf ahead and to either side, but his inner self was weary and saddened and suddenly afraid. There was something strange in the forest. He could feel it, smell it, sense it in the quivering of his nerves.

He had opened his mouth to call for the others to pause, when there came a shrill signal from Ku. "Come and see! This is most strange! Not-Gashta have been here!"

Not-Gashta? What could the boy mean? There were only Gashta and the predators, as all his kind knew too well. Silver-Fur caught his *zatku-hodda* defensive position and hurried toward the shadows that were the shapes of his family.

Ku had stopped, as a sensible Gashta should, well short of his find. He pointed, as the eldest came up to him. "See! *Zatku*, all dead. But not dead as Gashta kill them, and not eaten. Just killed and left to spoil! No creature that we know does that."

The oldster moved closer. Four—five—six *zatku* lay there, in a loose pile. Their heads had been crushed, but not in the manner of any Gashta he had ever known. And they were beginning to go bad. He could smell the thin breath of taint that rose from them.

He looked all about. There was nothing near. He could hear so much as the breathing or any predator, even the smaller ones, and there was no sound of that kind. Then he went forward and prodded the pile with his *zatku-hodda*, turning over the topmost one.

The others gathered about to see, for the light was very dim there in the shadows of the trees. He hunkered down to examine the under-shell of the *zatku*, pushing the others out of his way with the tip of his weapon.

And then something so strange, so unexpected, and so terribly alien happened that he had no words in his mind to describe it. Something rose up under all their feet with a great swish, scooping his entire family up into a sort of huge net-bag. They were all dumped, willy-nilly, into a heap with the dead *zatku* mixed in among them. He found himself lying on top of Ku, with Bud's face pressed into his left ear. Ik seemed to be under all of them, panting for breath from the pressure.

No matter what happened, Silver-Fur never lost his head. Now he must get his family sorted out and into positions that wouldn't stifle any of them, until they could find a way to escape from this peculiar thing that had caught them.

"Bud," he said quietly, "can you wiggle around so that I can remove my weight from Ku?"

She said nothing, but he felt her squirming. Then her weight was gone, and he saw that she had caught onto the net at the side of the bag-like thing and was holding herself off him in that way. He did the same, followed by Ku, and Ik was able to haul himself upright. Then they all managed to stand on the painful and insecure bottom of this out-sized bag, peering out through the meshes. The prawns were softened enough so that Silver-Fur could push them through the holes below with his feet, and they were soon freed of that unpleasantness.

The string-stuff that the bag was made of was tough. Neither teeth nor flint knives could do more than fray it a bit. When Ku climbed up to the top of the net, he found it to be secured with something too hard to move. And the holes, while big enough for semi-decayed *zatku,* were entirely too small to permit any of their own bodies to pass through. They were trapped.

They stood there for a long time, watching Gozzo move across the sky. Silver-Fur's mind was working swiftly, as it always did in times of crisis. He was sorting through all the things that he had seen and the things he had been told, the traditions, such as they were, that his kind had passed on to him.

At last he spoke. "This is a made-thing," he said, very softly.

"This one was thinking that," came Bud's voice from beside him. "Nets do not grow on vines. They must be made by those with hands. But such big-big hands would be required to make this net!"

"The old tales say that those who will come from the stars are big. Bigger than we, at least," said Ik, beyond her.

"Those who come from the stars, if they ever come, will still be Gashta. And Gashta do not kill *zatku* and waste their meat. No, this thing was made with hands by those who are not Gashta." Silver-Fur stopped, appalled at his own words.

The others did not speak again, and he retreated into

his thoughts. This was a thing that he could not solve. He could only wait.

The night was long, but eventually the sky lightened in the east. Before the sun rose, the thing that was not a *gotza* came humming down the sky and sat down in a clearing a short distance from the spot where his family hung beneath a big *rogo*. The Gashta had dozed, even in their uncomfortable positions, but this woke them immediately. Something on the side of the thing opened, and a—Gashta? NO! A not-Gashta—got out of its inside. Another evidently got out of the other side of it, and the two of them came toward the tree where the captives hung.

They were making noises. Silver-Fur listened with all his might, but there was no sense in their talk, though he memorized the sounds.

"About time! We got us a haul, Raul. See, the bag's full!"

"Mallin better be pleased with this bunch. I'm sick of this job. Sooner be on Niflheim!"

It was rational language, Silver-Fur decided. Pitched far down the scale, it made his insides feel shaken, but it held the patterns of speech. And the creatures were not, he now realized, entirely unlike Gashta. They were upright. Two arms. Two legs. Head on top instead of out in front as in the beasts. But so huge! He, large among Gashta, would come hardly above the knee of one of those things. And they had no fur. Something covered them, but he reserved judgment as to what it might be.

He could feel Bud shaking against his side. They were fearful, he knew. Yet he felt a quiver of excitement. His species had never thought that there might be another of the thinking kind. Yet here they were.

Even as they bundled the frightened Gashta into their bags, Silver-Fur felt his curiosity overcoming his fear. Wherever he was being taken, whatever the purpose of this strange occurrence might be, he was about to learn something of much importance to his people!

iv.

From Ernst Mallin's private Diary:

Today I received, through safe intermediaries, four healthy adult Fuzzies. After the fiasco of the escape by Holloway's group, I was extremely careful to see that they were secured effectively. We had prepared a room without windows whose door was secured with a safety-lock requiring a key at all times. Remembering the habits of those others, I had blankets placed inside, though I withheld any sort of tool or toy. That will come later.

These were captured in the wild by two hired trappers. They had in their possession at the time four of the wooden implements that they use in killing land-prawns, as well as two well made knives chipped from flint and a coupe-de-pointe axe. This fills me with misgiving. It is not going to be either easy or pleasant to deny sapience to creatures that make such readily-identifiable tools.

There are three males. One is slightly larger than the others and seems to be older. His fur is a silvery-white, though I haven't enough data to determine if that is a sign of advanced age. He has very large green eyes and several streaks or patches of scar-tissue on his skin, though those had to be discovered by manual examination. The fur conceals such scarring, as well as the genitalia of both sexes. Only by a minimal mammary development can one distinguish the males from the female.

The two younger—or perhaps I should say smaller—males are both of a golden color. They are active, inquisitive, and they are not nearly as terrified as they should be so soon after being taken from their natural habitat.

The female is no smaller than the smallest of the males, seems to be as strong and active, and is consulted often by the others. Her eyes are amber-colored. It *appears, from preliminary examination, that she has had several offspring, though there are no young with this group. Predators? Possibly.*

They were brought into the farm-lab yesterday afternoon. After securing them in their quarters, I spent the afternoon watching them through the one-way wall. After examining the room in painstaking detail, they sat in a circle on the floor and seemed to take part in an earnest discussion . . . but only shrill yeeks were audible. This lack of language is the strongest element in the case I must make, but I can see already that Ruth Ortheris is going to be a problem in my pursuit of the Company's goals. She insists that they communicate in words and that we simply don't understand how to detect that. A code, perhaps, she suggested. If there were any way in which I could detach her from this project, I would do so. I can foresee, already, that some of the methods I intend to use will upset her entirely too much. But she has been involved with these creatures from the first, and to send her away would be too obvious.

When I had the visible light turned off and the infrareds on, I watched them again through the night-scope. Their night vision seems to be excellent, for that did not seem to inconvenience them too much. They were evidently tired, however, and soon they shook out the bedding we had put there for their use, piled into a heap, and went to sleep. No sexual activity was observed.

I cannot, as yet, make many inferences. They do not behave as animals should, that is obvious. I cannot allow them to be found sapient. Tomorrow's tests should determine their level of ability, which will, in turn, suggest a methodology for unsettling them to the point of irrationality.

I have sent Margroge out to Delta Continent's observational lab. She is obviously becoming attached to the creatures already. I can see that any basic psychological work aimed at disturbing their psyches would find resistance there.

I only wish that I could send Ortheris with her. Jimenez is not so closely involved in the day-to-day

*work, so he can be kept ignorant of much that we do,
but Ortheris is another matter. She has made it obvious
that she will oversee everything meticulously. I can't
have that. I must invent some highly sensitive project
that will take carefully selected portions of her time.
And a lot of off-duty time? Yes.*

*I am keeping this journal of private observances and
thoughts upon the progress of the Fuzzy problem. It is
quite probable that I will destroy it, when the task is accomplished.*

*For it is already clear that extreme pressures will have
to be brought to bear on these creatures, if I am to gain
my—and the Company's—ends. There are methods and
techniques that reputable psychologists study, as a part
of their training. And shudder at. And never dream of
having occasion to use.*

*Men can be driven mad quite easily, when the proper
leverage is applied. These small creatures are certainly
no less subject to traumas than our kind. I will drive
them mad.*

*If, later, they should be found to be sapient (a matter
of time only, I should think) there will be no trace of
what I have done. I shall cover my tracks carefully in the
labs, and I shall also burn these notes, when their purpose is served.*

V.

There was no doubt at all that these big people came
from the sky. That, however, was no guarantee that
they came from the stars, as Silver-Fur knew quite well.
They possessed wonderful things, true, but they were
not at all helpful to Gashta. With regret, he laid aside
any belief that he had ever possessed in the tales he had

heard all of his life of help coming from the stars. These *toshki-hagga* were engaged in something that he couldn't comprehend.

The first day and night had been passably secure. Except for the fact that they had been caught in a net and put in bags and taken away from their own place, there had been no overt attempt to harm his family, or even to frighten them. Soft things had been in the space where they were, so that they could sleep comfortably, and he had taken heart from that fact. Perhaps, later, he might try to communicate with one of those out-sized creatures.

Even the second day had not been too bad, though they had all tired very soon of the childish games required to gain access to food. And the food itself had been none too good. The fruit and raw vegetables were passable, though not entirely fresh, but the *zatku*-meat had all been dead. Any child knew that *zatku* began to decay the instant they died. If more than a short time passed between the killing and the eating, the meat was tainted and useless. They had discarded it with disdain, placing it in a pile in one corner. It would soon become a problem, he knew, but there was no way he could think of to get rid of it.

He had learned one thing. The big people were terribly uninventive game-players. The combinations they had devised to complicate the getting of food from the various containers were boringly simple. Even when they made them a bit more difficult, it had been a matter of minutes only before Bud had deciphered the combinations of colored things to touch in order to bring fruit tumbling into their laps. She, being so young, had retained her interest in the entertainments longer than he and the other two, so they had allowed her the pleasure of getting food for all, once each was sure that he knew the way.

The third day had been another kind of thing. The big creatures had come into their room and caught him, stuffing him, once again, into a bag. He had gone away, his heart grieving at the thought of separation from his family. They had put him into a long and narrow passage, just large enough for him to go through with his head bent. At intervals, there were barriers across the way, with narrow right- or left-bending slots through which he must work his way.

Seeing no reason why he should trouble himself, he had tried to go back to the starting point, but something had burnt his feet on the smooth floor, forcing him to go forward. That angered the old male considerably, but like all his folk, he was philosophical about things he couldn't change.

The trip through the crazy ways was a bit difficult the first time, but he found himself emerging into a cage at last. A pile of mushy fruit waited there, but he sniffed it and turned up his nose. Then one of the big people took him out, carried him away, and put him into the tunnel again, at the same point at which he had begun the stupid game.

That was ridiculous! He flew through the ways, remembering with total accuracy every twist and bend, every dead-end and loop. Before the big creature had reached the end of the maze, Silver-Fur was standing in the cage, shaking the sides of the mesh, and speaking more harshly than he had done in many years.

But that had not been the end of the matter. They had sent him through several more mazes, which grew more and more complicated with each change. The last had six hands of turn-combinations to remember. Not difficult, but very frustrating when no good purpose was being served by the activity.

At last they had returned him to the room where his family was. Each of them looked cross and weary. Not one had found anything decently edible in any of the cages. They sat in the Circle, talking vigorously for a long time.

"These *toshki-hagga* are not-wise!" Bud said, shaking her golden mane. "They make us work and work for nothing, and they do nothing but stand and watch and make motions with their hands on a thing like a flat rock, using a stick. But they don't make patterns, or the

Spiral. They make little scratches like bird-tracks in dust. I saw when one of them picked me up. I bit him," she added proudly. "That was when he brought me back here."

Ik heaved a sigh. "It has been a long day," he said. *"Ja'aki fessi.* Are you hungry, too?"

They agreed that their exertions had made them very hungry, indeed. One by one they lined up at the spot on the wall where the colored things appeared, at times. They looked at it hopefully. In a moment, a white panel slid back, and the knobs were there.

They were all tired to the bone. Their tempers were short, too, and when they found that the combination had been changed again they thought of some very uncomplimentary things to say about the *toshki-hagga.* Silver-Fur, his old legs aching, let Bud decipher the new combination.

"But do not get our food for us. You are hungry and tired, also. Tell us, and we will get our own," he said.

She punched at the knobs. As each correct contact was made, the thing gave a click so slight that only Gashta ears could have heard it. As Bud found the way, she repeated it aloud, knowing that each would remember her words faultlessly.

"Push the red one twice. Then go over to the other side and touch the white one. Then the green . . . one, two, three times. Now the yellow . . . once only. Ssss! Not yet . . . oh! Go back and push the red one twice more. And there it is!" The opening at the bottom swished, and there was fruit, together with a kind of bread. Enough for one only.

Wearily, each of the males took his turn, going through the complicated pattern without hesitation. When all had their portions, they sat together and ate, talking all the while about their experiences of the day.

Silver-Fur ate and talked as well, but he had an eery feeling that he was being watched. One who has grown up in a forest full of predators knows those things unerringly. There was no place in this space where anything could hide. Nothing could be seen at all. But something was watching them, just the same.

He lay on the blanket, when they had all finished and gone to rest, thinking and thinking about it. These people had strange possessions. Among them must be a thing that let them see where they were not. Interesting. More interesting!

vi.

From Ernst Mallin's Diary:

The testing has run overtime. They have mastered all the standardized tests at least as quickly as pre-adolescent humans would have. As the tests were made more difficult and complex, they have kept pace. And last night, when they were returned to their quarters, the female went to the food wall, punched out the newly altered combination without one wrong move (as if she could somehow sense when the internal relays engaged), and yeeked at the others. They, in turn, used the new combination flawlessly and with far greater speed than she had done.

She had told them the new pattern.

This is appalling. They communicate verbally, therefore they are sapient. But they are not men. We are mankind, the only really highly developed sapient species found so far. I will not accept that these furry little beasts are our equals. Their excellence at the tests and programs we have tried must be found to be a quirk of chance—or the capacity for such excellence must be eliminated. The fate of the Company's investment depends on that.

The Company's welfare is paramount. Not only the livelihoods of hundreds of thousands of people on Zarathustra depend on that, but also those of millions

*of others across the galaxy. My own work is tied to the
Company, and my future depends upon the success of
this project.*

*I cannot prove the Fuzzies non-sapient. I must drive
them mad.*

*Of all the unethical things that I have done in the
name of the Company, this will be the most difficult.*

vii.

Silver-Fur shivered. Something was being done to him,
and it was a really bad thing. Even the small inconveniences of the past days seemed desirable, now, as he
floated in what seemed to be nothingness.

There was no light. He could feel nothing against any
part of his skin or his fur. His ears strained against the
fluid in which he floated, but there was not even a
gurgle of sound. He had never in all his life been placed
so that there was nothing to see or hear or feel or
smell—or even taste. Something within him wanted to
panic. To scream, even at the risk of letting that fluid
that was not quite like water get into his nose and
mouth.

But that was not the way of the Gashta. His people
endured whatever came to them. Those who had faltered, who had lacked the judgment and stability to
cope with the terrible world they lived on had been
eliminated from the species, both deliberately and by
chance. Now he, the child of all those generations of
survivors, clamped his teeth against his closed lips. The
pain was good. He could taste blood, too, and that was
a good thing.

There was no time, where he was. He couldn't determine if he had been there for hours or for days. Attuned

to the suns and moons of Zarathustra, the small person
felt removed even from his world, lost amid a nothingness so terrible that he shivered again. How could he
survive a long time of this? His mind felt as delicate as a
zatku-shell, ready to crack into slivers.

Then he gave a shuddering sigh. His big green eyes
closed, and he deliberately relaxed every muscle, from
scalp to heels. If a thing could not be endured in one
way, then there must be another that would work for
him.

He thought of a time so long ago, so far away that he
had forgotten it in the stresses of surviving. Once he had
been called Climbs-Swiftly. Yes, back in that Valley that
had almost been forgotten by all of his people, he had
lived as a child. There had been a mate—his first. What
was she called? Ah—Root-Grower, and their child had
been Leaf, a tiny pale-furred thing, even more silvery
than his own fur had been, then. They had played and
laughed and worked together for a time.

He remembered his decision to go out of the valley,
even though he would not have been forced to go. He
was of the *Haigun-sha* by nature, and Stargazer would
not have sent him away. Yet he had seen that matters
would get only worse, there where the rains were failing.
Root-Grower had not been convinced. She had thought
that time would heal their weather again, and that she
and the little one would be safe and happy there.

He wondered what had happened to them. Leaf
would be a woman of many summers, now. Root-
Grower would have found another mate. He could
barely remember how they looked, and he concentrated
upon bringing their faces clearly to mind. Lost in that
effort, he forgot his situation.

His face smoothed; the lines of stress left his forehead
and the area around his nose and mouth. He was
remembering, making every part of his life return, complete, to his mind. He could see and smell the place
where he had been born. The giant feathertrees, the big
rogo, the thorntree barrier that protected the wicker

houses with dry-scented arms that were needled with ferocious barbs. He could see the stream that watered the gardens . . . as it had been when he was young, before the rains failed. And the mountain that loomed over the Gashta. The mountain . . .

What had the old grandfather told him about that mountain? There had been so many tales, and he hadn't known which were tales of real happenings and which were imaginings.

The mountain stood above the spot where the Ship was buried. That was the thing he remembered.

"Long, long ago, before the oldest Gashta now alive had been thought of, our people came here in a great ship," the old Stargazer had said. "And the mountain caught the ship from the air and crushed it. But our ancestors sent out a message to the place that was their home. That is why we who are Stargazers look up at night, watching the blue star and the white one. When we see lights there, we know that the time for help has come. Help from the stars, from our own kind who live so far—so very far—that it will take them many Gashta-lives to reach us."

Silver-Fur could see the old Gashta's face, hear his voice. The smell of the stone they sat on came to his nostrils, sharp and sweet with fresh dew and green things growing at its base. He looked up, once again, at the pattern the old Stargazer had pointed out to him. He could see, quite clearly, every point of light in the night-sky. As if he stood on a high place, free and alone. Space opened out about him, but it was not frightening. It took him into its arms of darkness and comforted his spirit.

He floated in the sensory-deprivation tank. Hands lay peacefully on the heavy fluid. His chest moved with quiet breathing; his eyes were closed and his face calm. Silver-Fur slept.

From the diary of Ernst Mallin:
The sensory-deprivation tank has been a total failure.

Remote sensors record that though there is accelerated heartbeat, frantic encephalic activity after immersion, this lasts for only a short time.

Even the youngest of these Fuzzies calmed herself quite quickly, using, apparently, some relaxation-technique not unlike yoga. After the initial deep breathing, the subjects lost all symptoms of stress, though there was indication of increased mental activity for some time after the relaxed state was achieved.

Very gradually, the indices smooth out, as a sleeping state is achieved. Few human beings can cope with long periods of sensory deprivation. The Fuzzies have endured, quite comfortably, as much as seventy-two hours at a stretch.

How am I going to manage to unsettle their minds? We cannot use physical violence, not only because I personally disapprove of that, but also because it would leave traces that hostile witnesses might detect. There must be a way!

viii.

The large, smooth-faced Hagga was the one to study, Silver-Fur decided. It was he who barked at the other big people, and every time this happened they did another uncomfortable or unhappy thing to his family and himself. He had slick white not-fur, and the fur on top of his head started far back, so that his big face looked as if it began on top of his scalp.

After weeks of experience with this strange creature, Silver-Fur decided that he was quite mad.

This was a concept almost lost to the Gashta. Matters

that did not occur in the day-to-day lives of the people tended to disappear from their minds, under the demands of survival. But, there in that dark place with no sound, Silver-Fur had remembered many-many things. For Stargazer, though old and long retired from his post in favor of the new Stargazer, had been his own grandfather and teacher.

After the *gotza* had mangled his leg, Silver-Fur recalled, the old fellow had volunteered to watch the young one who had been himself. He had kept Silver-Fur amused with his tales, his intricate patterns, and his almost-forgotten songs, which he said were once known to all Gashta in the valley.

There had been a time, the old one had told him, when some Gashta were not-wise. There had been a rule among the people for many generations, that when a Gashta is seen to be not-wise, he must be quickly and mercifully killed. But that had not happened since any could remember.

It was evident that the Hagga practiced no such precautionary measure. This big one was more than not-wise. His mind seemed twisted in some inexplicable way. Why else would one choose to torment small people who had never posed a threat to him?

The dark-place-time ended. For a day or so, the Gashta were left to their own devices, which was boring, yet a relief, also.

Silver-Fur spent this time in re-examining the room in which they lived. He was curious. The dead prawns that they had put into a corner on that now-distant first day—what had happened to them? They had been gone when the white lights came on again, and the red light was so dim that it was hard to see what went on.

Then there was the white stuff that crinkled underfoot. That had been put, fresh, into the room every morning, replacing that which they used for relieving themselves. It was not as sanitary as a hole dug into the ground, perhaps, but far better than fouling the place where they must eat and sleep. It, too, vanished every night, though no Hagga came into the room.

Things did not go through solid places. That was plain to the smallest intelligence. So there must be an opening in or near that corner of the room, through which the dirty-stuff was taken away. It need not be very large to let a Gashta go through, too.

Yet Silver-Fur hesitated to try escaping. There was much to learn here, though that was made unnecessarily difficult. He was curious about the smooth-faced Hagga, too. One so bent invited study.

The old Gashta prowled about the corner, his nose almost touching the walls and the floor. His family was used to his curiosity, and they paid no heed. The watcher beyond the one-way wall, though the Gashta could not know it, had dozed. So when he found hair-line cracks, shaping a square in the floor-tiles, nobody noticed his nod of satisfaction. If things became terrible, there might be a way out. That was a good thing to know.

ix.

From Ernst Mallin's Diary:
Nothing has worked. It seemed, for a time, as if repeated electrical shocks from the floor and the food-buttons in the room might shake these creatures. They were extremely nervous and upset for several days, not knowing where the next shock might come from. The female almost gave up eating entirely, until the old male noticed and began securing her food for her.

That white-furred male is incredible. He stolidly endured extremely painful bursts of current, pushing the correct buttons no matter how frequently the combination was changed, never flinching, after the initial involuntary jerk. The others became short-tempered, as a result of having their sleep interrupted with randomly-timed shocks. They lost weight, ate less, and seemed in a fair way toward going the route I intend them to travel.

The big male called them into a circle last night. After he had yeeked at them for some half-hour, they shook themselves, groomed their fur carefully, and hugged each other! After that, no matter how intense the shocks, they only jerked. It seemed not to make them nervous anymore.

There must be something they fear. I shall ask Victor Grego to find out.

The bush-goblins are evidently the worst predators of Fuzzies. Grego tells me that remains of several have been found in the forest, evidently killed by the creatures.

This is the information that may make my task possible. Tomorrow I shall requisition one full-grown bush-goblin. The hunters should have no trouble in finding one. I understand that they are abundant in the forests on Beta.

The beast has arrived. It is the size of a large dog—perhaps even as large as one of the smaller of the big cats. Its ferocity is apparent, even when it is full-fed. It is amazing that beings as small as the Fuzzies have been able to survive at all in a place that practically teems with these creatures. It makes me, however reluctantly, respect their abilities. And their courage.

However, enough of that. Tomorrow I shall take the young female and place her in a cage. Then I shall allow the bush-goblin to roam free in the room. The cage has been constructed with the measurements of the beast in mind. She will be able to escape his claws only by pressing herself flat against a far side of the cage, when the beast reaches for her with his paw.

Terror can break the best of men, given time and the proper application. We shall see if the Fuzzies can withstand this treatment.

X.

Silver-Fur knew that the time had come when Bud was brought back into the room. She had been taken out early the evening before, and he and Ku and Ik had worried quietly for a night and a full day, according to the schedule of the lights, which was their only source of timing, now.

She was put down on the blanket. Her entire body was shaking violently, and the old male thought that even the Hagga who had carried her felt sorry for her. He patted her shoulder and pulled a corner of the blanket up over her. When he had gone, the three males gathered about her and took her in their arms, all hugged into a close bunch. Their warmth and closeness seemed to help her. After a time, she had subdued her reactions to a quiver. Then they all cuddled together, sitting very close. She sighed, and Silver-Fur knew that he could ask her, now, what had happened.

"They put me in a thing—like the thing that caught us, only the mesh was hard and stiff. It was large—I could take four steps across it, each way, and the top was two-Gashta tall. There was nothing to eat, and the mesh hurt my feet. I waited, and this one . . ." she looked at the old Gashta a bit hesitantly ". . . this one was afraid."

He patted her and stroked her mane. "Any Gashta would be, in a thing like that. Go on."

"After a long-long time, a square opening came into a wall. And . . . a *toshki-washa* came in."

The group about her straightened with a single galvanic jerk. Silver-Fur could hear harsh breathing from the other two males, but he said only. "Go on, Bud. Tell us."

Her small face was less rosy than usual. Even her fur seemed to have paled from its deep golden hue. She was still quivering, as if her very bones were shaking inside her. But she held onto the old one's hand tightly and spoke.

"There was no person there but the smooth-faced Hagga and one other. Not the kind female. Not the other males. He put me inside the cage and went away. The *toshki-washa* reached into the sides of the cage, but it could not reach far enough. If I pressed myself tight-tight against the other side, only its claws raked my fur without scratching my skin. It stood on top of the cage and reached down, and I lay flat and it could not get me from there, either. It was frightened and hungry, I think, and it tried for a long time. Then when the red light came on it rested for a while. If it had not, this one would not be here alive, I think." Her amber eyes were full of tears. She shook again as she remembered.

Silver-Fur put his arms about her and hugged her to him. She sighed and began again. "I rested, also, while it slept. But I felt someone watching me all the time. And I fell asleep in spite of myself . . . the thing was clawing at me when I woke, and I only just rolled away in time. It was a terrible time. That smooth-faced Hagga is a *toshki-Hagga*. Those others who put us into the mazes and made all the games we were forced to play were not cruel. They were not—do you realize, *Pa-ha-izza,* they were not in the place where they put us into the dark? Only the smooth-faced one and that other who was there with me did that. I think that they are not *toshki-Hagga*. Only that one, *Mallin*, and the male who brought me back here. And even he seemed sorry."

Ku and Ik stroked her fur, and Silver-Fur thought deeply. "I think that we can escape," he said, at last. "There where the wastes are taken away at night. There must be an opening, for every day the fouled white stuff is gone. When the red light comes, we will watch, and if it opens, we will go through the space."

"But we have no weapons!" Ku said, his big eyes frightened. "How will we protect ourselves, once we are outside of this place? Or kill *zatku?* It is terrible to be weaponless in the forest!"

"We will find sticks and stones. We will make more weapons, as we have done before this. True, none of our kind has ever been in a group that possessed no tools at all, but we will manage. We must go, for I can see that the Mallin is dangerously not-wise. It is more probable that we will die here than in the forest again.'' Silver-Fur patted Ku, then Ik, and hugged Bud again. "We will survive . . . if we can only escape.''

It was late. Before long it would be time for the red light to begin their "night.'' They waited, tense with expectancy, and watched the square of white stuff in the corner. But they had no chance to put their plan into effect. Heavy footsteps clacked outside the door. The things inside the door clicked and whirred, and the panel opened. Four men stood there, together with the kind female.

She was saying, "Is it necessary to take them tonight? They need to rest. Dr. Mallin tells me that they had a somewhat tiring testing yesterday and the day before. I was off-duty, but I am certain that it would be better to take them tomorrow.''

"They must be in Mallorysport in the morning,'' the very tall and slender Hagga said. "They're needed as soon as possible. Please see that they are—caged or bagged or whatever is needful for transporting them. And Miss Ortheris . . . the Company is not at all happy with your attitude during this entire experiment. Remember that.''

"I will remember that, Mr. Coombes,'' she snapped, and even Silver-Fur could tell from her voice that she was angry and upset.

They were put into cages again—small ones that held two Gashta. And then a strange thing happened. They were carried out onto a wide flat place and put into another flying-thing. This time they could see through a space of transparent stuff. Tansha was halfway up the east, Gozzo just rising. The forest waved in a light wind, its warm-winter-smell familiar in their nostrils.

Before they realized what was happening, the thing rose into the air, and they could see the square of the place where they had been kept. It was surrounded by trees, and the forest glimmered in the moonlight below them, as the lights of the place dwindled.

Silver-Fur was shaking now. Bud, in the cage with him, had recovered, it seemed, from her fright. Now she cuddled against him, holding his hand and crooning into his ear.

"No matter where they take us, we are at least together," she said. "You cannot know how terrible it is to be faced with a thing like that *toshki-washa* without any of your family to help or to comfort."

It was a long night. Now they could see only sky and stars. Occasionally the flying thing would turn so that one or the other of the moons would peep at them, but by then Silver-Fur had calmed himself and the two males. They all slept most of the night, as the thing carried them away into the unknown.

They were waked by rough noises like none they had ever heard in all their lives. Many Hagga-voices blended with hoots and whirrs and screeches and all manner of sounds unfamiliar to their keen ears. Their cages were hustled out of the flying-thing onto a flat surface. Then blankets were flung over them, and nothing could be seen as they were carried away into a bustle of alien activity.

It was still dark when the blanket was removed from the top of the cage. Silver-Fur noted with astonishment that the top was open, as well. The Hagga who took away the blanket must have unfastened the inaccessible catch. He stood, his head just clearing the top of the cage, and looked about. Beside him was the other cage, and Ku was just thrusting his head out to see where they were.

That was a question. It was like no place he had ever seen before, even the big boxlike place where his family had been imprisoned. Something like a gorge rose about them. There were no Hagga to be seen . . . it was still fully dark . . . but the place stank of them and their hot-smelling things that moved by themselves.

Silver-Fur climbed out of the box and turned to help Bud. Soon all four stood beside their former prisons, looking cautiously down the unfamiliar way.

"No trees or grass or bushes," hissed Ku.

Silver-Fur called them into a circle. Before they dared to move, they must plan.

"This is a strange place. We must go cautiously, quietly. If any Hagga shows itself, we must hide if that is possible. We must all look for anything that we might use as a tool or a weapon. Listen carefully for Hagga-voices—they talk a great deal, and that should warn us if they are coming. And sniff for predators, though I am sure there will be none worse than the Hagga in this place.

"Feel the wall beside us—this is a made-thing-gorge. Not stone and soil and growing things. These are all Hagga-places, not natural things. There will be things we do not know. There will be things that frighten us very much, but we must keep our heads steady and our nerves calm. Smell . . . very carefully . . ." he stood and raised his head, nostrils moving.

They all did the same, sniffing deeply. On the fetid wind, faint but true, came the scent of growing things. Of dirt and trees. It was distant, that place, but they knew that their noses would lead them there, if they could only survive their moving through Hagga-territory.

They went silently, between the walls of this not-gorge. And now they found a path, wider than any ever made by the hooves of *so-shi-fazzu*. On either side were the big boxes, but they were spaced widely, not forming a cliff as those in the gorge had done. There was grass about them, as well as some bushes. There were no lights, no voices. The Gashta ventured into one of the grass-patches and looked about. A blanket lay on the grass, smelling of Hagga. Ku folded it neatly and tucked it under his arm. At least they might sleep comfortably.

They went on, beneath the paling sky. Now there was a stirring in the Hagga-places, so Silver-Fur burrowed them into a hedge that grew close to a stone wall. There they dozed away the day, undisturbed except by a small animal that sniffed at them and barked once, then went away wagging its tail.

Night brought them out again, moving between the

houses. Another grass patch yielded a soft thing, square and thick. Ik took it. And Silver-Fur saw, lying on a bench, a thing that glinted in the light of the two moons. A tool such as he had never dreamed of, hard and sharp enough to hurt a *toshki-washa,* if necessary. Far better than any of their wooden *zatku-hodda.* Holding it, he felt more secure than he had since being taken captive.

Now they went more quickly. Their noses detected a real world now, that had spoken to them from afar. Trees. Growing things. Even small beasts.

They moved faster. Then Bud cried out, "Oh, see!"

It was almost like a Gashta small-one, sleeping beneath a bush. It was furry and white, though she soon saw that it was spotted with black. She bent and touched it with gentle fingers. It looked up into her eyes, its own bright in the gleam from the sky, though those eyes were far smaller than Gashta eyes. Instead of huge round pupils, those had long slits. Strange. All the Gashta gathered around for a moment to see.

"Mew?" it said.

She was charmed. It was no real baby, true. Its face was furred and different, but it was warm and soft in her arms. It seemed content there, and it set up a vibration inside itself that soothed her jangled nerves.

Silver-Fur watched. It seemed good to him that Bud should find one to nurture—she had no living babies, and it was sad for a mature female to be without.

Yet their escape was not to be so easy. Day came too soon, and the place they could scent as a refuge was still at a distance. And now Hagga were abroad. He hid his people, only to be flushed from hiding by inquisitive Hagga, small and large. Once they darted into an enclosure and found there what could only be a baby-Hagga. It was their own size, though soft and smooth-skinned, and they were pleased with its look and feel. It tried to talk to them, but its soft little words meant nothing. And then what could only have been its mother came out of her box and shrieked like a *gotza.* They fled again, their hearts pounding with terror.

Never had they dreamed of so many Hagga. The wide

places teemed with them, and all seemed intent on catching any Gashta they saw. Once there was a terrible noise, worse than lightning striking a nearby tree, and something whizzed above their heads. That was the final terror. They streaked into a brushy place, wriggled along for a long time, and finally emerged into the edge of a true wild-place.

The noise of the many Hagga was left behind with all the hard-paved ways and the boxes like cages. Here was a ravine that wound upward through trees and vegetation. They found a secure camping place, just as light faded from the sky. Relieved and exhausted, they burrowed into their stolen bedding and slept deeply.

It was a good place. There was no sign of anything harmful; even *gotza* did not circle overhead. They rested, finding *zatku* in fair numbers, as well as round-fruit and a few beanvines. They did not grow careless. This near to the haunts of so many Hagga, they felt exposed and imperiled. On the next day, a flying-thing swooped back and forward over their camp. The Gashta scattered into the brush.

Many Hagga appeared from down the ravine. They fled up it, leaving their blanket and weapon and cushion behind, though Bud clung to her new-found baby. There was the sound of voices above. They dispersed into cover. Silver-Fur found himself grabbed by one of the huge creatures that popped up from nowhere.

Before he could do more than cry out, both Ku and Ik were also caught, hugged into big arms, though he noted with surprise that the huge creatures were taking care not to squeeze them tightly. They seemed to be talking to him in soft voices.

He looked up, frantic, into a strange face. It was partly smooth. Scraggly white fur grew on the head, and a crossbar of it divided the face into two parts. A pair of strange-colored eyes was regarding him with surprise.

A cry distracted him, and he looked away downhill. Another Hagga was coming, carrying Bud. It also had her little animal, and it seemed to be treating them with much care.

There was a lot of talk, but this time his family was not bundled into bags. They went into the flying-thing and it took them into the air, very high. Silver-Fur was terrified and delighted. What things there were here to learn! But what, oh what, would happen to them now?

BOOK V.

Gashta and Hagga Make Talk

~~~~~~~~~~~~

When we slide down rocks
to splash into streams,
we keep one eye on the sky,
one on the forest.

When we play hide-and-find
we laugh and are happy,
but we must be cautious
or we may die.

When we steal-the-pebble
from our companions,
snatching and running,
still we take care.

Where is there a place
to play in safety?

i.

Little Fuzzy had loved riding in Pappy Jack's flying thing. The sensation of going right up into the air and looking down on the trees and the grasslands and even the mountains had made all his senses tingle. Now he was in a thing much finer even than that other one. The men here were dressed all alike—something like those who were Pappy Jack's friends, yet different. The colors and the patterns were not the same. And they had a thing that went up so very high that the whole world was there beneath Dark-Fur's eyes.

The forest was like fur on the curve of the world. The big water shimmered silver-blue. And there were other land-places than the one his people had thought to be all there was of the planet. Nothing like this had happened to any Gashta—or had it? He still retained dim memories of tales of a great ship and his people who traveled between the stars. He had thought them to be imaginary things, but now he was wondering if they might not be true.

It was frustrating that he couldn't ask those kindly men the things he wanted to know. Where they were going, for one. Other worlds would be very, very far away, he suspected. And only two places existed nearby to which they might be heading. Only the moons rode near to Zarathustra. Gozzo and Tansha had been his nightly friends all his life. Never had he thought to visit one of them, but he had a shrewd suspicion that that could be the only goal of a journey that went so extremely high into the sky.

The family was so excited that they bounced from one port to another, looking into the windows as if they were screens at home that made pictures. But Mama Fuzzy, as usual, felt uneasy about the entire project, and she had let her mate know it very plainly. Yet Dark-Fur could not feel any danger. Strangeness, yes. An odd feel in his legs, as if they were too strong for the weight of his body. A bit of dizziness, now and then.

"Baby is safe. All of us are well and happy. There is nothing to worry about," he told her, as the strange flying-thing came to rest inside a big-big room that had opened its mouth to receive them inside it. "There is much to see here, much to learn. Be happy, *Pa-ha-uka!*"

In spite of herself, she had taken his advice. Once they left the big ship, they found themselves in a place so unlike any they had seen that it enthralled them all. Made of the stuff that the Hagga called metal and glass and plastics, it smelled very odd. But it was filled with machines. Small ones went "paff-paff-paff." Big ones went "Cha-walla! Cha-Walla! Cha-walla!" The air was not like the air of the forest or that in the place they had escaped from. There was no way to see what might be outside, for there were no windows.

When the Hagga wanted to see outside, Dark-Fur noticed, they looked into a screen much like Pappy Jack's. When he discovered this, he tugged at the not-fur of the Hagga who seemed to be in charge of the Gashta family. While the big fellow didn't hear or understand what Little Fuzzy was trying to tell him, he did understand emphatic pointing and gesturing. With a laugh, he led the excited Gashta into a room and closed the door, so as not to have all the other Fuzzies all over the equipment.

"That's Zarathustra," he said, pointing to a wide ball that filled one screen. "See . . . the sun is almost down, and you can see the edge where it's night already. And that's a ship homing in on the other moon—it's around the curve of the planet, so you can't see it yet."

The big hand pointed, exactly as if the Hagga expected the Gashta to understand what he was saying. And the frustrating thing was that Dark-Fur did, indeed, comprehend much of what he was seeing, as well as quite a bit of the language.

"And that?" he asked, putting his small hand against the screen that showed a barren landscape of rock and hard-edged light and shadow. "Is that the outside, here?"

It was almost as if the big creature knew what he had said. He looked down at Little Fuzzy sharply. Then he pointed to the screen, to the floor under their feet, and outward, toward the wall.

"*T'ho!*" cried *Lo-Shta*, jumping up and down in his glee. "Yes! Yes! That is outside this place. We are on a moon! On Gozzo? Or Tansha? Oh, how I wish I could talk with you!"

Lieutenant Ybarra looked at the small person with amazement. The little guy knew what he had said—or at least the gist of it. He would have sworn that. Now how in Niflheim was he going to find out what the Fuzzy was trying to tell him? He'd bet anything that their vocal range was outside that detectable by human ears. First thing tomorrow, he was going to run some tests.

There would be special equipment needed. He could see that now. Much of it would be within his sphere of authorization, but he suspected that there would be some that even the chief Navy psychologist on Xerxes couldn't swing. He'd have to talk to Commodore Napier about that.

And they'd have to work fast. Down there on Zarathustra things were coming to a boil. Jack Holloway was charged with murdering Kurt Borch. Leonard Kellogg was charged with murdering Goldilocks. And the entire charade was being staged, if the truth were to be known, over exactly whether these were sapient people or dumb animals.

The Navy had known quite well that the Chartered

Zarathustra Company would not give up the world's Class III status without a fight, though it had obviously been granted in error. The existence of the Fuzzies hadn't even been suspected when the Company's charter had been approved. Now it was threatened, and the difference between undisputed ownership of a planet and mere tenancy under a civilian government was enough to drive the Company to extreme measures. The financial incentive was only part of it.

He had to hand it to Alex Napier. He had kept on top of this new development all the way, monitoring transmissions on the planet to keep up with the status of the situation from start to finish. Having Ruth Ortheris in place with the Company had been a stroke of genius, too. Without her instant and on-the-spot help, these little people might well be in a sticky mess. Ybarra respected Ernst Mallin's work. As a practicing psychologist he had to. But he hadn't an ounce of liking or trust for the man himself.

Ybarra's work was cut out for him. And he'd better work fast, too. Judge Pendarvis was famous for his rapid scheduling of trials, and the trial of Holloway (or of Kellogg, whichever came first) would be the proving-ground for the task he had been set. He knew that he must find a way of proving the obvious sapience of the Fuzzies and find it fast.

The little fellow tugged at his pants leg again, pointing to the door. He wanted to go back to his family.

Ybarra smiled and opened the hatch for him. He didn't actually believe, once they got started, that it would take very long at all to find a means of mutual communication with Little Fuzzy and his bunch.

ii.

The Gashta were ecstatic. They had been given a room all to themselves. In it were many-many tools and toys and other interesting if incomprehensible things. It had a screen that they could turn on and off whenever they wanted. It had little beds set into a wall, one above the other, so they could wrestle up and down, as well as on the padded floor. And they had just discovered that the strangely light feeling that they had noticed on coming to this place had wonderful uses.

At the moment KoKo and Cinderella were bouncing from floor to ceiling, making graceful turns in the air. Mike, always the clown, was leaping, turning head-over-heels in mid-air, and landing on his feet. Mitzi was bouncing sedately in one corner with Mama Fuzzy. And Little Fuzzy was trying what it was like to jump from his hands, using his elbows for flex instead of his knees. An amazing sensation.

They had had a wonderful sleep in those soft beds. The temperature had been just right, so that they didn't need to burrow into the blankets provided. They had been given a breakfast of esteefee, which had started their day off well. Now, as they played, Little Fuzzy was waiting for the one he already thought of as Unca-I-ba'ra. Play was wonderful, but he had a conviction that his people had been brought here for more serious purposes. And without quite knowing why, he felt inside himself a compulsion to get on with whatever that purpose might be. He had a feeling that he would be helping Pappy Jack in some unexplained way.

When the hatch opened and the big man entered, Little Fuzzy sailed from hands to feet to Unca-I-ba'ra's arms in one slow and graceful motion. Ybarra laughed and set him on his shoulder.

"Come on, boys and girls," he said, turning toward the opening. "We've got work to do this morning. Things are about to pop, down there, and we've got to keep ahead of them!"

The chattering group followed him down the passageway to another of the odd doors. There he stopped and motioned them to enter. Then he stepped inside and closed the hatch behind him.

A number of Hagga were inside the room, sitting at tables or standing by screens that were not quite like those that made pictures. They turned, as the group came in, and stood silent.

"These are the Fuzzies, Men. Rather, these are specimens of Fuzzy Fuzzy Holloway Zarathustra, the last-discovered sapient species in human history to date. It's our job to find a way to communicate with them—in speech, of course. They get their meaning across pretty well right now, and I think they understand a lot of what I say to them. What we've got to do is to find a way to bring their vocal range into our hearing range. Not too difficult, I should say."

It was a fascinating day. The Gashta talked into things that hummed back at them. They listened to things that made clicks and sputters and odd noises, or groans and hisses and shrieks. And all the while those screens made lines or patterns of dots (that interested the Gashta very much. Patterns were their abiding interest, as had always been true) or smooth curves of color.

When they were tired of that, they were taken into a big room with many long tables and fed *hoksu-fusso* of many kinds. But always there was esteefee to climax any feast. And there were Hagga all around, watching them eat and making marks on their flat things.

Little Fuzzy wondered if he might learn to make the marks-that-talk soon. That would, it seemed to him, make everything much easier. But when he had a chance to examine some of the writing for himself he saw that it would be much tougher than he had thought. First he would need to learn the meaning of the little bird-tracks. And then he would need a good understanding of the language it stood for. No, that would be a wonderful thing to do, some day, but it was no short-term project.

So he threw himself into the interesting games that the uniformed men devised for the entertainment of the

Gashta. After all the talking-and-listening tests, his family was taken into a place full of lovely things. There was a table entirely filled with things-that-screwed-onto-things. Some were like the nut and bolt that Pappy Jack had given him. Some were more like the jar and the canister. But there were many-many others, too. Long thin rods with different-sized balls that threaded onto them, each ball fitted to a different-sized part of the rod, which varied in thickness, thin at one end, thick at the other. There were round things that screwed into other round things, all colored beautifully, all fitting inside one another, so as to fill up the hole in the largest entirely, when put together correctly.

Dark-Fur just about exhausted his interest in things-that-screwed-into-others that day. As did his family. They had a wonderful time, though, punctuated by snacks of esteefee and intermittent tickling-and-tugging matches with the Hagga who stood about writing on their note-pads. These were fine-fine big people. They loved the Gashta, it seemed, almost as much as Pappy Jack and Unca-Ben. Every day, they provided several new games for them.

There was a wonderful game, indeed, that they played together. Small screens lined the walls of a room. Below each was a keyboard with buttons to punch. When you fingered the buttons, bright images came onto the screens and moved as you continued to touch the buttons. It took Little Fuzzy about ten minutes to realize that when Unca-I-ba'ra (who was now turning, gradually, into Unca-Panko) sat down and touched the keyboard beside him, he could put still other images among those Little Fuzzy was manipulating. At once, the Gashta made a connection. This was like a game of steal-the-round-fruit, or who-has-the-pretty-pebble. He could play with those other images, using those beneath his own fingers. What a *hoksu-washa,* indeed!

They played for a long time. And when they were tired and had stopped to eat and wrestle a bit, Unca-Panko said to one of the other Hagga, "The little devil beat me three times out of six. Not bad for someone who has never seen a game of hockey, would you say?''

Most of his words were meaningless to Little Fuzzy, but his tone was very proud. That told the Gashta that the man was pleased with him. It made him feel very warm inside. Pappy Jack might be proud, too, if he ever found him again.

But that was a thing that he couldn't get across to the Hagga at all. There were no gestures that meant Pappy Jack alone. Other men had hair across their faces. Other men wore the round-things-to-see-through. Other men used guns to shoot bad things. It was a hard thing, but, Gashta-like, he bore it philosophically. He could see that these men were working very hard to find a way to make-talk-with-Gashta. When some way was devised, then he would ask Unca-Panko where Pappy Jack was.

In the meanwhile, he was enjoying himself to the fullest. The games with lights and images, the sessions with sounds, were wonderful. And best of all was the fact that a table full of bright beads and beautiful stones and bits of odd but attractive stuff had been put into the Fuzzies' room. When everyone was tired out, they could all sit and make patterns while they rested. Such patterns had never been dreamed of by their kind before, Little Fuzzy was certain.

They were almost too lovely to take apart and redesign. He was absorbing his very best one, one evening, when Unca-Panko came up behind him and looked at the pattern. The big creature bent over it, studying every detail of line and curve, of color-gradation. He put out a gentle finger and touched the Spiral that rose through the center of the design.

"I wish I knew what that means," he said. "All of you use it so often, and it's always the same. No long skinny spirals. Not a single end-on view of a spiral. Every one just the same, something like a nebula . . . a nebula? . . ." he paused, staring at the colorful display. Then he shook his head.

"Getting notional," he said to the Gashta, who had watched him closely. "What would you kids know about astronomy, except what you can see from planetside? Not a telescope among you!'' He laughed, and Little Fuzzy climbed him and sat on his shoulder.

He was beginning to realize what Baby had found so wonderful about sitting on heads. When you were knee-high to everyone else, a point of vantage was very handy, indeed.

Ybarra raised his hand and patted the silky fur against his neck. ''Just about there, old son. A couple more days, and I think we'll be able to sit down and talk.''

iii.

Memo to Commodore Napier from Lieutenant Pancho Ybarra:

Sir:

As a result of the past week of testing, my colleagues and I have determined beyond any doubt that Fuzzy fuzzy holloway zarathustra *is, indeed, a sapient species. Their present paleolithic level of technology seems, in fact, anomalous when compared with the quickness of observation and ratiocination that can be observed in the actions of these beings.*

Specific: When introduced to various kinds of fasteners, openings of differing types such as latches, locks, doorknobs, and twist-pegs, they solved the problems almost immediately. Anything using threaded parts that screw together was already familiar to them, no matter how seemingly unlike the specimens we used might be. Other ''principles'' were studied, mastered, and applied even to matters that looked different but were, in fact, the same.

Specific: We set up an electronic center and introduced them to a number of games from all over the gal-

*axy. They understood the idea very quickly and became
adept at a number of things, including hockey,
checkers, weightless handball, and coordinate tic-tac-
toe. They have at least the same level of spatial imagination that* Homo sapiens terra *possess and can, when the
rules have been digested, beat us at the games they like
best at least half the time.*

*Specific: The extra-sensitive sensors indicate that
their speech is in the ultrasonic range. From testing, I
feel that a sort of hearing-aid might be developed that
would bring it into our audio range. Is there someone on
Base who has any expertise in hearing-aid construction
or repair?*
Signed
Ybarra, Lieutenant, TFN

Orders
Camber, Luis J., Chief Petty Officer, TFN
*Pursuant to the request of Lieutenant Ybarra, Psych-
ologist, you are being detached from present duty for
work connected with secret and urgent project. You will
need any equipment in your possession that will aid in
altering hearing-aids for specific uses.*
Signed
Olliver, Lieutenant, TFN
for Space Commodore Alex Napier

iv.

Dark-Fur had a feeling that things were about to
change. He was beginning to understand quite a lot of
the Hagga-talk about him, and the people who worked
with Unca-Panko were excited about something. And
that something had to do, he could understand, with

talking to his family. They were trying little buttons in
their ears, turning switches on and off, dancing up and
down as if they were Gashta.

"Hear that? By the Great Ghu's Grandfather, Lieutenant, I think we've done it! Listen to them chatter!
Sounds almost like Japanese. Yoshiko, doesn't it sound
like that to you?"

That was the new Hagga, the one Unca-Panko called
Cam-ba. He had been very busy with tiny things that he
adjusted and adjusted, then listened and listened, then
adjusted yet again, as he talked to the Gashta.

The black-furred Hagga he had spoken to was shaking her head. "It sounds like Japanese, Chief, but it
isn't really that. There aren't any words that I understand, though I'll have to admit that I haven't heard the
language since my grandfather died. But it's a language.
Hear the repetitions? It contains words, without any
doubt. Here, Love, come to Yoshiko . . ." She held out
her arms to Cinderella, who jumped into her lap and
hugged her.

Dark-Fur sat on a stool and watched as the woman
tightened the thing in her ear and started to talk with the
young Gashta. It was quite evident that she was hearing
what Cinderella said. These clever Hagga had made a
thing that did that. *Hoksu!*

But Cinderella was not the one to talk to. She had
been with big people only a short time, compared with
himself. She had not concentrated on learning Hagga-
words, as he had done. She, in fact, was less interested
in that than any of the rest of the family.

He hopped down from his stool and went over to
Cam-ba, who also had one of the little-bug-things in his
ear. Reaching up, the Gashta tugged at the leg of the
man's trousers until he looked down. Little Fuzzy
touched his own ear, pointed to Camber's. Then he motioned toward the bench along one wall. *"Mosh
ja'ne'ti!"* he said, indicating that he wanted to sit on the
man's lap. "We will have to talk, *t'ho?"*

Then he thought very hard for a moment, as the big
fellow settled himself onto the bench and made a lap.

He knew many-many Hagga-words, now. He should be able to speak something the man would understand.

"Fuzzy talk now—you hear?" he said carefully.

"By the Great Ghu!" said Camber so loudly that Ybarra came from the other side of the room to investigate.

"The little guy just talked English to me!" said the startled technician. "Say something for the lieutenant, Kid!"

"Lit-ta Fuzzy say he-yo, Unca-Panko."

Ybarra drew a deep breath. Then, military discipline be hanged, he whooped in triumph. "He-yo yourself, old Scout!" he boomed. "You've been learning our language—our words—all along, haven't you?"

"*T'ho*. Yes. Pappy Jack, where is? All Fuzzies worry much for Pappy Jack. Hagga take Gashta in flying-thing, no see Pappy Jack again."

"Don't you worry about your Pappy Jack. You and your people have just proved that you're not animals, and that's the main thing he needed to have done. We'll be going back planetside in a few days, and then you'll see him. Wow!" The young officer grinned widely. Then he recovered his dignity a bit and drew himself up.

"Report this to Commodore Napier at once, Stone," he said to the yeoman at the door. "Tell him that we have cracked the main problem. Now it only remains to learn what we can of their language before we have to take them back to Mallorysport."

As the yeoman stepped through the hatchway, Ybarra looked around at the excited group in the workroom. "Let's get cracking, boys and girls," he said. "Everybody, put a Fuzzy on your lap and record every sound he or she makes. If you can guess meanings, that's fine. If not, put them down anyway, phonetically. We'll compile a Fuzzy dictionary that will blow Victor Grego and Leslie Coombes and Leonard Kellogg entirely out of the water. Not to mention the Chartered Zarathustra Company!"

Dark-Fur had looked and listened with interest. And when the excitement died down, he sat on Unca-

Panko's lap and talked to him for a long-long time, telling him things about the Gashta and the Hagga, things about the world below and the beasts that prowled its forests and mountains. But most of all he tried to tell the big Hagga about the patterns, the Spiral, and the tales of his childhood that were becoming, more and more, to seem true, rather than imaginary.

"Once, very-very long ago," he said in Gashta, "the far-back-fathers-and-mothers of the Gashta went in ships across the sky. Like Hagga flying-things. But far-far—off into the sky. Came here on a ship. It broke on the mountain, and the Gashta lived there for long-long. Gashta still there? *Lo-Shta* feels it is so. For help will come from the stars. That is the thing all Gashta believe. Hagga come from the stars, it is true, but Hagga are not Gashta. Gashta will come from the stars!"

But of course the man didn't understand, and the small person on his lap simply had not the vocabulary to tell him the tale in his own tongue. Still, it was fun to see him making the marks that meant Gashta-words. That was enough, for now.

BOOK VI.

Hoksu-Washa

~~~~~~~~~~~~~~~~

Was there a Valley, long ago?
Is that a dream or a made-up-thing?
The old ones sing songs
and tell stories to the small ones,
and we stay close to hear.

They say that help will come,
and they look up
at moons that say nothing,
stars that wink secretly.
The little ones shiver.

Was there a Valley?
We almost remember . . .
Does one in that Valley watch,
even now?

i.

Never had Silver-Fur dreamed that Hagga could be so
kind and loving. Even those good ones, before in the
place where bad things were done, had not been allowed
to cuddle and spoil the Gashta as these new ones did.
The flight from the camp had been full of fear, it was
true, but that was only because he had had no idea that
such wonderful things were coming.

Now his family had been brought to a *hoksu-mitto* of
the very finest sort. There was soft-pretty on the floor.
Fine beds and finer food were here, and toys and tools
and strange-things of so many kinds that it was hard to
know which to examine first. And on the walls of this
place were large patterns that made pictures of real
things. This excited his family greatly. So ingrained was
the Spiral in their pattern-making that none had ever
thought to try making shapes-that-look-like-real-things.

Bud (the Hagga, for some strange reason called her *Id*
Not a bad name, really. He rather fancied his own—
Superego. It had a ring to it. And Ku was *Complex*, and
Ik was *Syndrome*. The Hagga did have a gift for finding
interesting names) was most interested in making pictures with bright things. They all, when weary of playing with their new things or of cuddling or wrestling and
tickling with the Hagga who took care of them, spent
much time experimenting with the idea. But the Spiral
was so native to them that they soon went back to their
older methods.

Best of all, however, was the screen there. They had seen the big people in the laboratory using the things, turning them on and clicking them off, speaking through them to others of their kind, but the Gashta hadn't been allowed near them. Now they could make the button click and watch as much as they liked. And it showed much more interesting things than simply talking-Hagga. There were many-many things happening there, all the time.

It was a good place; Silver-Fur (he often forgot to be Superego for a bit) felt secure there, and he knew his family was, at last, safe from mistreatment. Even Id's kitten was thriving under the combined attention of all of them. The small thing was, in some way, more fun than a baby Gashta. It could take care of its own sanitary needs, for one, and didn't have to be cleaned up many times a day. The box of sand that the thoughtful Hagga had brought in for it was all it needed. It was a large box, so the Fuzzies shared it with him, and to their delight it was removed twice a day and replaced with a clean batch.

Sometimes at night, when the Hagga were all asleep and old habits kept the Gashta wakeful, they would go into the middle of the big-big room and play with the kitten. It would bounce sideways across the circle, make a swift dart at one or another of its family, and roll away toward another before anyone could move. Then there would be a wonderful free-for-all, and at its end they were usually tired enough to sleep. The kitten took turns sleeping on chests or in the curve of arms or knees. In this alien place, fine as it was, the small creature comforted them all. For it was totally happy and unworried.

One day after they were brought to the new place, the Hagga who had spoken so gently to them brought a real baby Gashta to visit. What delight there was in that. It had been a long time since any of them had seen a living young-one that they all wanted to hold it, to talk to it. But Baby Fuzzy was too busy to sit in anyone's lap. Or even on anyone's head.

The kitten caught his attention at once, and it was ob-

vious to his elders that the notion of having someone of
his own size excited him greatly. Superego and his
family had to sit down and laugh very hard, for the
small-one wanted very badly to touch the kitten, and the
kitten wanted just as badly to stay out of his reach. At
last Bud-Id caught the furry beast and held it in her lap
while Baby Fuzzy approached it. He seemed to have
learned in the scramble that abrupt motions would send
the animal flying. So he crept up quietly to Id's side and
laid a questing finger on the black and white fur.

He watched, his big green eyes solemn, as the female
showed him how to scratch the creature's ears and make
it purr. In a short time the kitten was in his lap, while
he, in turn, sat in Id's lap. It was a wonderful, peaceful
time.

Once Baby and the kitten were used to each other,
things flowed smoothly for a long time. And then
another family of Gashta came into the big room. They
were with several of the Hagga, and there were a lot of
them—a hand and two fingers, Syndrome counted,
before calling it to the older male's attention.

Though Superego had begun to realize that there was
literally no end to the fine things the Hagga possessed, it
made him a bit nervous to have so many more come into
the territory of his family. And to make it worse, the
newcomers were entirely too interested in the family's
kitten. That little creature seemed to find instant ac-
ceptance among any Gashta it met.

Bud was disturbed, and her unhappiness unsettled the
others. The new ones were polite and well-behaved and
didn't frighten the kitten by fighting over it, but nevertheless things grew tense for a time. Then Silver-Fur
thought over the situation, called the entire group into a
circle, and settled things in a Gashtalike manner.

"There are many-many of us here. Seldom have two
hands and two fingers of our people stayed in the same
place for more than a little time. But you can all see that
this is a very large space, filled with more fine things
than all of us can play with or eat, even if we never slept
at all. Our Hagga all are friends, as you can see by ob-

serving their behavior. They provide the *hoksu-fusso*, the clean blankets, the toys and the games for us. If they have no worry, why should we?

"Our small beast is the only thing that is just-one. He is a part of our family, it is true, but all Gashta feel love for him. He does not object. As long as all are careful not to hurt him, we should be able to share him. Let us all be Gashta. This one believes that the time when only families existed among our kind is over. It may be that a time is coming when all Gashta are of the same family, on this world."

His voice stopped, and the others sat quiet, thinking over what he had said. Then Bud stood and handed her kitten to the female across the circle from her.

"It is good," she said. "Gashta should never be angry with one another. We will be friends, as our Hagga are. *T'ho?*"

"Yes," answered the female, and the word traveled about the circle swiftly. After that, all was harmony among his kind, and Superego was content to observe the new things, the Hagga, who came and went, played and watched. It was quite clear to him that they were all waiting for something. There was a tension in their bearing and in their voices.

One morning, all the Hagga were gone. Only those who lived in this place and brought food and did the cleaning were about. Silver-Fur felt his fur bristle. Surely this meant that the thing they had been waiting for had happened—or was happening.

He listened when the cleaning-Hagga spoke.

"Judge Pendarvis is a fair man, they tell me," said the female to the male. "Still, this trial is going to mean a lot to these little guys. They ought to let us testify, when it comes to deciding if they're intelligent or not."

"That's the truth. We're right here with 'em every day. I've cleaned up after people who were a lot dirtier and a lot less polite. You notice the little one over there? One they call Id? I just took out the sandbox, and she came over and thanked me. I'd swear it to Niflheim and back."

"Well, they'd just better do the right thing. After the Company tried that scam, getting the little girl to testify that a bunch of Fuzzies had beaten her up, just about everybody realizes that they don't intend to let the Fuzzies be declared sapient if there's any way to stop it. And trying to get those bums over in Junktown to hunt them for their furs! Now that was low!"

"What do you think'll happen if it goes against the little people here? Can the Company still trap or hunt them for furs? I don't know . . . it just seems wrong that anybody so bright and loving should be called animals."

The male nodded, wielding his mop vigorously.

Superego watched them work, but he was thinking of the garble of half-understood and incomprehensible words he had heard. He had gleaned from that conversation a hint of threat to his people. Not just to his family but to all Gashta. He wondered about many things.

But the afternoon brought a change. Men came and led the Fuzzies into a waiting flying-thing that carried them above the many-many boxes that the Hagga called a *city*. It put them down at the door of a big-big place filled with people, and more men led them all inside.

And there was the one with Baby, his white fur shining distinctly among the darker-furred ones about him. The familiar Hagga were all there. Silver-Fur had been right. This must be the place where that important thing was happening. Silver-Fur touched Bud's shoulder, drew the two males toward him, and kept them in order as they were showed where to sit. After that there was a knocking sound, and all the people became quiet.

There came a lot of talk, then, that he couldn't understand. Then some men brought in boxes that he thought at first to be new toys. The things inside turned out to be little dark-colored bugs that the Hagga put into their ears and clicked something on their webs.

And then the Hagga all went mad. The baby on the white-furred Hagga's lap started talking to the big creature, asking him what was happening. And the Hagga heard him!

Superego was amazed. He looked closely at the nearby big people with the bugs in their ears. He leaned toward the nearest and said, in Gashta, "I do wish you'd explain what is happening. I feel terribly frustrated!"

And that one heard, also, though he evidently didn't understand the Gashta tongue. In the midst of his amazement, he became aware that the men had gone out again and brought in still another family of Gashta.

Then there was bedlam, indeed. Pappy Jack rose and ran toward them. They, in turn were shouting at him, "Pappy Jack, Pappy Jack!"

Ah . . . that explained why that Hagga had been so sad and quiet when the combined families played with the other big people. He had lost his family! And here they were back again. Superego smiled. He loved happy endings to hard troubles.

ii.

In the days since the hearing-things had been perfected, Little Fuzzy had taught Unca-Panko many Gashta-words. In fact, all of the family, even Cinderella, had become entranced with the idea of making the big people understand them. They had all worked very hard, trying to say words and show meanings to the Hagga who were studying their tongue.

The huge creatures were a bit slow, but they seemed determined. By the time the day came for going back to Pappy Jack, Unca-Panko could say in quite passable Gashta, "Day come, go back down. You ready see Pappy Jack?"

It might not have been the most grammatical and flowing Gashta, but it sounded wonderful to Little Fuzzy and the family. They jumped up and down, enjoying the light gravity for the last time. Then they took the lovely shoulder-bags the *hoksu-Hagga* in this place had given them for carrying all their things and packed them full.

He could almost feel sorry to leave this most interesting place. But to see Pappy Jack and Unca-Ben and the rest of the big people he loved! That was the best thing. He followed Unca-Panko into the shuttle (he had learned all the names of the different flying-things, now, from photographs) with a joyful heart.

In what seemed a very short time, he and his family were being led into a very big place that was full of people. At the front there were tables . . . and at one of them sat Pappy Jack, himself, with Baby Fuzzy on his lap.

Mama Fuzzy moved past him, hurrying toward her only surviving infant. And Baby was dashing toward her, leaping from Hagga to Hagga as if they were trees or stones. The two met in one tremendous hug.

Then Pappy Jack was there, and Little Fuzzy leaped into his arms, along with most of the others. The Hagga sat down on the floor, amid chairlegs and people-feet, and the family tumbled all over him. He was talking, and tears were running down into his moustache, but nobody minded at all. It was the most wonderful of times.

Everyone was trying to show him the new shoulder-bags at once, bringing out fistfuls of little knives and small tools that the Navy-Hagga had made for them. And he had one of the hearing-things in his ears and could hear all of them when they spoke. Indeed, he tried to make his voice high for their ears, though that wasn't really necessary.

Then Dark-Fur remembered the really wonderful thing that Unca-Panko had made for him. With the most nonchalant air he could muster the small fellow reached into his shoulder-bag and pulled out the tiny pipe the big man had given him. He packed it with tobacco from his small pouch, frowning as if he noticed nothing else in the room, though he felt all eyes upon his actions. Then, with a flourish, he brought out his *own* little lighter and flicked it into flame, touching it to the pipe bowl.

His taste for the dramatic was satisfied. As he puffed, he realized that he had made all the Hagga go quiet to watch him. And they were now beginning to talk again, sharp gabbles of sound. There was a great deal of talk, after that, but as far as Little Fuzzy was concerned it was anticlimactic. He was satisfied that he had stolen the show.

That night his family met the new Gashta and was told about the conference they had held. It was good, sound Gashta-sense, and Little Fuzzy agreed. But his family didn't stay in the big room with all the fine toys. Pappy Jack took them to his own room with him, and they chattered far into the night. Before they got too sleepy Little Fuzzy realized that they were beginning to understand one another a bit. Much faster than those up on the moon. Perhaps when people loved each other it helped, he thought as he dozed off.

The next day they all went back to the big place Pappy Jack called a *courtroom*. There were more than three hands of Gashta there, and all the Hagga seemed to be in a playful mood. There was a mighty tug-of-war with a long thing Mama Fuzzy found beneath a table. People of all sizes were laughing and calling to each other. It was a lot of fun, and Dark-Fur decided that he liked courtrooms very much. It was just as well, for several more days were spent there, though none of those were as much fun as the first had been.

Then one day everything had been changed. The tables that had been at the front were gone, and benches were lined up across the space where they had been. The Judge (a delightful Hagga, full of mischief and laughter) was sitting in his place, very solemn.

After a bit, Unca-Panko got up and talked a long time. Dark-Fur thought that he was explaining about thinking to all the other Hagga. That puzzled him for a bit, for most of them seemed to think fairly well, if slowly. But when he was done, at last, the Judge hit the table with his little hammer and spoke again.

Then Unca-Gus picked Little Fuzzy up bodily, held him high in the air, and shouted, *"The winnah! By unanimous decision!"*

Only after he had had a chance to compare notes with Superego did Little Fuzzy really begin to understand what that meant.

BY THE STREAM

Hai!
The small ones slide
down smooth rock
to splash into the pool.

I do not heed
the water on my fur,
the mud between my toes
as I watch them.

I see the sky—
no *gotza!*
I see the forest—
no *toshki-washa.*

This is a wonderful day
of sunlight and play,
with all the young ones
laughing.

iii.

To John Holloway, Commissioner of Native Affairs, Zarathustra:

You are authorized herewith and hereby to take up residence on Beta Continent, together with your assistants and necessary personnel, in order to locate and identify all possible native inhabitants, such inhabitants being identified as individuals of Fuzzy Fuzzy Holloway Zarathustra. Such additional construction as may be needed may be billed to the new government of Zarathustra, payable at such time as said government institutes taxation and disbursement agencies.

In addition, you are authorized to borrow from the present Constabulary Department personnel to the number of twenty, such personnel to assist in protecting the persons and interests of aforesaid Fuzzy Fuzzy Holloway Zarathustra. Such officers and men may be offered, in addition to regular pay, augmented rank.

It is suggested that you take advantage of all offers of assistance from the Navy, which has been most generous in the extension of such offers, in the use of manpower and technical skills.

At their request, Ruth Ortheris (Van Riebeek) and Gerd Van Riebeek are assigned to assist in psychological and physiological testing of the native people. Training in new lifestyles will also be within their (and your) province.

Being new at this position, I am probably forgetting to mention several matters that you will find it necessary to address. In the event that you find yourself faced with any such problem, immediate attention will be forthcoming from this office.

Signed:
Bennett Rainsford, Governor

Memo to Governor Rainsford:
Dear Ben:

As you have learned from our reports, we are becoming very crowded with new Fuzzies. The forest is full of them, literally, all coming south after land-prawns. Their grapevine must be highly efficient!

While, as we have long ago realized, the Fuzzies are very even-tempered and non-aggressive among their own kind, this overcrowding is beginning to wear on tempers, both theirs and ours. There have been some skirmishes already, and we know that we will soon have many times the number of newcomers that we now are taking care of.

After discussing the situation with Major Lunt of the Native Protection Force, I feel that we have come up with a viable plan for locating the Fuzzies in good and compatible homes. Would it be possible to set up a Fuzzy Adoption Service? While personnel for processing such a program might be expensive, it is nothing compared to the expense of trying to protect the as yet unmet population from those who will almost certainly try to exploit them as "pets."

If you have any ideas about this, I'd be interested to know what they are. As Fuzzies seem happiest when they have a family of their own (a human family, I mean), that seems to me to be the best and most pleasant way of handling the situation.

Our studies are continuing. No reason for the very low birthrate has as yet been suggested, but we're working on that as well as many other facets of Fuzzyology. You might come over to Beta at the first opportunity. You'll be amazed.
Signed
Jack Holloway

Dear Jack,
No time to pay visits. I'm up to my neck in crooked lawyers who want to open up the whole planet to exploitation as of ten minutes ago. Luckily, Judge Pendarvis

put the question on hold for a year, while elections are held and a real government gets into place.

However, that made me realize that the Fuzzy Reservation question must be settled immediately. I propose closing the entire continent north of the Little Blackwater River and the East Fork of the Snake to settlement. That gives the Fuzzies the entire northern part of Beta and much of the central portion. Should be enough, I think, but if you disagree, give me a buzz and we'll discuss it on-screen.

I'm thinking over the adoption question. Sounds good to me. I'm going to ask the judge his opinion as soon as I have the chance. Have the Van Riebeeks and the new doctor settled in all right?
Ben

Ben,
All going well here, except for overcrowding. Your specs for the Reservation sound fine to me, and I tried to show Little Fuzzy on the map how it would lie. The little fellow seemed to know exactly what I was getting at. He ran his finger down the topographic map we have here in the office, following one of the streams down from the mountains. I think he was telling me that that was how he came . . . there were a lot of bizzos in there. Anyway, he conferred with a bunch of the others, and, until we can get a larger Fuzzy vocabulary or they can get a larger Hagga one, they seem to approve.

They don't seem to have too much sense of property —that is, in a sense of land. Don't try to take one of their chopper-diggers away from them, believe me! But the idea of all that land being theirs and their people's seemed to interest them a lot. They sat down in a circle and talked for a long time. We got it on tape, but so far it's not intelligible to us.

That big male of Ruth's—you remember the one she calls Superego?—seemed to be in charge of that discussion, too. He's pale-colored, extremely bright and thoughtful. Makes me wonder if he was always that light-colored, or if that's one sign of old age. We haven't had much luck at guessing their ages. He doesn't say a lot, lets Little Fuzzy do most of the communicating, both with us and with the new Fuzzies. But I have a feeling that he's the patriarch of the whole shebang. Every new batch seems to feel so, too. They don't even play with him unless he shows that he's in the mood.

I keep trying to ask Little Fuzzy about their ages. I don't think any of them have had the time or the opportunity to keep track. And most of this continent has very little seasonal change, so they don't even say, "Oh, six winters ago I did thus-and-so." At least, I don't think so.

The one thing that we ask most often is the question about the pattern that keeps cropping up among their art works. That spiral bothers me. It's just exactly the same, every time. Viewed from the top, at an angle. Never from end-on, never from the side. As if you were looking down into a spring you were holding in your hand. Or into a nebula?

I can hear you laughing. I'll shut up and let you get back to work.
Jack

iv.

The family had never had such good hunting. *Zatku* seemed to lurk under every shrub and fern, and the excited Gashta congratulated each other on following the advice they had been given by other families, all of them heading southward.

They had never come so far before. Always their wanderings had stopped at the Deep-Gorge Water, north and west of this place. Actually, they had only been driven that far since the rains had become so irregular. In addition to making it hard to find clean water for drinking, the drought had sent the *zatku* away from their former haunts.

Now the oldest female stood, head cocked to one side, listening. Seeing her, the other four stopped rustling about in the undergrowth and raised their heads. There was a strange sound in the forest. Though it was just barely audible, even to their keen ears, they knew that it must be quite loud if you went near to its source.

She shouldered her *zatku-hodda*. "This one goes there. Something is happening that I don't understand. We must see."

The two young couples looked at each other quickly. Each knew that there was fear in all the Gashta's eyes, for new things were usually dangerous—or fatal. Still, the reason their kind had lived so long in this hostile place was that they were curious, cautious, and ingenious. With thumping hearts, they settled their net bags, shouldered their weapons, and set out after her. She had always known what to do in emergencies. They felt confident that she would also know, this time.

The forest was thick here. They had come up out of a gorge onto fairly level land. The beanvines grew in abundance here, and round-fruit dropped ripely, at intervals, into the quiet of the wood. They could hear the faint squish of its landing on the mulchy layer below the trees.

This was a rich land. Though there was sign of the passing of many-many Gashta, there seemed to be none about, and they wondered at that. Uncrowded as it was, it might be a wonderful place to set up a wandering-circuit. Even predators were very few. The single *toshki-washa* they had smelled this side of the gorge had been a half-night's march behind them. Those dangerous beasts, they knew quite well, were as prone to moving about as were the Gashta themselves, but for a time they might take advantage of the absence of such beasts.

The moons were both up, Tansha far down the west, Gozzo just coming overhead. The way was bright, and they found themselves following a path. The oldest knelt and sniffed at it, then laid her cheek close to catch the shadows of an outline.

"Gashta," she said, her voice wondering. "Not long —last night, maybe. But where are they, if they came so lately?"

Nobody could answer her. And now the noise had stopped, as the night fell completely. They might not have waked to hear it at all if a noisy *zatku* hadn't made such a loud sound below the tree they slept in. It had been clacking its pincers, sidling about before an admiring female. Both had been beheaded and eaten before their courtship could advance past the preliminaries.

The female stopped and motioned. Her companions also stopped. Then they slipped silently to stand beside her.

A strange thing lay before them. For a long way all the big feathertrees had been laid down on their sides. Some still had their branches, complete with fronds of leaves that were now wilted, dark in the moonlight. Others had been stripped of branches entirely and lay, long and bare in the clearing. Still others had been cut into sections that lay in a long line, as if some giant *hatta-zosa* had laid its string of dung there.

But what kind of axe could do such work? Their flint tools made hard work of cutting a sapling for making *zatku-hodda*. And what Gashta could wield such an axe if it existed? It was a real puzzle, and the family hunkered down in a circle to talk it over.

They could find no explanation. It was evidently a terribly dangerous place that they had come to. But many of their kind had come there before, as proven by the tracks they had seen, the privy-holes they had counted along their way. If something was in that strange place, devouring Gashta, others must be warned.

"We will go into the trees until light comes. Then we will be able to see across this bare spot. It is better so." The old female's voice was firm, and none of her family could find any reason to argue with her.

Morning came entirely too quickly. They had rested near the top of a good-sized *rogo,* just within the border of feathertrees that stood beside the devastated area. From that point they could see the entire place, from side to side and end to end. And that was more confusing than ever, for large things stood in the center of the clearing. Square things, long things, things with many arms. Even as they watched, a huge creature, shaped like a Gashta but many sizes too large, came from one of the square things, climbed up into one of the things with many arms, and the thing shouted in a very loud voice.

It was the sound they had heard, there wasn't any doubt of that. The thing crawled forward a bit, then rose into the air and descended on one of the bare tree-trunks. A hair-raising burring sound filled the air, and the small people cowered in their tree.

Now more of the big creatures were in the clearing. Some rolled away the sections of log. Others climbed into the different things there. And some of those things went up into the air.

"Gotza!" screamed the youngest female, burrowing her face into her mate's fur.

But the oldest was made of sterner material. "I see Gashta," she said, unclasping her small hands from the branch she had grabbed. "Look!"

It was true. Small shapes hurried about near the big square things, going into them, coming out of them. They carried brightly-glinting tools in their hands, and over their shoulders were the finest bags any Gashta had ever dreamed of. Not one of them seemed frightened at all. Indeed, one of them ran up to one of the immense creatures and gestured to be picked up! The thing reached down and set the small person on his shoulder. It was quite evident that they were talking excitedly. Then the big one put the small one down, and it set out across the busy clearing toward the spot where the family was hiding.

That settled it. The oldest female slid down the *rogo* a bit faster than was quite good for her fur and set out toward the oncoming Gashta. Long before she met him, he was shouting to her.

"This one welcomes you to the *hoksu-mitto!* This one is *Lo-Shta*. We have fine foods, fine weapons, and the Hagga are the finest thing of all. Come. *Bizzo! Bizzo!* Bring your family. I take you to see Pappy Jack!"

A bit hesitantly, the younger ones joined the matriarch. The stranger waited until they were all together, then he held out his weapon. "Look! This is a *chopper-digger*. And this . . ." he motioned toward his shoulder . . . "is a *shoulder-bag*. The Hagga will give some to you, after you eat breakfast and meet Pappy Jack and Auntie Ruth and Unca-Gerd. You come with me!"

Although their hearts were still thumping, the bright shape of the new weapon enchanted them. The hope of having such a fine-fine thing kept them at Dark-Fur's heels all the way to the office.

Pappy Jack was awake, sitting at his desk with a cup of coffee before him.

"A new bunch, eh?" he asked, as Dark-Fur brought in the new family.

The old female looked up at the big creature. Hagga? It seemed so. She turned to *Lo-Shta* and asked, "Is it that Gashta live here all the time? Get food and weapons? Are safe from *toshki-washa* and *gotza* and *so-shi-fazzu?*"

He gestured toward the big one. "Pappy Jack kills all the bad animals. Here they cannot get Gashta-meat. And all Gashta should come here. It's safe here, and there is much food and many-many games that you will like. We don't have to work so hard to live. Have fun all the time, if we want to."

"We might come here, stay and be family too?" she asked. "The big one would permit this?"

Dark-Fur turned to Pappy Jack, but he knew the answer to the question before he asked it.

When that was settled, he led the newcomers toward one of the big houses. There were big men there in blue not-fur. They seemed very glad to meet the family, and at once they made a game for them.

"Here, roll your finger on this, see?" The oldest female did as he directed, then watched in amazement as a small-small picture of part of her finger appeared on the white stuff he put her hand down on.

One by one, her family had their fingerprints taken. And then each of them was given a wonderful ornament. On a chain around each neck went a round thing that Dark-Fur called *"idee-disko."* With marks that he told them meant that single Gashta and no other, ever. Marvelous!

After that, another of the men passed out the bright weapons and the wonderful *shoulder-bags* to all of them. Bemused with their new riches, the family wanted to sit quietly and talk over the entire morning, but Little Fuzzy wouldn't let them.

"Best of all," he insisted, "is the *hoksu-fusso*. You will know that I speak the truth the moment you taste it. A most wonderful food!" And he led them away to a place that smelled of fruit and meat and other edibles.

He was completely correct. They knew when they sniffed the dark brown pieces the Hagga handed to them that this was a food that their bodies had craved for as long as they could remember. Though neither Gashta nor Hagga knew it yet, Extee-Three contained an element that cancelled out the hormonal imbalance that had caused so many stillbirths through all the generations of Gashta on Zarathustra.

But all these knew was the fact that this was the finest food imaginable. They ate small pieces first, then larger ones. When they were all stuffed to capacity, their host led them off to the shade of a big tree that had been left in the quiet part of the compound and let them sit, at long last, to examine their new things.

While they tried the temper of the chopper-diggers, delved into the mysteries of their shoulder-bags, Dark-Fur talked quietly to his new comrades.

"This is a new time for the Gashta," he told them. "Now we can live without worry-worry, run-run, hide-

hide. The Hagga have taught us many things, and they are good, though sometimes slow at learning the things we want to teach them.

"For long-long I have tried to tell Pappy Jack of the help that will come from the stars."

The oldest female looked up at him, her eyes suddenly misty with memories. "I remember the stories. I . . . lost them when I got older and busier, but I remember them. Are these Hagga, then, from the stars?"

"The Hagga travel through the sky; they go to the moons. The stars are in the sky, so the Hagga may come from the stars, that is true. But I think the old stories said another thing. *Gashta* will bring help from the stars."

"Gashta?" Her eyes were very bright, green and luminous in the morning light. "There was a story . . . long-long ago. About a Ship? A Ship that brought Gashta . . ."

Dark-Fur nodded.

"But they did not come. It seems as if our kind has been here forever, and no Gashta have come from the sky."

He sighed. "True. But how far away were they? And what kind of message was sent to them? It is far to the moon, and it is the size of my thumb. The biggest star I can see in the sky is smaller than a grain of sand. Very far! It would take a long time for a message to go and for help to come."

A small figure came scampering across the compound, followed by its mother. Baby Fuzzy, hurt at being left out of the welcoming committee, was making up for lost time. He went at once to the old Gashta and climbed up to sit on her head.

Wearing him like a hat, she looked down to find her lap occupied by a strange thing indeed. A black and white animal was there, kneading her fur with needled paws. The baby's mother was trying to hug her without unsettling either baby or kitten.

She smiled widely at *Lo-Shta*. "You have said this was a wonderful place, and that was true. You have named the wonderful food, and that was indeed true. It may be that you have named a thing to come. Help from the stars? Why not?''

She leaned forward, careful not to squash the kitten in her lap, and hugged Mama Fuzzy tightly. Over her head, she saw Little Fuzzy nod, as if satisfied with her answer.

AFTERTHOUGHT

"Gerd . . ."

"Yes, Ruth?"

"We have quite a list of words compiled, now. I've been going over the Fuzzy dictionary."

"Well?"

"You'll think I've gone funny!"

"What, me? Never!"

"At least, you'll think my imagination is running away with me."

"Come on. Out with it, whatever it is, however oddball it may seem."

"I've been doing a lot of work with Little Fuzzy. He talks a blue streak. And I think I've got a clue to what he's trying to tell me. Over and over. The same exact words, repeatedly."

"Which are?"

"As nearly as I can tell, he's saying that the Gashta came from the stars."

"Well, we just learned that when they found the traces of the ship and the bones of the survivors who got trapped in the cave up there. He's been talking to the Leader . . . Stargazer, they call him. He probably is all excited at the notion."

"I know that. No, it's not what Stargazer told him, it's what they found out from comparing old stories handed down through the years. He thinks his people will come in another ship. To help his people."

"*After all this time? Why should they think that?*"

"*Stargazer told him that a message was sent. But the tale he learned said that it was sent 'slow-slow' because the main engines of the ship were out. Sub-light speed? It sounds like it.*"

"*Hmmm. That would take a long time, sure enough, even if the Fuzzy planet were fairly close, and we know it isn't. Generations. A thousand years . . . or more. He's sure they'll come, eh?*"

"*Positive. He said, and this was quite plain, 'Gashta come when Gashta call for help.' And they do. I've seen it many times.*"

Gerd rubbed his chin. A grin dawned in his eyes before spreading to his lips.

"*What if one day a ship comes dashing in past Darius, past Xerxes. One nobody can identify, without any of the codes or the proper signals. And berths at Mallorysport. And two-foot-tall, golden-furred Fuzzies get out, wearing space-suits and asking awkward questions about the way things have gone for their kin-folk?*"

Ruth laughed. "*It would boggle a few minds. Particularly among those Khooghra who still try to kidnap Fuzzies for sale off-planet. And the crooks who want to confiscate the Fuzzy Reservation and mine the sun-stones there for themselves.*"

She looked at her husband. He grinned back at her.

"*I like it!*" *they said in unison.*

Appendix I

NOTES UPON THE CHRONICLING OF THE GASHTA

From the notebooks of Lo-Shta, known to Hagga as Little Fuzzy

It seems a very long time since the day I first met my dear friend Jack Holloway and was introduced to the persons and the ways of the Big People. It has been a good time for my people, although it has meant a great change in the way we live and even in the way we think. I like to think that it has also been a good time for the Hagga, even though our meeting as two sapient races has changed some of their ideas and their dealings unalterably.

Without the intervention of *Homo Sapiens Terra*, I think that we would soon have lost our precarious foothold upon Zarathustra, which is a world particularly unsuited for people of our size and strength. I know, also, that our race would have dwindled to a number far too small to ensure our survival, even had we found a way to conquer all the predators that find us so delicious. We owe much to the Hagga.

Yet, for all our mutual affection and trust, there has been a lack of communication on the most basic level. Even the Hagga who were our first and most devoted friends thought us simple primitives, although bright ones. The fact that for so long our very speech was above their hearing-range contributed to that. They found us physically appealing and childlike, and their instincts made them love us. But they had no idea that our culture might have degenerated from an extremely old and technologically advanced one, in our own world. And, of course, most of us had forgotten that we came from another world than this.

It has required years of research, study and preparation, but now I have chronicled much of the story of my people on Zarathustra. Not until those other Gashta come from the Home-World will I know the story that led to our ancestors' journey to this place, but such history as we have preserved by means of Circle-Tales and Songs I have gathered together. They are presented here for the first time, even to Gashta.

Our race has been fragmented for too many generations. Tales passed down in one family-group have been lost to all others except those into which members have transferred by mating-procedure. The years I have spent in learning the Hagga tongue and the ways of their writing have been matched by those I have invested in researches among my own people. In this the help of Jack Holloway has been invaluable, as well as that of his colleagues, Ruth and Gerd Van Riebeek in particular. The Colonial Government has put all its facilities at my disposal in this endeavor, and I want to thank Governor Rainsford for his constant encouragement. Victor Grego, also, has been of great assistance, along with most of his staff at Company House.

I feel that I owe some apology to the Charterless Zarathustra Company. It was by no fault of their own that they were granted a charter to a world that all thought uninhabited by sapient beings. Their reaction on finding that their claim was invalid was severe but, under the circumstances, I think that it was understandable. As things stand, perhaps the damage that each side did to the other in the dispute cancels out. Now the efforts of the Company in mining the sun-stones on the Gashta Reservation keep us all solvent.

Among the Gashta, there are entirely too many from whom I received tales and songs and traditions for me to be able to thank each individually. I hope that this record will be sufficient recognition for those who have provided its content.

There has been some comment, particularly from those who have traveled here from Terra in order to study our people, about the readiness shown by Gashta to adopt Hagga ways and their seeming inconveniences to our dignity as an intelligent people. That, of course, is no longer a problem, since the adoption program has proven to be so successful among both the Big and the Small people. It does deserve some consideration, however.

A species that evolves upon a planet usually finds that it has been provided by nature with the means of surviving there. Otherwise it succumbs to natural pressures early-on and is seen no more. Our kind evolved on a smaller world than this, whose native beasts and whose chemical balances were entirely suited to our survival and well-being.

We had not intended to come to Zarathustra. That much is clear from all the remaining traditions. This is a planet filled with creatures too large for us to deal with physically, and it lacks a vital element for our survival as a species. If our ancestors had not brought *zatku* with them for breeding-stock on their intended colony, and if our ship had not contained massive amounts of that element, titanium, in its hull, we would have been less than a forgotten footnote in the natural history of Zarathustra.

Thrown upon our own resources in only a few generations, we had to substitute wit for strength and subtlety for force. It was a life so hard that it is probable that no Hagga can approach an understanding of its dangers and its hardships. The loss of most of our cultural heritage was not only natural, under the circumstances, it was inevitable.

We were reduced to small groups of wanderers, dwindling year by year as attrition took its toll. And into this hopeless situation came the Hagga. Big, warm, loving, generous, they were our saviors and our friends. Somehow, we knew that from the outset. We saw them as such, even at the beginning.

Here, honesty compels me to insert a truth that some of our Hagga friends may find offensive. However, in an effort of this kind it is vital to include all the facts, however strange or uncomfortable they may be.

We were not entirely certain, at the beginning, that the Hagga were, indeed, more than a kind of clever beast. The fact that they had food, and shelter that they were willing to share with our kind, soon told us that they were people of a sort, but the insatiable game-playing they indulged in puzzled us as to their overall maturity and innate intelligence.

In thinking over the matter, these years past, I have reached a conclusion that may or may not be entirely true. We, as a people, were starved for the carefree and playful lifestyle that our kind loves so well and had been without for so long. The Hagga, in turn, had been sober and businesslike, humorless as a species to some extent. They, too, were missing, in some deep part of their characters, the joy of their childhood.

When we met we were, for many years, children together. We accepted their ways and their names and their protection because it was quite simply the only road that led to our survival. But it was not a cold or a calculating thing. We grew to love the big people, as they grew to love us. We seem to fit together beautifully. So, in answer to those who question whether our quick response was lacking in dignity, I say that it is better to lose a bit of dignity than to become extinct.

This is a long tale, for it concerns many beings, living and dead, human and Gashta. Some appear only once and then are lost in the dimness of time. But all the tales told here were important to those who lived them and to those who learned the songs or the chants to preserve them. All, I think, tell something true about my people.

In conclusion, I must offer my profound respect and gratitude to the Stargazers. Not only to him who is now the holder of that old title, but to those generations of *Haigun*, whose combined tenures cross a thousand years and more, back to the very coming of the Ship to Zarathustra. Without their oral history, the traditions they have preserved in the face of great odds, and their steadfastness in their duty, this history would not have been possible to compile in a form that is coherent.

Mallorysport
Year of the Pale *Zatku*

SUPPLEMENTARY
NOTES

On reading over this very long account, it occurs to me that there are some gaps in basic information that may make matters confusing to those not involved with the entire Hagga-Gashta story. For that reason, I have put together several different kinds of information, including a Glossary, for the benefit of those who have not yet taken up the study of our language.

I feel, also, an obligation to emphasize the inestimable role played in the recreation of parts of our early history by the oral tradition among our people. Having lost both technology and time for painstaking preservation of our written language, the Gashta did what many other peoples have done: They organized folk and family tales into easily-memorized stories and verses and songs.

The Gashta memory is highly retentive, as testing has proven. Proof of this came, most gratifyingly, when we descendants of the *Kampushi-sha* met, once again, with the *Haigun-sha* of the Valley. Our songs, the ones that we still held in common, were identical. Verbally, of course. Melody has always been a thing that varied from singer to singer.

A matter that puzzled the Hagga somewhat, from the first, was our habit of gathering into circles, not only for discussion, which was at first inaudible to our larger brothers, but also for word-games and singing, which were likewise above Hagga hearing ranges. But it was through these circles, both within single families and combining families met by chance in the forest, that tales and songs spread through our kind. Considering the dangerous lives that we led here on Zarathustra, many such stories and songs would certainly have been lost entirely, if they had been left solely to single families.

There are, of course, many more existing tales and songs than could possibly be accommodated in this single work. Those used here are either germane to the story I have tried to tell, or they are representative of their kind. It is my hope that some Hagga scholar may choose to make a study of Gashta culture, at some future time, and for the convenience of any such, I have compiled a large collection.

This might be a good place in which to make some comments upon our social and familial organization . . . though that is entirely too strict a term for the flexible arrangements that proved to be necessary to our survival as a species here. We had no "leaders" in the sense that the Hagga do. In the Ship, of course, there was the kind of hierarchy that is required for mutual safety and efficiency, and only Gashta with the natural inclination for such discipline were chosen for that sort of duty. Otherwise, we were individually autonomous. The ones we chose as nominal leaders were more in the position of advisers. Nobody had to obey them, and they were by no means required to continue any duty that became objectionable.

Such an arrangement seems strange to the Hagga, I know. Yet we are a very homogeneous race, unlike the mixture of kinds and characters that compose the Hagga. That makes for less stress and disagreement among individuals or groups. Not that we are or ever have been inhumanly perfect—we have squabbled among ourselves at many points and over many matters. But we seldom become really angry, and we have never become angry to the point of killing.

This brings up the matter of those early-day removals of irrational or unbalanced or otherwise dangerous Gashta. Such action was never a punishment, in any sense of the word. One does not punish a Gashta for being what he was born to be. It was a sorrowful thing, a terrible duty, and a practical necessity. And such executions were done with a minimum of fuss, without anger or recrimination.

We have also been questioned closely by our Hagga friends of a psychological bent as to Gashta sexual promiscuity. Most of those interested in this aspect of our lives seem to be singularly influenced by a Hagga called Freud, who lived many centuries before his kind moved out into the cosmos. This caused some terrible confusion, as some of their assumptions as to the cause of our periodic mate-exchanging made no sense whatever.

Having taken time to read somewhat deeply in genetics, now, I understand my own people's conscious decisions, in those distant days, with grateful clarity. Our gene pool was limited to begin with, given the entire complement of the ship's crew and the colonists. Once the landslide removed over half our number, that became a terrible problem, and one which our ancestors understood and moved to alleviate as much as could be done.

In the first generations, mates were chosen for life, and then the *Haigun* assigned temporary matings for the purpose of mixing heredities. These had no impact upon the partnerships formed by those who wanted to spend their lives together. Once, however, the families moved away from the Valley, it was a different matter. There was no *Haigun* to manage for us, but our ancestors had been taught that this was a thing that *must* be done. When Gashta are convinced of a thing, they follow that conviction totally.

So it came about that families habitually coalesced, produced offspring, even though most of those died, moved about the land, and eventually drifted into different partnerships and conformations. It seemed random, but such pairing and parting was done in obe-

dience to the training that all Gashta were given as
young ones.

We have found it difficult to understand Hagga atti-
tudes on this matter. Procreation is highly enjoyable, it
is true, particularly now that it leads to the birth of living babies. Yet we find eating and playing and learning
equally enjoyable. With the Hagga, we can only assume
that it is different.

I do want to emphasize that all the material con-
cerning Gashta who are now living, or who lived at the
time of our early contact with the Hagga, comes from
first-hand conversations, as well as correspondence.

Leaf and her family have been especially helpful in
this context. I might mention here that the Mirabeaus
have been granted a lifetime permit to continue their
farming within the Gashta Reservation. This protects
them from any problem that might have come about as
a result of their illegal homestead. Both Lem and Gus
added much to the section dealing with their finding of
Leaf and her child.

And of course Silver-Fur and his family have added
an entire dimension to the story. Ernst Mallin, too, once
he accepted the truth of the situation, made great efforts
to make amends, and has provided the sections from his
diary, embarrassing though it must seem to him. This is
the mark of a true scientist, as I feel you will agree.

There is much that I could add. Time and space are
now limited, however, so I must close with the observation that we of the Gashta have much to learn of
Hagga psychology, sexuality, and history. I hope that
we will deal with those subjects as kindly as the Hagga
have dealt with ours.

Dark-Fur
Holloway's Run

Appendix II

SOME OBSERVATIONS
ON GASHTA
NAMES

A close observer may have noted that in the early parts of this history, mention was made of the original families from the Ship. Unfortunately, the five names used in the section dealing with the sending-out of the early Gashta into the south are all that survive, as far as I have been able to ascertain.

The Family *Ginzu*. We have no translation for the parts of this name.

The Family *Zashi*. The derivation is from the word *za*, meaning like a shell (see *zatku*) and the word *shi*, resembling. Probably the fur-color predominant in that family resembled some shell-fish or creature on the home world.

The Family *Taki-yo*. This name probably also describes physical or mental traits usual in that family, but both root-words are lost to us.

The Family *Hasa*. This is quite easy to translate. *Ha* is the word for loved or beloved. *Sa* can mean work (or worker), make, or do, interchangeably. My rendition would be "The family that loves its work." An admirable trait.

The Family *Hashi-so*. *Ha* is love or beloved, *shi* means resembling, and *so* means you: this combination probably connotes a family of very warm and affectionate nature.

It is interesting to note that these names came down to us principally because of that last-calling-of-names. Some of the listening families recognized their old names, when they were called, and preserved them consciously. They became a part of their Circle-Stories, and were thus preserved.

Later, of course, names became less important. The babies were given simple names, like Seed or Pebble or Fruit, which served them through childhood. Then, as skills or distinctive coloration or personal traits became apparent, most of them took on their adult and permanent names. Though, indeed, some like Leaf clung to their original nomenclature. It was a matter of choice as much as of usage.

It has been a temptation to render our names, throughout this work, in Gashta. They are much more beautiful and meaningful in that language. Yet I have realized that that could make reading the story of my people a difficult thing for most Hagga. Thus, I have translated our names into Hagga-words that come nearest the original in meaning.

My Gashta name is *Lo-Shta*. It translates into Dark-Fur, which loses the connotations of "fur-seen-by-moonlight-at-midnight" that is contained in the original. It was not a name that I earned, as so many earned theirs, but one that nature managed for me.

It is obvious that most gained their adult names from the work that they chose to do. Root-Grower; the ardent gardener. Axe-Maker. Snail-Catcher.

Some had personal traits so remarkable that they set their seals upon their possessors. Remembers-Things. Sees-Far. Fast-Foot. And many more.

Perhaps the most famous of all those we have found in our history is Bad-Thing-Killer. Not only did he preserve his family name, *Hasa*, and heritage, but he was spoken about all through our history as the only

Gashta ever to kill a *toshki-washa* single-handed. Not to mention the fact that he was the one who chose that particular encounter. He must have been remarkable, and I have included elsewhere the Circle-Tale about his historic battle.

There is a book's worth of material to be gleaned simply from our names and the characters they delineate. Unfortunately, this is not a proper place for such things. So I will end with the observation that though the Hagga have named us strange things, and we have accepted those names at their hands for the sake of affection, we still cling to our original ones, among ourselves.

Appendix III

GLOSSARY OF TERMS

Aki	me
bizzo	come
do	how
dokko	how many
dovov	how not?
en	to make
etto	thought
etza	break(s)
fazzu	depart quickly (scram)
fe'h	golden
fe'ha	sun
fessi	hunger (hungry)
fusso	food
ga	people
Gashta	furred people (Fuzzies)
gotza	harpy (flying predator native to Zarathustra)
Gozzo	moon (Darius)
ha	loved
Hag	large (as in Hagga, large people, easily confused with *ha ga*, loved people)
Hagga	large people (*homo sapiens Terra*)
hatta-zosa	goofers (animal native to Zarathustra)
he	what
heeva	say

he-inta	what is happening?
hizzu	poisonous insect, native to Zarathustra
hoksu	wonderful
hodda	weapon (mutual root with *hudda*, death)
hok'e	flower (blossom, bloom)
hudda	death, dead
hudd'en	to kill
inta	happen(s)
izza	father
ja	to have (as in a need—*Ja'aki fessi:* I have hunger)
ja-aki	I have
josso	give
kashi	small predator native to Zarathustra
keef'i	quiet, soft, secret
kin-sha	leader, advisor
ko	heal
ko-so	healing plant
li	small
lo	dark
mitto	place
mosh	we, us
ne'to	talk
ninta	touch
noho	tell
noho-washa	Teacher (lit. "tells things")
nozzo	always
oko	friend
pa	well (much)
pa-ha-izza	beloved father
pokko	show
posse	give
rogo	species of tree native to Zarathustra
shi	like (resembling)
shta	fur
shokka	beautiful
siggo	like (appreciate)
so	you
so-shi-fazzu	run-like-hell (species of predator native to Zarathustra, called by Hagga a "damnthing")

Tansha	moon (Xerxes)
tai	my
t'an	silver
t'ho	yes
toshki	bad
t'ra	twigs (wood)
uka	mother
vov	no
waji	water
washa	thing or things
wi	to
zatku	food animal brought to Zarathustra by the Gashta, (called a "land-prawn" by the Hagga)
zeeto	small rodent native to Zarathustra

The Tribes of the Gashta

Haigun-sha	the ship people (crew and technicians)
Kampushi-sha	the colonists and their descendants

THE WORLDS OF H. BEAM PIPER

COLLECTIONS OF FANTASY AND SCIENCE FICTION